Killer Tuition

JERRY MOORMAN

College Professor Dr. Tarr Baldridge has been implicated in the murder of a fellow professor, with whom he had a physical altercation. While trying to unravel the murder and the reasons for his involvement, Tarr uncovers a large Mafia-controlled money laundering scheme involving the college where he is employed. With the help of his ex-Navy Seal brother and a security executive childhood friend, Tarr must rely on his secret past to sort out the players in this high-stakes money game.

Throwing in an exceedingly skilled assassin plus an aggressive police detective makes an untenable situation even more dangerous. Follow Tarr, his brother and their childhood friend as they navigate through this complex situation.

SELECTED CHARACTERS

Lucky Baldridge	Navy Seal
Tarr Baldridge	Marketing Professor
Philip Barberri, (The Barbarian) "Old Man"	Mafia Boss in Colorado
Dr. Daniel L. Karp	President of Thunder Mountain College
Kelsie Daggett	Finance Student
The Enforcer	Assassin
Dr. Arthur Gibbs	Finance Professor
Adri Korabit	Albanian Seal
Greg Manci	V.P. of Finance
Detective Orr	Policeman
Dr. Dondria (Doni) Rader	History Professor
Jack	Tarr/Lucky's childhood friend

Chapter 1

Dr. Arthur Gibbs looked at the documents on his kitchen table, all the while sensing death looking back. A dusting of anthrax powder would not have made them deadlier. The documents themselves couldn't kill him, but the story they told would make certain people want him dead. Like yesterday.

Did anyone know he had them? One person for sure. He'd have to deal with that immediately.

What should be done with the documents? The FBI and Internal Revenue Service seemed the most obvious recipients. But how could that be accomplished? What would be the best way to turn the information over to a federal agency?

Mailing them in anonymously might keep him from getting killed in the process. But mail to whom?

He couldn't exactly address the package "To Whom It May Concern." A name was needed. There was the professional friend who was a criminology professor at the University of Denver. Such a professorship obviously required law enforcement contacts. He'd call him at the office tomorrow.

For now, the information would be safe hidden in the freezer compartment of his refrigerator. Wrapped in aluminum foil, it would look like a beef roast or something. No one would ever think to look there.

Calling Kelsie was the next most immediate concern. Kelsie must be told not to talk to anybody about what she had discovered. Unless warned, she might accidentally blab about it to a friend.

Although extremely bright and certainly observant, she was, after all, only a 19-year-old college sophomore. Her interest in helping him was enthusiastic, but her judgment to not tell might be somewhat underdeveloped.

Her pride in getting the secret documents might create a need to share. At this point, sharing was not a good idea. As a matter of fact, it might become her last idea.

Chapter 2

"Slow down, take a deep breath, and tell me what the problem is." The voice on the other end of the line spoke in a fatherly, yet authoritarian fashion. "Just give me the basics and spare any commentary. I'll decide what needs to be done."

The excited speaker took a deep breath as instructed. He needed to relax if he wanted to celebrate another birthday. The voice on the other end of the line might sound fatherly, but anyone who knew him knew better. It belonged to a guy who could cancel all future birthdays with one snap of his fingers.

"Our anonymous donor files were accessed by an unauthorized person this afternoon. A hard copy of an updated set of files was taken. It was the file copy duplicated for transfer to the Aspen Ranch vault." The speaker physically flinched as if about to be struck, even though separated from the other speaker by 250 miles and two major mountain passes. The fatherly voice was currently relaxing in a well-appointed study in Denver.

It was stressed by an underlying anger. "I see. Do we know the identity of this unauthorized person?"

"We are almost positive it was a young work study student who has been working in the financial area of administration since the beginning of the semester. We've had her under surveillance since she left campus about 4:30.

"After making one stop, she went straight to her apartment. She's been there ever since."

The fatherly voice responded without hesitation. "I don't care what it takes; I want those files back in our possession before morning. Send a couple of guys to toss the apartment and also the place she stopped. The files have to be at one of them.

"Also, bring the girl to the Ranch. If I leave now, it'll take me about 45 minutes to get to the airport and another hour to fly to Aspen. It's 6:15 now; meet me at the Ranch no later than midnight. Don't disappoint me; I expect to see you there with the girl." The line went dead.

Chapter 3

"Dr. Gibbs, this is campus security. Someone broke into your office and trashed the place. We need you to come down immediately and tell us what was taken."

Art Gibbs did not believe much in coincidence. He was, after all, a highly trained academic. Proper academic preparation taught that a coincidence was when two related activities came together by chance occurrence. No, this was no coincidence. Someone thought he might know something and wanted to find out what. Because of that knowledge, his life depended on what he did in the next few days.

Dr. Arthur Gibbs had been on top of the world only a few days earlier. His study into private college finance was progressing well, especially with a trusted student supplying information from the office of financial affairs.

He hadn't really been trying to get secret information; he had merely wanted to impress his Dean with how much he knew about the college's finances. Never intending to tell the Dean how he knew, Gibbs had simply planned to bring up tidbits of knowledge at appropriate times.

It would appear that he possessed such knowledge because he was smarter than other faculty members. Since the Dean was not trained in finance, it might then make sense to fill the vacant Associate Dean's slot with yours truly.

Gibbs had been studying higher education finance for a couple of months now. Although learning quite a bit, he had been unable to gather any specific information about how Thunder Mountain ran its financial affairs.

That had all changed with the discovery of a young finance major working in the financial area of administration.

Convincing her to help had not been that hard. After all, no one was getting hurt, Dr. Gibbs just wanted to have a better understanding of how the college handled its finances. Shouldn't that be public information anyway?

Offering her an "A" in an independent study class had cinched the deal. Until this afternoon, however, she provided him with little useful information. He had pressured her by holding the grade over her head. Get information that only the V.P. of Finance knew or she could forget the A. Boy, had she come through.

Gibbs grabbed a light jacket and headed for the door. As was his compulsion, he checked the lock twice to make sure it was locked. Gibbs didn't really think the documents were in danger of theft, but what the heck? Whoever had torn apart his office thought he had the documents there. What fools!

Dr. Arthur Gibbs had always been the smartest guy around; what had changed? Nothing, as far as he was concerned. It was bothering him, however, how someone got onto him so quickly.

It had to be Kelsie. Someone must have seen her take the files. Someone who knew she was one of his students and had been spending a lot of time with him lately. Stupid bitch. He should have known he couldn't trust her. Now, he was in big trouble, bigger than ever before in his life.

He'd figure a way out, though; he always did. No one could outthink him. Most people were stupid. He had always operated on that premise and not ever been disappointed. Why should this time be any different? The only difference was the stakes. Somehow, that excited him.

As Dr. Gibbs was backing his car out of the drive, two men sat watching from a vantage point about half a block away. Since it was dark already, their presence went unnoticed by the neighborhood.

"Looks like the fake burglary worked." The driver smiled at his passenger. "Let's go; campus security said they'd keep him for at least an hour at his office."

"I've got five bucks says the good doctor put the files in the freezer or at the bottom of his dirty laundry basket." The passenger smirked even though it went unseen in the darkness of the car.

"That's a bet I wouldn't touch with borrowed money. Guys like that always think they're smarter than everybody else just cause they went to college forever."

As the driver continued talking, he squinted while trying to see his partner. "Well, I just hope the professor has them. Since they weren't at the kid's apartment, this is our last shot. I really don't want to tell the Old Man, at the Ranch tonight, we got nothing to show for our time. Do you?"

"Not me," came the reply. "Let's do it. The little coed in the trunk won't stay knocked out forever."

Chapter 4

It was a little after 11 pm as the three-car caravan rolled through Aspen. The town was quiet. Ski season hadn't started yet. When it did, the small town would get a lot busier. Tonight, though, it was almost dead. You could count the number of cars they encountered on one hand.

The cars passed through town heading east. The ranch was about fifteen minutes outside town. To outsiders, it was rumored to be the retreat of a very wealthy and very private corporate executive.

Inquiries about the ranch were referred to a law firm in Denver. The permanent staff kept to themselves and never went into town. All food and anything else needed were delivered.

Rumor also had it that the true owners were a family who controlled one of the biggest retail companies in the world. They always arrived in a private jet after dark. The jet was met by a limo with darkened windows and the passengers driven away immediately. They left in reverse fashion.

The rumor had been planted several years ago as a way to explain the tight security. It didn't take a rocket scientist to see that no visitors were allowed. The entire 180 acre ranch was surrounded by a split rail fence with prominent "NO TRESPASSING" signs spaced every ten yards. Signs also warned of attack dogs and electronic deterrents.

Unseen were the motion detectors twenty feet inside the fence and roving guards. What the owners didn't know, though, was the motion detectors were never turned on because of the abundant wildlife wandering around inside the fence.

The main house sat on a hill surrounded by ten acres of rolling meadows. The 17,000 square foot main house was part of a compound that also included two large log houses, an irrigation house and a 5,000 square foot garage and shop.

The permanent staff of 20 was spread between the two log homes. Guests stayed in one of the five suites in the main house.

The positioning of the compound was not by accident. It had been designed to occupy high ground which could not be approached without traveling through almost 10 acres of open meadow.

The ranch was surrounded by spectacular 14,000 foot snow-capped mountains. The land itself was a combination of high mountain meadow, aspen groves, spruce and fir forests, plus a year-round stream that crossed the property. An additional buffer zone was provided by national forest on three sides.

A large 20-inch underground irrigation pipe connected the stream to a two-acre pond close to the compound. With its own water supply and four large generators, the ranch was very self-sufficient.

The three cars slowed and turned on a small paved road marked by a very large sign saying it was private and violators would be prosecuted to the full extent of the law. Twenty yards down the road was a very sturdy gate built from heavy iron bars anchored in stone walls.

Just in front of the gate, the road broadened and gave the appearance of a small cul-de-sac. Its purpose, no doubt, was to provide an area for the curious and lost to turn their vehicles around and head back to the main road.

The gate was positioned in such a fashion that a vehicle had to make a hard left out of the cul-de-sac to pass through. Obviously, there would be no running starts and smashing the gate.

The driver of the lead car slowed to a crawl and maneuvered slowly up to the gate. A uniformed guard stared at him through a thick bullet-proof window of the property's gatehouse.

Putting the car in park, the driver got out and looked up at a surveillance camera.

A very hard looking man carrying a semi-automatic shotgun with a short barrel suddenly materialized from the other side of the gate.

The driver jumped ever so slightly at his appearance. "I wish you would make some noise or something. Every time you do your magic appearing act, I jump and move for my gun. One of these days, I'm going to shoot your ugly butt."

"Yeah, sure you are. Who you got with you tonight?"

"Me and two soldiers up front, two Bosses and a soldier in the middle, and two soldiers and a cute little coed bringing up the rear."

As the gate started to open, the shotgun was replaced by a cell phone. "I'll tell 'em at gate two, nine of you are driving up in three cars."

"I'm going to shoot you next time you do that to me." The driver pointed his finger at the hard man on the other side of the gate as he drove through.

Putting the cell phone in a side pocket, he laughed. You'd shoot your only brother. What would mama say?"

The hard guy flipped off the driver and disappeared into the darkness. The driver smiled. Seeing the kid reminded him he hadn't called home this month.

A few minutes later the small convoy slowed as the drive made a 90-degree turn and emerged from the forest. The guard at gate two was waving them through. As the cars drove into the openness of the meadow, a thousand twinkling stars blanketed the sky.

The brightly lit house could be seen in the distance. Passing a fair sized irrigation pond complete with a bigger than expected pump house, the cars began the gradual ascent to the circular drive. Straining a bit toward the top, the convoy leveled off and pulled in front of the house. Even with three full-size cars parked in the drive, its size made it appear near empty.

Three armed men waited in front of the house. No doubt, one or two more were watching from the shadows. Chances were never taken at the ranch.

As the men went into the house, the Bosses headed to the library; the rest of the group broke up. The girl was taken to a secure area in the basement where she would be chemically interrogated.

Long gone were the days of slicing and dicing the victim until they talked. Drugs were quicker, cleaner, and inherently more reliable. Within the hour, they would know everything she knew.

The Old Man was waiting in the library for the two "Bosses." Philip Barberri knew everyone referred to him as the Old Man. He didn't care; he kind of considered it an honor. There were a lot of men in his profession who never lived long enough for such a nickname.

Philip (The Barbarian) Barberri had come to Colorado 30 years ago for his health. Because Chicago was too damp for the arthritis that had attacked his body at an early age, his Mafia family approved the move. No one could ever have guessed how very lucrative his arthritis would prove to be.

He had made his reputation and picked up the nickname early in his Mafia career by demonstrating horrifying and barbaric methods in his work. The bloodier the work, the better it suited him. The conversations usually went something like, "This job could get pretty bloody, better send the Barbarian."

Because Phillip Barberri never hesitated to maim, kill, or destroy everybody in his path, he was feared both within and outside the organization. Even though he no longer took a personal part in the bloody aspects of the business, everyone knew he took a very vicarious interest in such things. Most thought him still perfectly capable of the work himself.

As the Bosses walked in, the Barbarian stared at them.

"Well, do we have the file back?"

One of the Bosses looked at the second in deference to his obviously superior rank. The second spoke while still walking forward. "We got it. After grabbing the girl and coming up empty searching her place, we had campus security get the Professor back to campus. You know, the one she went by to see this afternoon.

"You wouldn't believe how stupid he was. Thought no one would look in the freezer. He must have skipped the class that explained how to hide stolen files."

"Did you bring the girl?"

"She's in the basement. We ought to know something in a few minutes."

The speaker relaxed as he saw the Old Man smile, sit down, and point toward the bar. "Get us a drink. We need to have a little talk about security on that college campus of yours. If a student can get information so easily, think what a trained undercover cop could do. This had better never happen again."

Both Bosses felt a shiver pass through their bodies. Neither thought it was from the air conditioning.

Within 45 minutes, the girl had given up all information requested. She said she felt warm all over and very relaxed. After the questioning she was sent into a deep drug-induced sleep.

"So, the Professor wants to know about our financing, huh?" The Old Man was smiling. "Danny, I want you to call him in tomorrow. Tell him we're working with the FBI on a major sting. Make up something good. Ask him if we can use his financial expertise. Make him believe you think he is God's gift to financial analysis. Shouldn't be hard; all those academic pricks think they're the best at whatever it is they studied."

Danny was Dr. Daniel L. Karp, President of Thunder Mountain College, the Chamber of Commerce man of the year, and all around fair-haired boy down at the local Rotary Club. He was also a Boss in the Colorado Mafia Organization. The L. stood for Luciano, his mother's maiden name.

Dr. Daniel L. Karp was originally from Philadelphia, but one could never tell from his resume. Very little on the resume was real. Almost all of it had come at a high cost involving numerous payoffs. In reality, he was just a smooth-talking, well-dressed wise guy who had been groomed over a period of several years to be President of Thunder Mountain College.

"And tell him you know it's kind of a weird deal, but it'll all be over in a couple of weeks. Promise him an Assistant V.P. job if he helps. He's a greedy prick, so it will probably work."

The President looked at the Old Man in a questioning fashion. "By tomorrow, he'll know the file is gone. How do I handle that?"

The Old Man scrunched his eyebrows in deep thought. "He probably won't volunteer any information about the file. Just tell him to be careful. The bad guys are watching everybody and know a lot about what is happening on campus. He'll probably think they took the file."

Greg Manci was the other Boss in the room. He had doubts about Danny's ability to pull the whole thing off. "Why don't we bring somebody in for the meeting with Gibbs. Say a fake FBI guy with a badge, credentials, and the works. Gibbs will be drooling all over the floor to help."

Greg was Greg Manci, V.P. of Finance at Thunder Mountain College. Much like Danny, his background was also the fictional creation of payoff money.

Daniel Karp concentrated on Manci as he talked. "That's not a bad idea. It'll certainly seal the deal. I've got a question though. Why don't we just kill Gibbs and get it over with? We're only buying a couple of weeks."

"That'll be enough." The Old Man was once again smiling. The smile, however, had no warmth. "By then, The Enforcer from Newport Beach will have resolved the issue. Gibbs is going to die; there is no doubt about that, but it has to look like something other than what it is."

"What about a bad blood killing?" Karp could hardly contain his enthusiasm. There's another faculty dick-head I'd like to unload and this would be perfect. He had a very big and very visible shouting match with Gibbs a few days ago. This'll be perfect."

"Okay, Danny, that sounds like a plan. I'll have our friend from California give you a call for the details. Now for the girl." The Old Man seemed to savor whatever was going on in his mind.

"Oh, and Danny, tomorrow have somebody hack into her e-mail. Send a message to friends, relatives, and the works saying she is tired of school and is heading to California to chill out. Also, have the Registrar drop her from school as if she had requested it. Have security clean out her apartment and lose her car and belongings where they will never be found."

"What about her?" Karp thought he already knew the answer.

The Old Man's face seemed almost flush with excitement. "Oh, don't worry about her. She'll be our guest tonight. No doubt, before morning she'll be just another disillusioned college student heading west to seek her fortune. People will be asking, 'Why doesn't she call?'

"Little Miss Coed has taken her last class. What's left of her will never be found."

Karp and Manci didn't even want to think about what the Old Man meant. Each said a silent prayer that he would never be on the receiving end of the Old Man's vengeance.

Chapter 5

The Enforcer had arrived in Grand Junction, Colorado more than a week ago. His timing had been chosen to coincide with the surge of hunters pouring into the area hoping to bag an elk.

The "hunter" had changed hotels three times already; with each hotel, he had changed his appearance. It really wasn't that hard!

Most people saw what you wanted them to see. During hunting season in the mountains of Colorado, people saw hunters. If you dressed and looked like a typical hunter, that's what you became to most people. Very few looked beyond the camouflage pants and down vest.

The Enforcer had chosen to drive a white GMC truck with a camper shell and Texas plates. Since half the hunters were from Texas, he felt the vehicle would create a certain vehicle anonymity. It had worked. Already, he had seen three almost identical trucks.

At the first hotel, he appeared wearing a padded body suit, a long black hair wig, and full beard. By throwing a couple of "y'alls" and "yes ma'am's" at the desk clerk, he became a middle-aged, 200-pound Texas hunter with unstylishly long hair.

The second hotel checked in a 200-pound, clean shaven Texan with well-trimmed brown hair. Other than the clerk and restaurant wait staff, the Enforcer never spoke to people. If someone spoke, he merely smiled and nodded in acknowledgment.

The third hotel clerk looked up from her computer to see a heavyset, clean shaven middle-aged man with short blond hair. The "Texan" rented a room for one night and paid cash in advance.

He needed to leave very early the next morning to meet up with his hunting guide and did not want to stop at the front desk. Since this request was common among hunters, the clerk never gave it a second thought.

The Enforcer took the room key, thanked the clerk, and walked outside to the parking lot. His white GMC was parked in the side lot between the hotel and the local Denny's restaurant.

He opened the truck door and climbed inside, being careful to notice if anybody was nearby. Reaching behind him, the Enforcer retrieved a small overnight bag. It was on the floor partially concealed under the rear bench seat of the king cab truck.

Opening the bag, he took out a latex glove like those worn by physicians. He slipped it on his left hand and got out of the truck. Firmly closing the truck door, he double checked to make sure it was locked.

With his left hand in his pocket, the heavyset hunter walked toward the motel room. This would be his last night in Grand Junction.

The motel was located right off Interstate 70 about a mile from the local airport. It sat on a commercial strip lined with several other motels, assorted fast-food joints, numerous restaurants, and a couple convenience stores. All in all, a good place to hide.

The room was on the first floor with an outside entrance. The Enforcer liked that; it would be easy to come and go without attracting undue attention.

As the Enforcer glanced back at the parking lot, he could see two other GMC trucks. Although not white, they were close in appearance to his. Even though he was too far away to make out the license plates, he figured at least one was probably from Texas.

Tonight, there would be untold trucks similar to his driving around the town. No doubt, several would carry Texas plates.

If he accomplished his job as it was planned, the number of Texas trucks would become a moot issue. If he screwed up, they would become critical to his escape.

Using his body as a screen, the Enforcer pulled the gloved hand from his pocket. It held the room key which he quickly used to open the door. Slipping through the opening, his elbow was used to close the door.

After flipping on the light switch with the gloved hand, he carefully placed the overnight bag on the end of the room's king-sized bed. Being cautious to not touch anything, he opened the bag and removed another glove for his right hand. There would be no finger prints left in this room.

Even though neither he nor this room would probably ever be associated with the crime planned for tonight, he was not one to take chances. Twenty-seven kills over the past ten years with no association to him attested to his cautious nature.

He planned to sleep six hours before leaving for the evening, but not before giving the room a lived-in look. The last thing he needed was a suspicious maid talking to management about a room that had not been used.

In the bathroom, the shower was briefly run and a towel used to mop up the moisture left in the tub. Soap was unwrapped and run under water; shampoo was poured down the drain; a wash cloth was dampened and thrown on the edge of the tub along with the damp towel. It would appear tomorrow morning as if the "hunter" had showered at night so he could get an early start.

The Enforcer put the overnight bag on the dresser and threw back the bedspread. On one side of the massive king bed, he laid out a complete change of clothing. It included shoes, socks, underwear and everything else. All the items had been purchased two weeks ago in Vegas and were still in the original packages.

The Enforcer remembered being lectured on such things by his mentor, a mob button man whom he stupidly tried to mug one night. After taking his knife and knocking him on his can, the button man had laughed.

Apparently, the mobster saw something he liked in the ragged, half-starved, unskilled young mugger. He took him home. That had been almost 20 years ago.

The kid never really knew what kind of crime the mobster was involved in until the button man showed up one night about 11 years ago with a bullet in his back. Knowing he could never exercise his special brand of crime again, he began to teach his adopted son the trade.

As it turned out, the unskilled mugger was a natural in the "Murder, Inc." business. After a year of training and with careful planning help from the old hit man, the mugger turned professional killer had successfully done his first piece of work.

There was no remorse or guilt after the kill. It was, after all, just business. Business had been brisk ever since.

One of the Enforcer's first lessons had been that a kill must be absolutely sterile and without the remotest chance of finger print evidence. That meant all clothing and other tools of the hit could never be handled without gloves.

If there were a problem with the job and something went wrong, then there would be zero probability of prints connecting him to the crime. So far, that had never happened, but you never knew when the unexpected might happen.

The Enforcer lay down on the bed opposite the clothing. He set his mental alarm to wake him in six hours.

Chapter 6

Tarr Baldridge, Professor of Marketing at Thunder Mountain College, was going on a date. He had arrived at *The Sanctuary* a few minutes early. Being habitually early was one of his well ingrained personality traits. Not many things created stress in his life these days. Being late was one of them.

He was also a little nervous. Tonight would be the first date he had in over a year. Dating had never been easy for him. A loner lifestyle seemed to suit him better. That didn't mean he was alone, though. He had lots of students, professional colleagues, friends, and his brother to keep him company. At the end of the day, however, he always enjoyed the solitude and comfort of his condo.

After seeing the newest History Professor in August at the College's back to school meeting, he had been re-evaluating his lifestyle. She was a tall, slim creature with a bunch of thick dark red hair that hung to her shoulders and framed sky blue eyes.

Tarr had gotten to know her on the Academic Policies Committee. He had been on the committee for three years; she was the newest appointee. They met the second Tuesday of every month at 3:30.

Colleges are the worst form of bureaucracy one could possibly imagine. Nothing is done without being studied and talked to death. Tarr and all the other college professors had to serve on what seemed to be an endless list of committees. Finally, a positive impact from all his service, though; he had a date.

He had asked her to join him for dinner while walking out of the building following their meeting on Tuesday. With the smile that seemed to come so easily to her face, she had accepted.

She agreed to meet him at the restaurant about 7:00; she had something to do that could run late. Tarr knew that was just a polite way of showing up in her own car. He knew that if the dinner went poorly, she'd make up an excuse and leave early. That was okay. It left him with the same option.

Tarr didn't consider the arrangements deceitful, just smart. A boring date could seem like an eternity if you picked her up at her door, had dinner, and then had to drive her back home.

Tarr liked her better already. She obviously was a good thinker who planned ahead and thought well on her feet.

His thinking was jerked back to present reality by the maître d' escorting his date to the table. Tarr rose from his seat and smiled as she was seated.

"Hello, Dr. Baldridge." She returned his smile as she adjusted the chair's position more to her liking.

"Hello, Dr. Rader." Tarr reciprocated with the same level of formality she had used. It was not at all uncommon for professors to refer to each other by their academic titles. Probably in recognition of the many years of study required to achieve them.

"This is really a nice restaurant, Tarr; I've been wondering what it looked like on the inside." She was gazing around the small dining room at the original art hanging on the walls. Apparently it was alright to drop the formality.

"So, this is the first time you've been here."

"Yes, it's a little out of the price range of a new non-tenured Assistant Professor. A tenured Full Professor like you probably comes here on a regular basis." There was no sarcasm intended; she was, however, making a small joke at his expense.

"What's good here?" The beautiful redhead asked as she studied the menu.

"The fish is fresh and the steak tender. They also have some of the best escargot this side of France, if your taste buds crave snails."

"Oh, I love escargot, especially in mushroom caps. If that's the way they're served, I'd love to split an order. I also love all kinds of fish. Since you're the regular in here, why don't you order for both of us?"

"Trusting your stomach to me may be risky, but if you insist, I'll go for it."

"I insist." she said.

A very stuffy looking and very proper waiter dressed in a tuxedo had approached the table and was looking at the couple. "Hello, my name is Melvin and I will be assisting you with your dinner this evening. Would you like a cocktail before dinner? Madame?"

"I'll have a white wine, house will be fine."

"Sir?"

"I'll have Jack Daniels straight, on the rocks. Thanks."

"If you would like to go ahead with your dinner order, I won't have to disturb you for a while. I'll send it to the kitchen in about 15 minutes."

"That would be great." Tarr had laid the menu aside and was giving the order from memory. "We'll start with escargot in mushroom caps followed by Caesar Salad prepared table side. We'll cleanse our pallets with your premium Champaign sherbet and then have baked Monk fish. Also, two more glasses of your house white wine served at the same time as the meal. Thanks."

The waiter took their menus and walked briskly away.

Tarr looked at his lovely dinner companion with somewhat of a perplexed expression on his face. "You know, I've been seeing you in the Academic Policy Committee meetings and around campus for almost three months now and I still don't know what to call you. Do you prefer Dondria or something else?"

"My ex-husband insisted upon calling me Dondria, all my friends call me Doni."

Tarr laughed, "How bout I start the evening calling you Doni? If my charm doesn't impress you and we don't make it to after dinner coffee, I'll switch to Dr. Rader for our future committee meetings."

"Sounds like a plan to me." She had a directness about her that, no doubt, had intimidated many men in her time. "So, tell me about Dr. Tarr Baldridge. You can start with your childhood and work forward, then I'll do the same."

"Do you want the abridged version or a bit more detail?"

Tarr smiled as he studied her face for clues to her personality. He was curious if directness was just her natural style or, instead, some kind of defense mechanism.

"How about abridged for the childhood and progressively more detailed as we get closer to the present? Especially about ex-wives, prison records, sexual perversions, textbooks written, and why a guy your age has to walk with a cane." She seemed as comfortable with Tarr as she would with any friend of long standing.

Tarr laughed out loud. This was definitely a different kind of lady. "Okay. Fifty years ago an eleven pound five ounce boy was born. I joined an older but much uglier and far less sophisticated brother."

She was smiling at his joke as he continued. "While we were still in elementary school ..."

Chapter 7

Tarr was smiling as he turned from his building's drive into the underground parking garage. His date had lasted almost three hours.

He was still smiling as he pointed the car toward one of three reserved parking spaces that had his apartment's number very prominently stamped both on the floor and wall in front. He had two vehicles, but one of them required almost two spaces.

Around town, Tarr drove a ten-year-old Cadillac. It had low mileage and was very dependable. For the road, however, he drove something a little bit bigger and heavier. It was too big to drive around town conveniently, but nothing could beat it for long-distance travel or off-road needs.

Dr. Tarr Baldridge had two extravagances in his life. One was his penthouse apartment in Monument Towers, the only high-rise residential building in Grand Junction, Colorado. The second was his one-year-old tan turbo diesel Hummer.

At 72 inches wide with 16-inch ground clearance, his "truck" was usually the baddest non-commercial, non-military thing on the road. Originally, he had needed a vehicle that could get him to his brother's house and back. Depending on time of year, the trek could involve ice, snow, sand, mud, and water or all the above.

Since switching to the Hummer, he had never been stuck. It was also a comfortable fit for his 6'4", 240- pound body. He had very little body fat thanks to a very good weight room, but he was still a rather sizable specimen.

Getting out of the Cadillac, he locked it and glanced over at the Hummer. Ever since he got it, people had asked, "Why a Hummer?"

Well, first of all, it can go almost anywhere. Even with 16 inches of ground clearance, it is virtually impossible to turn over because of its width. It can drive in up to three feet of water and its weight will insure safety in almost any type of collision, even head-on.

The most important reason, though, was probably because he fell in love with its uniqueness the first time he saw one. As he was driving through west Denver, there it was on the north side of the interstate on an elevated lift for him and the world to see. Three months later, he had one in the underground garage.

Tarr walked across the garage to the elevator. As was his nature, he quickly scanned the brightly lit area for anything out of the ordinary. In a previous life, such behavior was a result of intensive training. In this life, it was probably somewhat paranoid. He laughed to himself as his thoughts reminded him of what an old mentor had once said about being paranoid.

"Just because you're paranoid, doesn't mean they're not after you."

What did a middle-aged college Professor like Tarr have to fear? Very little, he hoped.

All he saw was the garage attendant waving at him from the comfort of a small, glass-enclosed booth. He knew the booth contained a video monitor that covered the part of the garage out of sight of the booth.

Supporting much of his weight on the silver and ivory handled cane in his left hand, he used his right index finger to press the elevator button. It opened almost immediately.

Instead of pushing a floor button, Tarr used a key to activate the penthouse button. Most floors contained six to eight apartments; the penthouse floor, only two. The elevator rapidly rose from the garage level, past the lobby level, and up seven more levels to his floor.

Tarr hardly ever went to the lobby other than to greet an infrequent guest or more likely a consulting client. The business spaces available never failed to impress.

The lobby itself was very opulent by almost anybody's standards. It was lavishly furnished with richly polished dark oak paneling and leather furniture. The three main sitting areas each had an expensive oriental rug on the granite floor. On the main wall was a six foot high native stone fireplace.

The stairway leading up from the lobby was wide and curved. It sported a highly burnished brass railing which gleamed in the overhead chandelier. Tarr had often wondered who polished the thing.

To get inside the lobby from guest parking, a person had to be buzzed in by a doorman who occupied a heavy antique desk within sight of the front door. He communicated with them via an intercom built into the outside wall and connected to the desk. No one was permitted entry without the doorman finding their name on a visitor's list or first calling the resident being visited.

Residents almost never used the front door. They usually came up from the garage. Its entry was protected by a floor to ceiling electronic gate. Full-time attendants who staffed the garage 24 hours a day made sure it was never left open. They also provided security in the garage and manned a car washing bay. The card used to activate the garage gate could also be used to enter the building's front door.

The building's security was top flight and very unusual for a western Colorado town with little random crime. The building had been constructed many years earlier during an oil shale boom in the area. No expense was spared.

Initially the building, named Monument Towers, had been built for East Coast executives who needed a part-time home in the area. Now, years after the boom had turned into a bust, it was home to mostly California retirees who had discovered the area.

The building's tenant association had maintained the high level of security, not so much to prevent crime, as to insure privacy and exclusivity. Tarr had moved to the building because it suited his lifestyle and because it had a great view off his patios. The view west from the large patio was of the Colorado National Monument; the view east from the master bedroom patio was of the Grand Mesa and Mount Garfield.

Tarr also liked the health club like amenities on the lobby level of the building. There was a large swimming pool, complete weight room, billiard room, four guest suites for visitors and four mini-conference rooms available to conduct business.

Since he traveled quite a bit when the college was not in session, Monument Towers was perfect. He never had to be concerned about his home while out of town.

Monument Towers was the most expensive condo building in Grand Junction. Most of Tarr's colleagues at Thunder Mountain thought he could afford to live there and drive a Hummer because of the extra income he made from two top-selling textbooks and his corporate consulting.

Tarr did make an extra hundred grand or so a year from the outside activities, but that plus his salary would not pay for his current lifestyle. The real truth was that he earned another $150,000 a year in interest income from a trust established by his mother before her death. His brother, Lucky, earned the same amount.

There was also the $50,000 tax-free he received as disability income from the federal government. When all was said and done, Dr. Tarr Baldridge had an average annual income in the neighborhood of $400,000 a year.

Living in Monument Towers and owning the Hummer were expensive pieces of his lifestyle. Each did, however, make life easier for him.

The elevator door opened to a small lobby. Two ornate

doors faced each other from opposite ends of the tastefully decorated space. Each led to a penthouse.

Tarr lived in one and Mr. and Mrs. Jay Chesterfield lived in the other. Currently, the Chesterfields were on a yearlong cruise around the world. For the next few months, Tarr had the top floor to himself.

He pulled keys from his right front pocket and unlocked the door. Stepping through the doorway into the foyer, Tarr flipped on the lights and stepped to a security panel with a flashing red light. Entering a series of numbers, the light turned green. Entering another series of numbers, the light went off.

Tarr's home security system was a step above most and had been installed by his brother. Knowing a good technician could bypass the electronics of the basic system, a backup was installed. It was almost impossible to detect. If either were tripped, a silent alarm was activated both at the alarm company and the doorman's desk. A not-so-silent alarm was activated in the apartment.

"Probably overkill," Tarr thought to himself. "Why would anyone come after a college professor?" His brother, Lucky, had insisted on the security, though. So far, it had not been needed.

Tarr's walking cane made a slight noise on the cherry-wood floor as he made his way out of the foyer and past the kitchen. The apartment was much more than he really needed, but he liked the space. He considered a nice home and a nice vehicle to be the rewards of life.

He had the apartment completely gutted and remodeled before moving in. An interior decorator may not have agreed with what he had done, but it suited him.

Adjacent to the foyer, sliding tempered glass panels on stainless-steel tracks separated the state-of-the-art kitchen from the two living areas. One area, a large library, was enclosed by a wall of tempered glass. It was sparsely furnished in an oriental style.

The other space was a large living room. It was furnished with distressed leather chairs and contained a built-in gas fireplace.

On each end of the living space was a bedroom suite with a king-size bed, small sitting space, walk-in closet, and a full bath. Both bedrooms had built-in bed platforms and granite baths. Each bath contained an oversized Jacuzzi tub and separate walk-in, twin-head shower.

The master bedroom had a few extra features Tarr and Lucky had added after the contractor left. The most important was a concealed six foot by two foot by one foot safe in the bed platform. Tarr kept some cash and a few private items there.

The overall decor had a kind of western Colorado flair combined with oriental influences. It was made even stranger with his minimalist approach to furnishings. Not exactly something prompting Architectural Digest to come a calling, but it was comfortable.

Since the apartment occupied the entire south end of the floor, a large wrap-around patio was attached. It could be accessed from either bedroom or the living room. If truth be told, Tarr probably spent more time on the patio than inside.

After pouring himself a double brandy, Tarr undressed and settled in to a hot bath with the jets on high. His left knee was reminding him why he walked with the aid of a cane.

As the hot pulsating water worked on his knee from the outside and warm brandy from the inside, Tarr laid his head back and relaxed. His mind drifted back to Doni and his date.

Chapter 8

The place for their date was *The Sanctuary*, arguably the best restaurant in Grand Junction, Colorado. It was located in an old stone building that had, at one time, housed a Catholic Church.

The old auditorium of the church was now a large dining room that could easily handle 150 diners. For those desiring a cozier ambiance, a half dozen small dining rooms such as the one seating Doni and Tarr, were available.

Reservations were almost always required at *The Sanctuary*, the food was delicious, and the service excellent. It never failed to deliver a most satisfying dining experience.

Tarr continued to answer his date's questions.

"While we were still in elementary school, our parents were killed. Our lives took a decided change at that point. Lucky and I came to live with our mother's father west of here up in the Glade Park area."

"Lucky? Tarr? You guys have unusual names. What's up with that?"

Tarr took a breath and continued. "Lucky is a nickname for my brother's given name, Luckley. Tarr is my actual given name. We were both named after our mother's side of the family. Her maiden name was Luckley and her mother's maiden name was Tarr. Our mother was concerned that her family names not be lost to future generations."

"Your parent's death and subsequent relocation to the mountains must have been very traumatic on you two." Doni's expression revealed sincere concern.

"Well, we were young enough that we got over it quickly; the way kids do. The hardest part was leaving the city and moving in to what we thought was a cave with a man we had never seen."

Doni's expression changed from concern to curiosity. "A cave? A man you had never seen? You're joking, right?"

"Not really. Our grandfather was a government engineer who traveled all over the world. I later figured out that our father didn't care for him, so other than coming to see each of us when we were born, he did not visit. He had just retired and moved to Colorado when our parents went down in a plane over the Swiss Alps."

"But, what about the cave comment?"

Tarr allowed a somewhat sneaky grin to work its way out. "Well, it looked like a cave to small boys. In reality it was a house built into the face of a granite cliff. Back in those days, it was very unusual.

"Using explosives, grandpa had created a big space back into the rock. It must be 3,000 square feet. He then used the granite blasted out to enclose the entire front. It has two large windows for light and a door.

"When he got through, you could never tell anything had been done. A large outcropping of rocks creates a natural wall about twenty feet in front of the opening and conceals the house.

"It also creates kind of a naturally enclosed patio out front. There's just enough space between the rocks for a man to squeeze through.

"Further down the cliff face he blasted out a garage and storage space. He didn't put windows in the garage, though, just an industrial type overhead door. After he painted the door to match the surrounding rocks, it was hard to see.

"A stranger could never find the place. Grandpa was just as unusual as his house! He was a loner who never remarried after our grandmother died. He wanted to live his life in the solitude of the mountains with no interference.

"In preparation for retirement he searched all over the west for the right kind of location. He found it up on Glade Park with a 5,000 acre piece of land with little more than granite hills and scrub brush.

"Lucky and I were obviously not a part of the plan. He took us in, though; educated us, taught us to hunt, fish, and live off the land; and loved us enough to make up for the loss of our parents."

"You said he educated you?"

"That's right," Tarr replied to the beautiful redhead. "He homeschooled us before it was a trendy thing to do. There was really no choice; the closest school was in Grand Junction. You've got to remember this was a long time ago before the roads were paved. Even today, it's still difficult to get to the ranch without serious off-road transportation."

Doni was caught up in the story by now. "You talk about this place like it still exists. Does it?"

"As a matter of fact, my brother and I still own the place. You've got to remember, we were both raised to be loners. It took more with Lucky than me. After he retired from the Navy, he came back home. He lives in the house much like our grandpa, no doubt, intended when it was built."

Doni watched Tarr as he spoke. "Well, that explains why you have your own loner reputation. A couple of my colleagues in the History Department couldn't ever remember you socializing to the extent of actually going out on a date. To what do I owe the honor?"

Tarr let out a laugh befitting his size. A diner across the room turned to stare. "I religiously go on at least one date a year to maintain my heterosexual standing in the community. You happened to be the closest female around when I thought of it."

"Flattery like that probably ensures you have a lot of first dates and no seconds." She threw her red hair back as she laughed.

Tarr was laughing as he watched his dinner companion.

"This one might be worth a second date," he thought.

"I suppose I've got to do better than that, huh? Well, I travel a lot and spend most of my time consulting or writing. Dating hardly ever seemed worth the effort.

"When I saw you at the back to school meeting in August, however, I reconsidered. It's taken me this long to plan my approach. My initial reaction is that you could well be worth the effort."

Her eyes were smiling, but at the same time boring into his. "Try again, Professor. There's something else. Some girl broke your heart or you're a pervert or something.

"I know! You've been married and divorced and she took you to the cleaners after running off with your best friend. Or maybe you prey on all those young, pretty marketing students."

"None of the above," Tarr replied in a jovial but more somber tone. "I was married, though, back in my twenties."

Doni had detected the slight change in Tarr's demeanor. "I'm sorry, Tarr. I don't really know you well enough to joke like that. I apologize if I strayed into sensitive territory."

"That's okay; it was a long time ago. I was married when I was 22. She died three years later. I've never remarried."

Doni reached across the table and touched his hand. "I'm sorry, I have a tendency toward directness that isn't always polite. Do you want to tell me what happened after that?"

"I went back to school, got an MBA and then doctorate. I went to work for the feds in the Federal Trade Commission for a number of years, got fed up with Washington, was lucky enough to get a job back home at Thunder Mountain College, and have been here ever since.

"Because of the federal work, I'm able to get about all the consulting work I want. Those contacts also helped me get my first textbook contract. Because it sold well, I got a second. Those things allow me to ask beautiful redheads out to dinner at *The Sanctuary*.

"Let me think, have I forgotten anything? Oh, yes, the cane. That is courtesy of a car wreck which shattered my left knee."

Tarr had not kept count. Was the story about his knee lie number two or three?

She glanced over the top of her wine glass with an embarrassed expression. "This is probably why I don't have many second dates. My ex-husband used to tell me that directness was cute in a small child but not so much in an adult. He told me it brought to mind the word, bitch.

"I'm sorry if I come across as a nosey bitch. I don't mean to; it's just that your story is very interesting."

Tarr was watching her with increasing attention as he unsuccessfully tried to suppress another belly laugh. "I'm sorry," he said as the diner across the room once again turned and stared. "Your honesty is so damn funny and refreshing at the same time. Is there anything else you want to know?"

"Well, you forgot prison records and sexual perversions."

"What a lady!" Tarr thought.

"I've never been in prison," he said, "but the cane does have alternate uses."

As her complexion reddened to almost her hair color, she looked at her obviously entertained companion. "I guess I deserved that."

Thankfully, dinner was starting with the arrival of the escargot. Conversation turned to the college and people they had in common there. Doni asked Tarr numerous questions related to his department and what he taught.

Conversation ceased as the salad chef performed his show tableside. As the Monk fish was served, conversation returned to questions for Tarr.

"So," she said between bites of the fish. "What's this I hear about you living in a penthouse and driving a Hummer? Is that true?"

"Yes, both things are true. I expense out a great deal of the penthouse cost as business. I not only write there, I also deal with consulting clients. It's really more for business than anything else."

Tarr didn't think another small lie would hurt at this point in their relationship. It obviously wasn't the only one he had told tonight. There were some things about his past that were still classified information buried very deep in a government computer somewhere. Lying seemed the best course of action.

Her raised eyebrow, in response to Tarr's answer, told him she didn't completely buy his story. She didn't say anything, though, so he continued.

"The Hummer is just an expensive toy that I justify by saying it's necessary to get back and forth to the cliff house."

"Now, a truthful answer." Her expression was one of curiosity. "How big is the thing?"

He told her.

"How much does one cost?" She asked even knowing it was a rude question.

"Mine cost about 80 grand."

"What kind of gas mileage does it get?" Obviously a safer question she thought.

"Well, mine is a diesel. It gets about 14 miles per gallon."

"Is there anywhere it can't go?" She was intrigued by this point.

"Water more than about three feet might stop it, but little else.

"How fast will it go?"

"Only about 90; speed is not its forte. Strength is."

The Monk fish was gone and the table cleared. Both declined dessert, opting for an after dinner coffee. As the coffee was served and the waiter walked away, Doni looked at Tarr. "My turn now?"

Tarr nodded his head in an affirmative response to her question.

Her story took up the better part of an hour. As she was winding down, she did what any good teacher does, she summarized the story for Tarr. "So, in summary just in case you missed something, I'm a farm girl from Ault, Colorado. We farmed beets just south of the Colorado – Wyoming border.

"My high school sweetheart and I went to college at the University of Colorado in Boulder, graduated together and got married. While he worked on his law degree, I started graduate school in history.

"He got his Law Degree; I got my Masters. We went off to Denver to start the American dream. The dream ended about ten years later.

"We woke up one morning, looked at each other, had a heart-to-heart talk, and decided to go our separate ways. I went off to get a doctorate and he went off to become Denver's best criminal defense lawyer.

"I got my degree last May and my first teaching job at Thunder Mountain College. My ex is indeed the best criminal defense lawyer in Denver. My only regret is in not asking for alimony."

The date was nearing its end as Tarr and Doni walked through *The Sanctuary's* massive oak front doors. The cool air refreshed them both as they walked across what used to be the church's parking lot toward their cars.

Tarr looked down into her blue eyes as they stopped by her Honda. "You know, for a self-proclaimed bitch and fiery redhead, you're really lots of fun. How about the elusive second date?"

She looked up at his dark form and grinned. "How can a girl turn down such a charming offer? You should have been a poet. It's worth a second date just to hear more of your romantic oration. Give me a call."

Tarr held the car door as she climbed in. This was quite a woman.

Chapter 9

The Enforcer's eyes popped open. Glancing over at the bedside clock, he smiled with satisfaction. He had been asleep for five hours and fifty minutes. His mental alarm had never failed him.

Working quickly but efficiently, the Enforcer undressed and placed his clothing in the overnight bag. Standing by the bed as naked as the day he started life, he slipped into black underwear, a snug fitting, long-sleeved black cotton tee shirt, black pants, black socks, and black sneakers.

Around his waist, he attached a slightly oversized black fanny pack. Into the pack, he placed the only non-clothing items he had brought into the room. First, a state-of-the-art prototype pair of night vision glasses was put in an outside, easily accessed pocket along with a cell phone and a sap glove.

Second, a lock pick was put in the large center pocket. It was a device resembling a small gun in shape. He could defeat any home-type lock within 20 seconds. A small flashlight and lock-blade pocket knife joined the pick.

In a special concealment compartment next to the back of the pack resting against the body, the Enforcer placed a small-frame five-shot 357 magnum revolver. The pack was one of the new ones designed to conceal a handgun. It had been created for the large number of citizens who legally carried concealed weapons.

He hoped the new fanny packs didn't catch on very well. An armed citizen who knew how to shoot was a criminal's worst nightmare.

The Enforcer dropped the truck keys into his pocket. Picking up the motel room key, he headed for the bathroom.

Using the still damp towel, he carefully wiped away any prints. He didn't want any prints left at the hotel. Keys were easy; it was the registration form that was always the hardest.

The Enforcer left nothing to chance. If he somehow made a mistake and was traced to the hotel, the trail would end. There would be no prints.

Most unskilled criminals forgot about the prints on the registration form. It was almost impossible to sign the thing without leaving several good prints.

The Enforcer had developed a system years ago. He would walk in to the motel, inquire about a room, and hand the clerk a phony credit card, which he had just removed from his wallet.

When the clerk made an imprint of the card and presented it for a signature, the Enforcer simply laid the wallet on the form and used it as a rest for his left hand. Then he signed the form, took his credit card back, and put it back into his wallet. No prints.

The pen he used was not a concern for two reasons. First, its round surface made getting a clear print almost impossible. Second, within an hour, a dozen other people would handle it.

When he paid cash for a room, he signed nothing and the cash disappeared into the register, never to be associated with him again.

Throwing the room key onto the dresser, the Enforcer opened the door and stepped into the dark. He had a stop to make before the main event.

Chapter 10

Art Gibbs was sitting on his back patio having a drink. It had been almost two weeks since he had first seen the file. The night of the burglary at his office had been a weird one. When he got home after spending almost two hours with campus security, his house had been broken into.

The file was gone. Obviously, whoever took it knew he had read it. He didn't know what to do, so he left home and spent the night in a motel. He needed time to think.

He showed up at his office early the next day intent on calling the FBI. Convinced he was about to be killed, there seemed to be no other option.

The phone next to his desk was ringing as he walked in. The caller ID indicated the call was coming from Dr. Karp, President of the college. He had never spoken to the President other than at receptions and public functions. He certainly didn't know him well enough for a personal call.

Tentatively lifting the phone to his ear, he spoke into the mouth piece. "Hello, this is Dr. Gibbs."

"Dr. Gibbs." The voice on the other end was very pleasant and very female. "President Karp asked me to call and see if you could meet him in his office at 8:30 for coffee. He said it wouldn't take long."

"Of course, I'll be there. Thanks for the call." Gibbs was visibly shaking as he returned the phone to its cradle. Sinking in to his chair, he tried to clear his head. What could the President want? Did he know about the file? If he did, why was he being so nice?

At 8:20, Gibbs left his office to make the five minute walk

to the President's office. Walking across the college quad, he encountered several students from his classes. If the day had been normal, he would have ignored them as if they were unseen. Being a very abnormal day, he ignored them because they were unseen. His mind was totally focused on the meeting.

Gibbs walked up the long concrete ramp and into the building. Turning left, he climbed the short flight of stairs taking him up to the mezzanine. Immediately he stepped through the door on his left.

A middle-aged secretary looked up as he walked in. "Dr. Gibbs?"

"Yes, I'm Dr. Gibbs."

"The President is expecting you. You may go on in." She was gesturing toward an open door, which no doubt led in to the President's private office.

Gibbs walked into the office to find three people waiting. The President he knew by sight as he did the second man, Dr. Manci, V.P. of Finance. The third man, he had never seen before.

Manci was a very unpleasant surprise. They must know about the file. But why were they all smiling? Something was going on and he wasn't sure it would be a good thing for him.

What Gibbs didn't know was that the men had just gotten back into town from Aspen. It would have made him soil his pants to know that he had been the topic of conversation most of the way.

Not being satisfied with the original explanation for the files missing from his house, they had brain-stormed different scenarios for their disappearance.

The reason for the three men's smiles was a better plan. A plan that was ironclad. One that would keep the very nosey Dr. Gibbs quiet for the next two weeks. After that, he would be quiet forever.

All three men stood as Gibbs walked tentatively into the

plush office. Gibbs was not in the mood to admire the dark green carpet and custom crafted pecan furniture. He didn't even notice the wall of photos pairing the President with state and national politicians or the wall full of plaques and certificates noting an almost endless list of honors.

Gibbs was interested in one thing and one thing only. Surviving the next ten minutes with his job intact. Furnishings held little interest for him at the present time.

"Dr. Gibbs, thank you so much for joining us on such short notice. Like my secretary said, this shouldn't take very long." The President spoke with a smile and a style polished over years of meetings and public speaking engagements. "I believe you know Greg Manci and this is Gordon Teter, Special Agent for the FBI out of their Denver office."

The President used his most sincere and patronizing smile as he continued. "Have a seat Dr. Gibbs. May I offer you a cup of coffee?"

Art Gibbs was so nervous he knew he could never handle a cup of hot coffee. "No thanks, I'm fine."

All four men sat down as the President continued. "Dr. Gibbs, you are a part of something that probably needs explaining. I think it best that Agent Teter fill you in on what is going on including the burglary of your house last night."

Gibbs felt his very structured life spinning out of control and knew that a fatal crash was imminent. Instead of speaking, however, he merely turned his head in the direction of the FBI agent. It took all of his training and will-power to appear calm on the outside while a hurricane of immense proportions was circling around his gut.

Agent Teter held Gibbs's eyes with his own as he spoke. "Let me start from the beginning. At the beginning of the semester, we placed an undercover agent in the finance office. You know her as your student, Kelsie Daggett.

"Agent Daggett's assignment was to investigate a possible

money laundering scheme being developed using the college and its European campuses. An informer had put us on to the operation. He told us the college comptroller was the inside man, but he didn't know the outside connection.

"Our investigation drew a blank for the first month, but then you entered the equation. Agent Daggett developed a plan using you that she thought would lead us to the outside connection. Washington approved the plan and we put it into motion.

"The plan was simple in its design. Agent Daggett would keep her eyes open for some sort of information that appeared sensitive. Once she found something that looked promising, she would steal it.

"She would then pass the information on to you. After that, we would just sit back and see who crawled out of the woodwork. You were never in any danger; we have had you under surveillance since the files were delivered to your house.

"We knew we had hit pay dirt when Agent Daggett's apartment was searched while she was at your house. The burglary at your office on campus was staged to get you out of the house. It was imperative that you be safely out of the way.

"Two very scary guys showed up at your place not long after you left. It took them about ten minutes to find the files and leave. We were glad you didn't take time to hide them.

"To make a long story short, we followed the three guys to their contact, a wanna be wise guy from Denver. All four are now in Federal lock-up. Their college contact is being picked up at his house about now.

"So, as you can see, the whole thing is over. We apologize for using you in our case, but we felt it was the most expedient way. Let me assure you that your safety was never compromised. We've had a protective team on you from the beginning.

"Agent Daggett is on her way back to Washington and everything around Thunder Mountain can get back to normal. I felt it would be best if we explained all this to you before you got nervous about the burglary and went to the police.

"Since the press will no doubt get on to this in a few days, we wanted to ask you not to comment to them or speak to anybody about your involvement. It is doubtful that you will have to testify or have further involvement at all."

Gibbs was dumbfounded; he had been too shocked to speak during Agent Teter's recount of the case. He was still shocked. What was the College going to do to him? He had, after all, gotten College records in an unethical way. Illegal? Probably not, but unethical nevertheless. "Of course, I won't discuss this issue with anybody. What about my job though? What I did wasn't exactly kosher. Am I in trouble?"

Agent Teter and V. P. Manci both broke into broad grins as the President responded. "In trouble? No way. Agent Daggett told us you just wanted to know more about college finance. She made it clear that you had the best interest of Thunder Mountain at heart and under no circumstances did you have a criminal motive.

"She was very impressed with your knowledge and told me that you were being wasted on a classroom assignment. After the way you have handled yourself, I have to agree.

"If you can keep everything said here today confidential, I will personally guarantee that beginning next semester; you will be the new Associate Dean of the Business School. You will have proven your loyalty and it will have been rewarded.

"Now, I know you have a class starting before long. I also know you must have a lot of questions. Why don't we all just sit tight for a couple of weeks and let things sink in? After that, I'll have you over to the house for dinner and we can talk about your future."

"I don't know what to say." Gibbs was visibly flustered and at a loss for words. "Thank you for your faith in me; I won't let you down. Please tell Agent Daggett thank you for me."

All three men shook Gibbs's hand and thanked him in their most sincere manner before he was escorted out of the President's Office, through the outer office and into the hallway. Shaking his hand one final time, the President smiled and walked back into his office area.

Gibbs reversed his earlier trip and headed back across the open quad toward his office. He had no intention, however, of going to class. His mind was too preoccupied with grandiose thoughts about the future. The stupid clods masquerading as students were on their own today.

Boy was he lucky. Someone had handed him a pile of manure and he had crafted a pie of it. Associate Dean, what a deal. Tarr Baldridge and the rest of the Business Faculty pricks could eat their hearts out. His brilliance had finally been recognized.

Wait until they discovered he had been invited to the President's house for dinner. Dr. Arthur Gibbs's career had just taken a very positive turn. Immediately, he began to fantasize about what he was going to do to his least favorite faculty member.

As Associate Dean, he intended to make academic life very miserable for one Dr. Tarr Baldridge, Professor of Marketing. When he was through with him, Baldridge would be working the third shift at the local convenience store, if he could still get a job.

Chapter 11

The Enforcer slowed the pick-up truck as he neared the high-rise apartment building. It was nearing midnight and traffic was light. His plan called for him to get off the streets within the next thirty minutes. Small town cops have a tendency to pay attention to out-of-state vehicles prowling around after most folks are safely home in their beds.

It had been an hour since he left the motel. Changing the tires on the truck had gone exactly as planned. The new tires had been waiting for him in a garage located in a scrap yard down by the river. As he had instructed, no one else was around.

While wearing a pair of lightweight work gloves, he changed the four tires. The old tires went inside the camper shell; he'd need them later.

He drove away from the river and toward the apartment building. There was one thing left to do before going to Gibbs's house.

Turning into the public drive in front of Monument Towers, the Enforcer could see a new mini van parked in one of the spaces. That would be his "watcher."

The white GMC truck continued through the parking lot and back into the street. The Enforcer pulled to the curb a hundred yards past the apartment. Taking his cell phone from the fanny pack, he punched in a phone number. It was answered on the second ring with one word, "Yes?"

The Enforcer responded with three, "Is he there?"

The voice of the watcher was calm and detached. "He got home about 10:00 alone. He's been there ever since. The lights went off about 20 minutes ago. I'd say he's in for the evening."

"Call me if there's any activity or change." The Enforcer

punched the cancel call button, switched the ring option from sound to vibration, and put the phone in his front pants pocket.

It took exactly 14 minutes to reach Gibbs's house. The Enforcer parked on a side street where a dozen other vehicles were parked. He got out of the truck, locked it, and started walking down the sidewalk. To a casual observer, he was a guy coming home for the evening.

The Enforcer had parked here several times during the past week. By now, no one would think the truck out of place.

Each time he had done the same thing. Park, get out, and walk away. About a hundred feet from where he parked, a large shrub and tree created shadows. He stopped unobserved in the shadows. For 30 minutes, he observed the neighborhood and listened.

Satisfied that he had aroused no suspicion, he slipped the night vision glasses from the pack and put them on. Unlike earlier such devices which were large and uncomfortable, the new prototype wasn't much larger than a pair of prescription glasses.

The new size was made possible by the use of an improved generation of small batteries. The device was powered by three, each about the size of the nail on your small finger.

Taking his time not to make noise and following the path he had worked out days ago, he worked his way down a connecting alley and into Gibbs's backyard.

The Enforcer positioned himself next to a small storage shed within view of the rear of the house. The master bedroom was a short distance away.

The Enforcer left nothing to chance. By observing the house three times before, he knew where Gibbs slept and what lights were normally on at night. Tonight, nothing was out of the ordinary.

He settled in to observe, just as he had done on the previous visits. The observation would last until 4:50 am. The Enforcer believed in patience and observation. By 4:50, his senses would be fully tuned to the rhythms of the neighborhood and it to him. Any animals in the area would be accustomed to his scents and have accepted them as non-threatening.

At 4:50 he would make his move. Until then, he would be completely immobile. Like any other deadly predator, he would become invisible until the strike. Then with speed, cunning, and no mercy, he would seek out and kill his prey.

Chapter 12

Tarr stood in his darkened bedroom and gazed out the window at the moonlit Colorado National Monument looming a few miles to the west. The view, no doubt, accounted for the name of the apartment building.

All in all, it had been a good night. Doni had been a very pleasant surprise. He knew he could get a lot more interested in her, if he let himself. Maybe it was time to think about a less solitary life.

It had been a long time since he had anybody special in his life. The timing was good. He had a regular type job in a regular town. Danger was not part of his life any longer.

She seemed like she might like to get to know him better. At the end of the date, she had agreed to a second. Yes, it was time!

Chapter 13

Gibbs checked the front and back doors twice to make sure everything was locked up for the night. Pausing by the front door, he turned on a small nightlight. After checking the back door off the laundry room, he walked through the kitchen to the living room.

The master bedroom was right off the living room down a short hall which contained the bath. Stepping into the bathroom, Gibbs turned on another nightlight.

He then took the short hallway to the bedroom. Sitting down on the edge of the bed, he flipped on a small bedside lamp so he could check his alarm clock. Satisfied it was set, he turned the light off and lay down.

Within ten minutes Dr. Arthur Gibbs was fast asleep. Right before he dropped off he was daydreaming about the announcement of his new job as Associate Dean of the School of Business.

Chapter 14

The Enforcer rose from his position by the storage shed. Even though he had remained motionless for several hours, his body was relaxed and ready to go. Years ago, he had taught himself the art of relaxation without motion. It was a skill called upon again and again in his line of work.

There had been no activity from the house since about 3:30 when Gibbs got up and went to the bathroom. The flushing of the commode could be heard outside in the still morning.

The Enforcer had witnessed the same need for the bathroom on each of his earlier visits to the backyard. He also knew from those visits that Gibbs was not an early riser.

The wait had continued. It was now 4:50 in the morning and a time when a person such as Gibbs, who retired after midnight, was in their deepest possible sleep.

The Enforcer took one last look around the darkened yard. The night vision glasses gave everything a somewhat ghostly green cast. There were no obstacles between him and the back door that would make noise.

He carefully moved to the door. His total black appearance made him almost invisible. Standing with his back to the door, he paused a full two minutes and listened for sign of any movement inside the house.

Confident Gibbs was asleep, he carefully removed the lock pick gun from his pack and went to work on the lock. True to form and practice, it took him under 20 seconds to pick the lock.

Replacing the pick gun in his pack, he very slowly opened the door and slipped into the laundry room. Immediately, the Enforcer dropped into a type of crab position with hands and feet both on the floor.

If he encountered a person while close to the floor, nine out of ten people would look right over the top of him. Very slowly and deliberately he began a crab crawl toward the kitchen.

Once in the kitchen, the Enforcer paused to look around the room. The night vision glasses made everything as visible as if all the lights were on. Gibbs was a neat housekeeper. The sink was clean; not a dirty dish in sight.

Even though the Enforcer had never been in the house, he could visualize its layout from watching the bedtime routine. Lights each night went out in the laundry room, then the kitchen. A nightlight came on in the bathroom, then a small light in the bedroom. It went out almost immediately as Gibbs probably lay down.

The Enforcer was on the floor at the entrance to the bedroom. Using only peripheral vision, he could see Gibbs on the bed and hear a moderately loud snore. The snore was a good sign indicating deep sleep.

The Enforcer rose slowly from the floor and walked to the edge of the bed where he stared directly at Gibbs. He knew that if he looked directly at Gibbs, it would probably trigger some subconscious defense point in the brain causing him to awaken. Why? Who knows? But it almost always did.

That's why you never look directly at a person you are watching. Instead you look to one side using your peripheral vision instead.

The Enforcer wanted Gibbs to wake up. This had to look like an amateur killing, not a professional hit. He slipped his right hand into the sap glove he had in his pack. The glove was made of leather with powdered lead inserted over the knuckles.

As Gibbs stirred and started to sit up, the Enforcer hit him in the side of the head with a hard right hook. The weighted glove made little noise as it connected. Gibbs was immediately knocked out.

Dragging Gibbs from bed, the Enforcer propped him in a

corner of the room. Holding him with his left hand, the Enforcer repeatedly hit Gibbs in the face with his right sap glove-encased hand. The sap glove added enough force to each punch to make it appear that it had been delivered by a very large and very strong man.

Still holding the Finance Professor up with his left hand, the Enforcer delivered one final blow. It started at his waist and was an open palm strike upward into Gibbs's nose. The bone could be heard breaking just prior to starting its journey upward into the Professor's brain.

As Gibbs fell to the floor, the Enforcer repeatedly kicked him. The idea was for the murder to appear the result of extreme rage.

The killing took less than four minutes. In that time frame, Dr. Arthur Gibbs's dream of being the newest Associate Dean was over.

At precisely 5:00 am, the Enforcer let himself out the back door and relocked it. It took him another five minutes to get back to the truck.

Confident his actions had gone unobserved, the Enforcer started the truck's engine and drove around the corner in the direction of Gibbs's house. Turning his lights off, he pulled into the drive as if making a visit. He immediately backed out of the drive deliberately running the rear tires over the edge of the lawn.

Thirty-five minutes later, the white GMC with Texas plates crossed the Utah/Colorado border heading west on I-70. Eight hours later, the truck was pulling into a long-term parking lot at the Las Vegas Airport.

The Enforcer had stopped at a truck stop in Green River, Utah to shower and change clothes. Shortly after, he had deposited the black clothing and bag in a dumpster behind a grocery store.

Five gallons of gas and a lit match turned the whole thing

into an unexplained fire. All the hardware had found a resting place at the bottom of the Green River.

After locking the truck and heading to the terminal, the Enforcer dropped the keys into a trash can. He wouldn't be needing them again.

Within the hour, the truck would be picked up and on its way deep into the Nevada desert. The tires would be changed and it would be torched.

Nothing destroyed evidence like a good hot fire. As if he would ever leave any evidence. Before locking the truck, he had carefully searched it for anything left behind. Then he wiped it down to remove any finger prints. Even if found, the truck could never be traced to him.

Walking through the terminal, the Enforcer headed for a wall of airport lockers. Patting his pockets as if looking for the key, he glanced around to see if anyone was paying him any undue attention. Confident no one was, he slipped the key from his pocket and opened the locker.

From inside, he retrieved a plane ticket, ID, and cash. Pocketing everything, he walked away. Within three hours, the Enforcer was home in his own bed sleeping like a baby.

Experiencing guilt for the murder was not part of his mental makeup. It was, after all, just business.

Chapter 15

It took three days for Dr. Gibbs to be missed at Thunder Mountain College. Several more days passed before anyone got concerned enough to call the police.

A full week had passed before the police went to Gibbs's house. Seeing his car in the drive and not getting an answer at the door or on the phone, the officer forced his way in. Immediately, the stench in the closed house answered his question about the whereabouts of Dr. Gibbs.

The patrolman called the murder in and began to secure the crime scene. Leaving the front door open for the detective, he walked outside to have a look around. He looked toward the street as the sound of a distant siren snaked its way into his consciousness. Something didn't look quite right.

Walking out to the street, the patrolman approached a tire track in the grass next to the drive. Looked like someone missed the drive with one wheel. Probably nothing, but he decided to secure it as possible evidence. He moved the police cruiser close to the track to prevent another vehicle from pulling across the evidence. Dragging over two empty trash cans from across the street, he used them to form a protective barrier on the side of the track not shielded by the car. Important or not, the car track was now protected. Detective Orr could decide if it meant anything.

Detective Bruce Orr was the police officer investigating the death. It wasn't his first; he had been a homicide Detective in Denver for 20 years prior to retiring and moving to Grand Junction. Retirement lasted about a year before boredom began. He had been with the local department a couple of years now.

The patrolman was standing on the street-side curb as the detective's car pulled up. Opening the door for the detective, the young patrolman began speaking rapidly. "There's a dead body inside, sir. It's in really bad shape. I'll never be able to get the stink out of my system. I can even taste it. You should see it. Someone kicked the crap out of the guy and then kicked him some more for good measure. Plus, he's all bloated and stuff."

"Whoa, slow down son; is this your first homicide?"

"The first one like this. I saw a few dead bodies before, but nothing like this."

The detective walked around to the rear of the car and opened the trunk. Reaching inside he took out what appeared to be a flask of whiskey and two dust masks, the kind made out of paper with an elastic band attached. Handing one to the patrolman, he motioned with the flask. "Here, take this."

"Thanks, sir, but I better not drink while I'm still on duty. I will take the mask, though; it might cut some of the stink back in the house."

Smiling, the detective opened the flask and poured a small amount of the liquid on the mask he was holding. "Gasoline, he gestured with the flask. Old detective secret for ripe dead bodies. It'll take care of the smell and that taste you mentioned." Handing the flask to the patrolman, the detective headed for the house. "Throw the flask back in the trunk when you're through."

Quickly wetting his mask with gasoline and carefully putting the flask back in the trunk and closing it (He didn't think throwing it was such a good idea.), the patrolman hurried to catch up with the detective. "Sir, there's a tire track over by the drive that I marked off. I didn't know if it was important or what."

"You never know, son. Always better to err on the side of caution. We'll check it later. Now bring me up-to-date on what brought you over here and show me what you found inside."

"I got a call maybe 30 minutes ago from dispatch telling me to come to this address and check on a Dr. Gibbs. He's a professor at the College who hasn't been to work for a few days.

He missed a bunch of classes and didn't call in or anything. When I rang the doorbell, no one answered.

"I called dispatch and they told me to force my way in. After breaking the glass in the front door, I stepped just inside. You wouldn't believe the smell. After calling Dr. Gibbs's name a couple times, I decided to look around. Kinda had an idea what the stink was. I found him on the floor in the bedroom."

The two police officers passed through the front door of the house and headed toward the bedroom with the young patrolman in the lead. At the entrance to the bedroom the detective paused long enough to slip the gasoline-scented dust mask over his nose and mouth. As the patrolman did the same thing, the detective stepped past him into the room.

Turning partially back toward the younger officer, the detective's probing eyes took in the scene. "You touch anything in here?"

"No, sir, one quick look at the body told me what I was sent to find out. I could see him from the doorway and knew he was dead. I backed out of the room and called it in. With the stink and all, I needed some air so I went back outside. That's when I saw the tire track and secured it. No one's been in here till now."

Slipping on protective gloves, the detective stepped further into the room. "You go back outside and bring the lab crew in when they get here. Till then, no one gets in, understand?"

"Yes sir." The, by now, pale officer immediately turned and headed for the door. The gas in the mask had taken care of the smell, but it did nothing for the sight of the beat up body.

The detective stood for a good three minutes just looking at the bedroom. He mentally divided the room into sections and very carefully searched the space for visual clues to what had happened. After 22 years of working homicide scenes, his trained eyes missed nothing.

Next, he carefully stepped closer to the body. Bending down, his face was just inches from the remains of one Dr.

Arthur Gibbs. It was a mess. The left side of the corpse's head had absorbed a lot of blows. The nose was broken and at an awkward upward angle. Probably blows to the body too, but they weren't as evident.

He carefully examined the hands and arms for defensive wounds; there appeared to be none. Strange! Even the most unskilled person would normally hold up his arms to protect the head from blows. It was a natural reflex.

Detective Orr stood up and looked around the room again. There was no apparent sign of struggle. As a matter of fact, the whole room, other than the corner occupied by the body, was extremely neat. Dr. Gibbs kept a very tidy house. It was almost as if the deceased had meekly gotten out of bed, walked to the corner, and allowed someone to beat him to death, without fighting back or trying to defend himself in any manner. Very strange indeed.

"Detective Orr." The detective turned when he heard his name. The head of the lab crew along with the Coroner were standing just inside the bedroom. "You ready for us to come in?"

"Yeah, come on in. I've seen all I need to see for now. Take your time and get everything you can. There's something fishy about this. I don't know what it is, but my gut says this is not what it appears to be."

"You got it Detective." The head of the lab crew carefully moved further into the room and set down what looked like a large metal toolbox. He immediately opened it and pulled on a pair of gloves.

"Doc." The detective had once again looked down at the body. "I'll be outside. When you're through, I want any preliminary stuff you got. Even if it's just a hunch or a maybe."

"Sure thing Detective. You'll be the first to know." The coroner stepped to one side to allow the detective to pass through the doorway.

Once out of the house, the detective removed the dust mask and took in a deep breath of the chilled Colorado air. There was only so much gasoline filtered air you could breathe before it made you sick.

The patrolman was standing by his cruiser looking down at the tire track pressed into the ground by the driveway. "Is this the tire mark you were talking about?" the detective asked as he approached the young officer.

"Yes, sir, this is it. Do you think it means anything?"

The detective knelt down to get a better look at the impression. "It might. Looks like it's been here for several days. Did you notice that it seems to be bigger than the ordinary tire? We'll get the lab boys to make a cast of it just to be safe. Then we can check it out."

The detective stood up and allowed his 50-something- year-old knees to relax from the strain of kneeling. Gazing around the neighborhood, he pointed to a house directly across the street where an Old Man was standing. "I'm going to talk to that man over there. You get a couple more guys and start talking to all the neighbors to see if they saw anything. Don't forget the ones in back."

The Old Man smiled as the detective walked up. "What's going on over there? Somebody break in and steal something from that snooty professor? You gonna bring my garbage cans back?"

The detective held out his hand as he stepped closer to the Old Man. "Good morning, sir, I'm Detective Orr with the Grand Junction PD. Sorry about the cans. We'll get them back to you later. I was wondering if maybe you could help me out."

The Old Man stood up straighter in anticipation of the questions he knew were coming.

"When was the last time you saw anybody across the street?"

"Ain't seen that stuck-up Professor for 'bout a week now.

Not that it matters much. He's not exactly a friendly neighbor. When he first moved in, I went over to say, welcome. I'd probably gotten a better reception by pissing in his flowerbed. He just kind of dismissed me by saying thanks and closing the door in my face. Never waves or anything when I see him. Figured he must be out of town. Haven't seen him in 'bout a week." The Old Man repeated.

The detective patiently waited for the Old Man to finish. He knew that if you just said the bare minimum and listened to an old guy like this, he would ultimately tell you everything he knew. And usually guys like this knew a lot. They were puttering around outside off and on all day and looking out the window at all times during the night. An old man's prostate required several visits to the bathroom during the night. Any noise out of the ordinary would draw him to the window.

As the Old Man paused to take a breath, Detective Orr asked another question. "When was the last time you saw any activity across the street. Anything you saw might be important. People, a car, maybe just a noise that seemed out of place."

The Old Man rubbed his chin the way some people do when they think. "Well, it's been pretty quiet over there for 'bout a week now. I figured the Professor was off on vacation or business somewhere. There was something, though, 'bout a week ago.

"I had to get up early in the morning to drain the old lizard for about the fourth time that night. As I was walking back to bed, I heard an engine noise like maybe from a truck. Peeking out the window, I saw a big truck or something backing out of the drive over there.

"I wouldn't thought much of it, except it didn't have its lights on. It just backed out real quick like and took off. It never turned its lights on while I could see."

The detective glanced back over where the tire track was blocked off. Might be important after all. "Can you describe the vehicle or give me any information to help identify it?"

"Like I said, the lights were off. The only thing I could make out was that it was some kind of big thing. Might of been one of those SUV's or a big pick-up. I couldn't see real clear, I didn't have my glasses on."

"Can you give me an idea what time it was that you saw the truck?"

"It was about five o'clock. I remember being irritated because I had to get up and pee just 30 minutes before I get up for the day.

"When I woke up, I rolled over and looked at the clock. Since it was a couple minutes before five, I had a little debate with myself about whether or not I could make it to getting up time without going to the bathroom. I decided I couldn't. So it had to be about five or maybe a few minutes after."

"Thanks. You've been a big help. I'm going to have someone else come by and talk to you again later. If you can remember anything more at all, it would be a big help."

The Old Man pointed a finger across the street. "So, what happened over there; you never said."

The detective smiled briefly at the Old Man. "You can piss in his flowerbeds all you want and he'll never complain. He'll never wave either.

"Someone killed Dr. Gibbs."

The Old Man just stood there with a slack jaw as Detective Orr retraced his steps across the street. After a while the old guy turned toward his house muttering, "Well, I'll be damned. Couldn't of happened to a nicer guy."

The Coroner was standing in the yard when the detective got back across the street. "How's it going in there, Doc?"

"I had to get a little fresh air. With the smell in that bedroom, no one can stand it very long. That's as ripe a body as you're likely to see."

The detective tried not to sound impatient; he knew it was

tough work inside. "Any preliminary findings or thoughts?"

"Well." The Coroner was still taking in large gulps of the cool air. "First, there are no defensive wounds on the hands or arms. That seems kinda strange.

"He's got a bunch of broken ribs plus a severely broken nose. My guess is the nose is what killed him. Probably broke and the upper bone was driven into the brain. Helluva lucky punch or someone really knew what he was doing.

"Whoever did this was a professional fighter or he was just plain ole big. Had to be really strong or well trained to do that kind of damage with just fists."

"Anything else, Doc?"

"I'll know more when I get him on a table and opened up. One thing, though. Whoever did this is probably still showing damage on their right hand."

This last tidbit of info perked up the detective's interest. "What kind of damage, and why just the right hand?"

"The damage could be scratches, broken bones, dislocated knuckles, or swelling or all the above. You don't inflict the kind of damage seen in there with a bare hand and walk away unscathed.

"I believe it would be the right hand because all the damage was on the left side of the face and head. Unless he was being beat up from behind, we've got a messed up right hand somewhere. The body damage was probably done with a foot."

"Doc, do you think the damage to the hand would still be evident? The guy's probably been dead a week."

"Yes, even if nothing is broken, the hand would probably still be bruised and tender."

"Thanks, Doc. How about giving me a call when the autopsy results are ready?" The detective watched as the Coroner reluctantly turned and headed back into the house.

Chapter 16

Dr. Randy Haller was Dean of the School of Business. He liked his job at Thunder Mountain College (TMC). When he arrived five years earlier, he knew it would be a good place to finish his academic career.

One of the main reasons he had taken the job was the Business Faculty. All of them with one or two exceptions were outstanding professors. Not only were they an excellent teaching faculty, most were well published and widely known nationally in their respective disciplines.

The fact that TMC had an endowment of close to 300 million dollars had not hurt. Not bad for a small liberal arts college in Western Colorado. And it was still coming in.

President Karp excelled at fund raising. He consistently raised 20 to 30 million dollars a year in corporate contract dollars. The money was used to fund corporate training programs around the world. There was a special unit of the college with staff located around the world that did nothing else.

For the past five years, Haller's job had been a breeze, now this mess. One of his faculty members had been murdered and a police detective was on his way over.

When the police had called, he had immediately contacted the College President to let him know what was going on. President Karp had said to be fully cooperative with the police and not hold anything back.

The President felt the quickest way to get beyond the negative publicity of the tragedy was complete and total honesty. The college had nothing to hide.

The phone's intercom buzzing interrupted the Dean's thoughts. Punching the button, his secretary's voice softly invaded the space, "Dr. Haller, there is a Detective Orr from the police to see you."

"Send him in and hold any calls until he leaves." Dean Haller rolled his high-backed leather executive's chair away from his desk and quickly got to his feet. He had stepped around the desk as the door to his office opened. Detective Orr walked into the lavishly furnished office and took the outstretched hand into his own.

Passing the Dean a business card and displaying a badge, Detective Orr made a quick visual appraisal of Haller and his office. "Thanks for seeing me, I know you must have a lot of work to do dealing with the death of Dr. Gibbs. Hopefully, I won't take an excessive amount of your time."

Dean Haller had a concerned look tainted just a bit with sadness etched across his face. "Take whatever time you need. We've already made arrangements for Dr. Gibbs's classes to be taken over by another faculty member.

"Now, we want to do whatever we can to help in the investigation of this horrible crime. Can you give me any details? We were only told that he was murdered in his home. Was it some kind of home invasion or what?"

Detective Orr carefully listened to and watched the Dean. It appeared that his lack of knowledge was genuine. "Dr. Gibbs was beaten to death in his bedroom about a week ago. We found the body this morning.

There was no sign of forced entry. Right now, we're trying to interview as many people as possible that might have information about Dr. Gibbs. That brings me to the reason for my visit. What can you tell me about Dr. Gibbs?"

"Just the usual academic details, I didn't really know him on a social level. He was here when I came to TMC five years ago. He received tenure and promotion to Associate Professor of Finance last spring. He was a good scholar but not very popular with the students."

The detective took notes in a small, leather-bound notebook as the Dean talked. "I'll need a list of all the faculty members and staff in the Business School and also the students in his classes. Also, I need to know what, if anything, he was working on other than regular class stuff."

"I'll get my secretary to put together everything you've requested. She'll have it for you tomorrow morning by 9:00. And no, he wasn't, to my knowledge, working on anything special.

"Is there anything else?" Haller had never been interviewed by the police before. He didn't really know what to expect.

Detective Orr liked to put people at ease by asking for things he knew they could do. It was time for more difficult questions. "Can you tell me if anyone you know of had a problem with Dr. Gibbs? The kind of problem that might lead to violence?"

The Dean thoughtfully stared out the window as he pondered the Detective's question. "Well, judging from last semester's student evaluations, I'd say numerous students did."

Detective Orr looked up from his note taking. "What do you mean by numerous students? Can you be more specific?"

"Not really." The Dean reached for a fairly thick folder laying on the corner of his desk. "It's all in here, though. I had an appointment this week to talk with Dr. Gibbs about the evals. I guess it really doesn't matter now, does it?"

The Detective pointed at the file folder with his pen. "May I?"

"Why not, I guess they're no longer private. If you think there's a clue in here, be my guest." The Dean leaned forward so Detective Orr's outstretched arm and hand could grasp the folder.

Opening the folder, Orr looked down and then back up at the Dean. "How about a brief overview? I'll read these in detail later."

The question obviously made the Dean uncomfortable. "Dr.

Gibbs is dead, but I'm sure he has a family out there somewhere that doesn't want his name smeared. They could sue me for divulging this kind of information."

Detective Orr smiled inwardly. He was finally getting a glimpse at Dr. Arthur Gibbs, the man. If the evaluations were so bad the Dean was afraid of getting sued just for talking about them, they must paint a nasty picture.

"Anyone can sue anybody for anything these days. I doubt anyone will sue you for answering questions in a murder investigation. Besides, I assume your opinion is supported by the evaluations."

Small beads of sweat were starting to form on the Dean's neck just above the starched collar of his white shirt. "The evaluations paint an unpleasant picture of Dr. Gibbs. They're not the first either. Last semester was just as bad. As a matter of fact, they haven't improved much since his first semester here.

"The bottom line is that the students pretty much hated him. Consensus of comments in the evals indicates he was an arrogant, self-centered Professor who consistently berated students publicly in class.

"Statements are laced throughout the evaluations supporting the assessment. Comments were consistent across all his classes at both the undergraduate and graduate level. Students despised him. One particularly crude student referred to him as an 'arrogant asshole' who needed a serious attitude adjustment."

Detective Orr was taken aback by the blunt assessment. "I now see why you are concerned with lawsuits. Are there other Business Professors with these kinds of student evaluations?"

"No, as a matter of fact, the rest of the Business Faculty have some of the best student evaluations on campus. Our senior Economics Professor was even honored recently as the 'Professor Most Respected' by students on campus. Dr. Gibbs appeared to be an anomaly."

An uncomfortable silence hung over the office as Detective

Orr made what appeared to be lengthy additions to his notes. Finally looking up, he continued. "What about Gibbs's relationship with the rest of the faculty and staff? They love him, hate him, ignore him, or what? Any of them have a grudge you know of?"

The Dean sat up straighter in his chair as if he were preparing to lecture a naive student on some subject with which he had intimate and absolute knowledge. "Bickering, disagreement, that sort of thing is an everyday part of the culture of the Academy."

The eyebrows on the Detective's face seemed to jump upward and scrunch together. "The what?"

"The culture of the Academy." Dean Haller was obviously in his own backyard of knowledge and enjoying it. "You see, higher education has its own way of doing things. It's like a world all unto its own. We're different because at one level we are so homogeneous. We're different, yet we're the same.

"All of us spent many years studying until we attained the highest degrees possible in our respective disciplines. We are taught to be cynical and question the creation and distribution of knowledge. In effect, we are taught to question and be distrustful of each other.

"It's not really a mean-spirited thing. Just the opposite, most of us revel in intellectual banter with our academic colleagues. We enjoy the mental calisthenics required in defense of our various disciplines and theories. What might appear to be a heated argument to an outsider is considered good-natured discussion to those of us in the Academy.

"You will often see Professors nose-to-nose in heated debate over an issue one minute and the next they will be headed off for coffee together. As you might suspect, it is difficult to decipher good-natured banter from genuine dislike."

"The culture of the Academy, huh?" Detective Orr did not seem impressed. "You ever have one member of the Academy really get pissed off and pop another member upside the head? You know, clock him really good?"

The Dean's demeanor changed to show his displeasure at the crude, disparaging remark toward the Academy. He had to admit, though, sometimes the discussions teetered on the brink of physical contact. "There was a minor incident several weeks ago.

"It happened in the faculty dining room on a Friday, I believe. If memory serves me correctly, the discussion had to do with whether students were incapable of learning certain quantitative concepts or whether professors were not skilled enough teachers to transfer the knowledge.

"That's a long-running debate in the Academy. It's an oft debated issue of whether failing grades are the result of poor students or poor teaching.

"Dr. Gibbs was of the 'poor student' theory and Dr. Baldridge was of the 'poor teaching' theory. As I recall, Dr. Baldridge was the clear winner of the debate rallying most of the faculty in the room to his position.

"He seemed to be enjoying the debate and was not visibly angry. As a matter of fact, the opposite seemed true. He was laughing and joking and even told Dr. Gibbs to have a good weekend as he rose to leave.

"Dr. Gibbs, however, was not jovial at all. He had turned red in the face and was using quite a bit of profanity. Personally, I was surprised Dr. Baldridge took it so well.

"At one point, Gibbs referred to the Marketing Department where Dr. Baldridge is Senior Professor, as a bunch of bastards who couldn't count to 20 without taking their shoes off.

"Dr. Baldridge just smiled and got up to leave. That was when he told Gibbs to have a good weekend. Gibbs apparently wasn't ready to concede the point.

"As Baldridge made his way to the door with his back to the room, Gibbs almost jumped from his seat and rushed to catch

Baldridge. As he got within a couple of feet, he yelled for Baldridge to turn and face him. It was almost like a schoolyard fight.

"I'm not sure exactly what happened next. Apparently, as Dr. Baldridge stopped and turned, he accidently hit Dr. Gibbs in the left knee with his walking stick. He must not have realized Gibbs was so close behind.

"It caused a fairly significant injury. Gibbs fell to the floor clutching his knee in obvious pain. He limped around for two weeks after it happened. The Doctor said if it had been just a fraction harder a strike, Gibbs would have had a broken kneecap."

"Professors fighting," Orr chuckled to himself. *That must be right up there with a chick fight.* He continued, "What did Baldridge do after he hit Gibbs?"

The expression on the Dean's face told you he was mentally back in the faculty dining room. "He quickly apologized and tried to help Gibbs up, but Gibbs kept yelling that he had done it on purpose. With Gibbs yelling obscenities at his back, Dr. Baldridge simply walked out."

"You said this Dr. Baldridge hit Gibbs with a walking stick. What's the story with that? Does he always use one?"

"I've never seen him without it. He has a problem with his left leg, the result of a car accident I've been told."

Detective Orr had mentally gone back to the murder scene visualizing the beaten body. "Baldridge must have hit Gibbs pretty hard to cause the damage it did. How do you think that happened?"

"Well, Dr. Baldridge did turn very quickly, especially for a man his size. I suppose the severity of the injury could be the result of the speed of his turn and his strength. He might even have been off balance. That could have made him put more pressure on the cane."

Detective Orr looked up quickly at the Dean. "What do you

mean, a man his size?"

The Dean held a hand several inches above his head to indicate height and then used both hands to show width. "He's a very large man. Probably six-four or six-five; maybe 250, 260. Looks real strong like he used to be an athlete."

The Detective's insides had just done a loop. He had a dead body beaten to death. He also had a Professor who almost crippled the deceased a few weeks earlier.

The best part was the size and strength of the Professor. One member of the Academy, Dr. Baldridge, had just moved to the top of the suspect list.

"How do I find this Dr. Baldridge?"

Chapter 17

President Karp was sitting behind the desk with his back to the door. He was staring out the large window facing the quad. Vice President Manci was to his right sitting in a leather wingback chair and looking in the same direction. He was doing the talking. "Look at all those kids down there. We got over 5,000 students this year. Looks like most of them are on the quad this morning."

Karp glanced over toward Manci. "Does the 5,000 include our special international program?"

Manci rewarded the President with a smile. "Naw, we got over 2,000 of those. They just don't show up on campus much."

Both men let go with a belly laugh.

"How's the investigation into Gibbs's murder going?" Manci's eyes were following a blonde coed's progress down the sidewalk.

Karp's attention appeared to be directed toward a brunette several steps behind the blonde. "The police talked to Dean Haller about an hour ago. They're probably hot on the trail of our good Dr. Baldridge by now."

Chapter 18

"Dr. Baldridge?" Detective Orr was standing in the doorway to the office.

"Yes, I'm Tarr Baldridge."

Orr stepped through the doorway and toward the big man sitting behind an ornately carved antique oak desk. "Nice desk."

Baldridge smiled at the man standing in front of his desk trying to make small talk. He knew exactly who he was and why he was there. Word had spread quickly this morning about Gibbs. It was just a matter of time before they came to see him.

"I picked it up a couple of years ago at an estate sale. Legend has it that a Madame down on Colorado Avenue imported it back in the late 1800's for her office. Prostitution was a thriving business in Grand Junction then. I don't know if the story is true or not, makes for interesting conversation though. You a furniture buyer?"

"No, not exactly, I'm Detective Orr with the Grand Junction Police Department." Orr watched Baldridge for any physical response to his answer. There was none. Baldridge merely smiled.

"I've been expecting you since word hit campus this morning about Dr. Gibbs."

"What word would that be?"

Baldridge substituted the grin for a noncommittal mask. "The word that Dr. Gibbs had been murdered."

Orr waited for Baldridge to continue. He had learned years ago that most people are uncomfortable with silence. The knowledge had served him well on countless occasions. He stared at Baldridge and waited for him to continue. Baldridge merely stared back without continuing.

Maybe the old shock question would catch Baldridge off guard. "Did you murder him?"

Baldridge continued to stare at the Detective to the point of rudeness. "You're either not as smart as you look or smarter than your question implies. I'll go with the latter.

"Do you think I killed Dr. Gibbs over a philosophical discussion about teaching? If every discussion like ours that happens on campus were manifested in murder, you'd need a substation here staffed with 20 detectives. We'd be the murder capital of the world.

"If you want to play games with me, send over a copy of the rules and I'll get back to you once I've studied them. Minus that, ask me a reasonable question and I'll help you as much as I can."

Orr smiled at Baldridge. This was a cool professor. Maybe a bit too cool. One more trick question to see if he had rattled him at all. "Where were you the night Gibbs was murdered?"

Baldridge pushed back from the desk and tilted his chair toward the wall. His hands were laced together behind his neck. His look was one of amusement. "I told you I would need the rules if we were going to play with each other.

"Two things. First, when I heard Gibbs was dead, I assumed he had been murdered, but I didn't and still don't know that for sure. Second, if he were murdered, I don't know when and I doubt you do either.

"Word on the faculty grapevine is Gibbs had been dead for a long time when your guys found him. Since I watch a lot of *CSI-Miami*, I know that makes determining time of death almost impossible. If you're having trouble with this case, maybe you should check the show out for a few hints. You can catch it on Net Flicks.

"Now, if we're going to continue exchanging volleys like this, maybe we should change into tennis shorts and sneakers."

"Okay, okay; You're obviously way too clever for a college dropout Detective like me. Tell me about your fight with Dr.

Gibbs."

"It wasn't a fight; we were having a discussion about teaching and learning. I've had the same discussion with any number of colleagues."

"Tell me about you hitting him in the knee with your walking stick. Was that on purpose? Have you ever hit anybody else with the stick?"

"I hit him when I turned around in response to him calling me. He startled me some with his tone and I guess I turned more quickly than usual. I always lead with the stick when I turn around. If I don't, there's a good chance I will stumble. My left knee is pretty well shot.

"He was closer than I thought. The stick accidently smacked him in the knee. I quickly apologized and tried to help him up. He was very upset and said I did it on purpose, which of course I did not. There must have been a dozen witnesses, why don't you ask them?"

Detective Orr was carefully writing everything down in his notebook. "I will. Can you tell me who was there?"

"The Dean. You probably already know that. Most of the Department, I think. We all try to lunch together on Fridays. It helps promote collegiality, especially with the newer faculty. There were faculty from other departments in the room, but I don't know how much they heard. It's a pretty big room. You could probably ask around."

Orr was looking around the office. He spotted what he was looking for in a corner behind the desk. "May I see your cane?"

Turning to reach behind and to the right, Tarr grabbed the cane and handed it to the Detective, handle first. "It's one of a kind. If you're in need of one, you'll have to settle for something else. I saw a pretty good selection last weekend at Wal-Mart in their pharmacy."

Tarr knew exactly why the Detective wanted to look at the cane and it had little to do with a personal need for ambulatory stabilization. It was to examine it for dents or blood or something else that might be associated with the crime. The news was already on the faculty grapevine that Gibbs had been beaten to death.

The Detective merely smiled as he took the cane from Tarr. "I'll keep that in mind if I ever need one." He then held the cane in one hand just as a person might hold a club. "This thing has a sturdy feel to it. Probably make an effective weapon if someone knew how to use it. What's it made of?"

"It's a seamless aluminum shaft with an oak core. As you can see, it has an ivory and silver handle."

The Detective balanced the cane across his upturned open palm. "Nice balance. I bet you could beat down a brick wall with this thing and barely make a dent in it? He had phrased the last comment as a question.

Tarr reached forward and took the cane from the offering hand. "Maybe, but I wouldn't know much about that. Beating up on brick walls is not an activity of interest to me. It will support a 6'4", 240-pound Professor, though. Not many commercial canes will. A guy my size can put a lot of pressure on a cane."

The Detective was reviewing his notes. He looked up at Tarr. "Tell me again how you 'accidently' smacked Gibbs in the knee. Or was it more than an accident? Maybe even a skillful shot to the knee by a person trained in stick fighting?"

"Come now, Detective, I thought we were through playing games. It was just what I said, an accident. Why would I assault a colleague over a difference in philosophy? If Professors fought over such trivial issues, the Quad would have more fighting going on than a karate movie.

"Do you think I had something to do with Dr. Gibbs's death? If so, spit it out. Was he beaten to death with a walking cane? Is that what this is about? If it is, then forensic evidence should be analyzed and my cane either convicted or cleared."

Tarr was smiling his most cynical smile as he spoke.

Detective Orr returned the smile in a challenging manner. "I don't know if you had anything to do with the murder or not. My instinct says probably not. But I've been wrong before.

"There's something about you, something that's outside the lines. I just can't put my finger on it. You may be a college professor, but my gut tells me you're more. Maybe I should check you out just for the hell of it. What would I find, if I did?"

Tarr knew he was being baited. Detective Orr was very good at his job. He also knew the more he told of his background, the less likely the Detective would waste time in a background check. Tarr knew he could survive a cursory check. If the Detective were persistent, however, he would encounter a dead-end. That, in itself, might ignite an even bigger curiosity. Bigger curiosity, Tarr didn't need.

"Well, Detective, you'd find a widower professor somewhat liked by his students and colleagues who's been at TMC for about ten years. Before that I was a faceless bureaucrat at the Federal Trade Commission who investigated complaints of false advertising against retailers. After ten years of that drudgery, I lucked out and got a teaching job in my hometown.

"I'm a moderately successful textbook writer with an equally moderate consulting business. The only family alive is an older brother who is retired from the Navy.

"Minus a minor philosophical difference with Art Gibbs, I had little to do with him, certainly nothing that would even be remotely a motive for murder. I didn't kill him and I don't know who did. If I can help you in any way in your investigation, I will.

"If you promise not to arrest me, take me to jail, and beat a confession out of me, I promise to stop being a smart-ass professor and just shut up." Tarr held his hands up in mock defeat and displayed what he hoped was his most sincere smile.

The Detective held out his hand in an invitation to shake.

"Okay, I guess I don't need to beat a confession out of you today, but I reserve the right to do it later." He laughed and walked out of Tarr's office.

Somehow, Tarr didn't think he had seen the last of Detective Orr.

Chapter 19

It was Saturday morning, the day after Tarr was questioned by Detective Orr. He was having a cup of coffee on the largest of his patios. The air had a slight chill. The sky was the kind of clear blue found only at higher altitudes. It was cool enough to indicate the possibility of an early snow for the Colorado high country. The hot chicory-laced coffee was just what the Doctor ordered on such a gorgeous fall morning.

As Tarr sipped the extremely strong, milky sweet coffee, his view was drawn to the Colorado National Monument rising to a height of over 6,000 feet from the desert floor just a few miles west. He never ceased to be amazed by its grandeur. Looking at the Monument was one of his favorite ways to start a new day.

He put the coffee on a side table and reached for the morning paper laying on the chair beside him. The headline should not have been a surprise, but somehow it was.

TMC PROFESSOR BEATEN TO DEATH IN OWN HOME

A killing is a rare occurrence in Grand Junction; an unsolved murder is almost unheard of. There may be one every two or three years. So, when a murder happens, it's going to be the front page headline. Just like today.

It hadn't taken long for the Grand Junction Daily Sentinel to pick up on the murder. Like most good newspapers, the Sentinel had access to a majority of police reports before they were officially filed. The murder of Dr. Gibbs was no exception.

It never ceased to amaze Tarr how much information a police department was willing to share about an unsolved murder case. The Sentinel reported that Dr. Arthur Gibbs, Finance Professor at Thunder Mountain College, was found beaten to death in the bedroom of his home early yesterday morning. There was no sign of forced entry and nothing appeared stolen from the home. Dr. Gibbs had been dead for several days.

Although no motive had been clearly established, an official source close to the investigation stated it appeared to have been a murder perpetrated in a fit of rage. Also, because there was no forced entry, the murderer was obviously an acquaintance voluntarily admitted to the home by Dr. Gibbs.

The source also stated the murderer was probably male and above average in size and strength. The source was quoted as saying, "Whoever did this was very strong, probably very big, and most definitely very angry."

Well, Tarr now knew why Detective Orr had wanted to question his big meaty self, posthaste. It made sense now. Everything on the faculty grapevine had been accurate. Gibbs appeared to have been beaten to death by a big, strong, angry guy.

Tarr was a big strong guy. Occasionally, he was even an angry guy. When you added a metal cane to the equation, he could understand why detective Orr had come a calling. It was almost as if the murder had been committed with Tarr in mind.

There was something else too. Tarr knew a thing or two about criminal investigation. The Detective had already decided Tarr was his number one suspect. He had nowhere else to go. If the crime were not cleared in 36 hours, chances were it never would be without an extreme bit of luck.

Tarr could sense the Detective's feelings almost from the beginning. Why else show up unannounced and come at Tarr from a half dozen different directions. The Detective had only one lead and that was Dr. Tarr Baldridge. He was out there somewhere right now trying to make a case.

It all seemed so stupid though. First of all, who would want to kill Gibbs? Sure, he had been an arrogant, self-centered prick who only cared about his own career. He hated the students and loathed most of his colleagues. It was no secret that he wanted to be Associate Dean and would do almost anything to get there. But, so what. If you were to kill every Professor with those traits, you'd have several more bodies scattered around town.

No, it had to be something else. Maybe Art was messing around with the wife of a seriously deranged husband. What else could cause a person in Grand Junction to commit murder? The only two murders Tarr could remember in recent history had both been crimes of passion.

But beating a man to death. Now that was something else. Tarr knew a little about violence. As a matter of fact, he knew a lot about violence.

Beating a man to death was not something that happened every day, especially when committed by a jealous husband. No, beating a man to death with just your hands took professional level skill or immense luck.

Tarr didn't much believe in luck. So, that left skill. But professional skill meant the anonymity of a contractor. Who would pay to kill Gibbs? And who would want it to look like a crime of passion? A bullet in the eye was quicker and much more certain.

It did answer the question about the Detective's interest in Tarr's cane, though. A quick shot from a cane to the right part of the head could kill a man instantly. If the autopsy revealed any blunt force trauma to the head caused by something other than a fist, Tarr knew he would be seeing the good Detective again.

But Tarr didn't think any such evidence would be found, even though he hoped so. It would be too easy for Tarr to clear himself by letting the police lab examine the cane for trace blood evidence. Everyone knew you could never remove all traces of blood, even if you had a degree in cane cleaning.

As he stared across the rooftops of Grand Junction at the Monument, Tarr had a nagging feeling that the murder had somehow been staged to put his name all over it. But why?

What was this really about? Was he just being paranoid or was he being set up? He laughed as he thought about what an old friend had once told him. "If it walks like a duck and talks like a duck, it must be a duck.

Maybe being a paranoid duck was not such a bad thing. Several times in a past existence, paranoia had saved his life. Maybe the old instincts were not gone. Maybe they had just been dormant. Something was in the air and whatever it was could get a lot worse before it got better.

Tarr's biggest fear was that if he were arrested and charged with the murder, that piece of his life that was buried would be put on public display. Don't get the wrong idea here. He had never broken the law. It was just that he had not really worked for the Federal Trade Commission investigating false advertising.

In reality, he had worked for the Treasury Department in an area called FinCEN. FinCEN is an acronym for Financial Crimes Enforcement Network. At the time of his "retirement," Tarr had been a senior investigator working undercover operations involving large-scale money laundering. Actually, the job was a bit more than undercover; it was a black hole operation completely off the books.

Even though sanctioned by the government, it would never have been acknowledged as existing. The reason: sometimes drastic measures were required to stop well-connected, very influential, high-profile criminals. Tarr had been the go-to guy implementing those measures for almost ten years.

If you checked into his background, you would indeed find him listed as a past employee of the FTC. If you checked further, however, you would not be able to find a single FTC employee who knew him.

A guy like Orr would find that suspicious and check further. Further checking might ultimately lead to the real personnel file. That would not be good.

What file, one might ask? Well, everyone who has ever worked for the government and is now receiving a retirement check (like Tarr) has to have a file somewhere. Some files are more difficult to find than others, but a persistent investigator can eventually dig it out.

Some of Tarr's official activities were better left alone. He was no stranger to violence because he had been involved in more than his share. Sometimes giving, sometimes receiving, and sometimes involving fatal outcomes.

His left knee was a good example. Most who knew him thought the bad knee, requiring the assistance of a walking cane, was the result of a car wreck. It was one of several small lies he had told Doni on their date. What would she and his colleagues think if they knew the truth?

The bad knee was not because of a car accident, it was the result of a six-inch knife blade being thrust through it very violently. The blade was wielded by a guy Tarr had knocked to the ground in a New Orleans' back alley. What would everybody think if they knew Tarr had pulled the knife out of his own knee and left it buried in the left temple of said same assailant?

What would they say if they knew he had killed four men as a government agent? All killings were fully investigated and ruled justifiable. Justifiable or not, Joe citizen might not want little Susie or Bobby taking Principles of Marketing from a man capable of such violence.

So, Tarr had no legal concerns with his background, but the citizens in a small town like Grand Junction might find such a background uncomfortable. His biggest concern, though, was teaching. The thing he loved most in the world might be taken away.

It would not matter that he had been disabled for life and was receiving a tax-free full disability retirement from a grateful government. The only thing that would matter would be that he was a killer. After all, it wasn't like he had to do it in a war or something. Tarr did it because he was like the scum he had been chasing. You know what they say, "Takes one to catch one."

Something was going on here in river city and Tarr needed to be careful. The carefully crafted and immensely comfortable professorial life he was living was suddenly in jeopardy. Common sense dictated he keep his eyes open and do a little checking of his own.

Chapter 20

As Tarr shifted the Hummer out of overdrive, the massive tan vehicle began an effortless ascent up Little Park Road on the way to a mountainous area of Mesa County called Glade Park. Grand Junction is located in Mesa County, most of which is a high mountain valley located in extreme western Colorado bordering the Utah State line. Not a large city by any reasonable standard, it is the biggest city between Denver and Salt Lake City.

Grand Junction is a little big city that reminds old timers of what Sedona, Arizona, used to be like. As a city, it contains all the trappings of culture and sophistication. It has a symphony, a historic theatre showing art films, several venues for live theatre, art galleries, museums, and two institutions of higher education. In addition to TMC, there is Colorado Mesa University, a very well-respected public college.

A unique downtown district is the home for what seems an endless array of festivals celebrating cultural heritages, holidays, service club events, and anything else that sounds like fun. There's art on the corner featuring a revolving group of sculptures displayed year-round.

During the summer months, an upscale farmers' market occupies Main Street every Thursday night. On Fridays, an "Art Hop" is held where local artists set up and demonstrate their chosen media on Main Street. Open air restaurants and bars dot the downtown area. Antique shops abound.

Culture, however, is just the tip of the iceberg. Outdoor activities are plentiful for those so inclined. The name of the town, Grand Junction, is a reference to the junction of two major rivers in town. The Gunnison flowing from the mountains of the south joins the Colorado flowing from the mountains east to provide river rafting, fishing, and an endless selection of water activities.

Skiing is as close as 45 miles to the east at Powder Horn Resort, 150 miles east to Vail, 100 miles southeast to Aspen, and 100 miles southwest to Telluride.

Tarr wasn't really thinking about any of the reasons he and countless thousands of others lived in the valley, though. He was thinking about a murder and its unexplainable connection to him. He was also thinking about keeping the Hummer between the lines as he climbed the narrow road snaking up to the high plateau west of town.

Glade Park is a large geographic area west of Grand Junction and west of the Colorado National Monument. The monument is a majestic area of canyons and unusual rock formations framing the western edge of town. Many of the tourists who come to visit the monument each year say it reminds them of a miniature Grand Canyon.

By going up Little Park Road, Tarr was bypassing the Monument and any tourist traffic attracted to it. He didn't feel like crawling up a mountain road behind a 35-foot Class A motor home.

After 30 minutes spent negotiating switchbacks and cattle gaps across the road, the Hummer reached the Glade Park plateau. He soon intersected the only major east/west highway and turned left. That's west if you are interested.

He stayed on the two-lane highway for about ten miles until he came to a metal gated fence blocking a small rutted dirt road which meandered off in a northwesterly direction.

The gate sat about 20 feet off the highway allowing Tarr space to park in front and get out of his vehicle. The fence paralleled the highway in both directions for several hundred yards. A small sign stated that behind the gate was private property and trespassers would be prosecuted. He walked up to the gate and opened a very sturdy looking combination lock.

A couple of minutes later, he was through the gate with it relocked behind him. The small dirt road twisted and turned as it wove its way through small rock formations and scrub oak brush.

After crawling along for about 1,000 yards, Tarr encountered another gated fence which set behind a small rock outcropping not visible from the highway. As he exited the Hummer and walked up to the gate, a large sign proclaimed it to be the entrance to an experimental scientific facility.

Trespassers were warned that they could be endangering their personal safety by proceeding. It went on to say that the facility and surrounding 5,000 acres were protected by electronic deterrents. EXTREME CAUTION URGED.

Tarr passed through the second barrier as he had the first. He couldn't help but smile at the deception. How many times had he taught young marketing students that "a lie told 2,000 times becomes the truth, and a perception left unattended becomes reality?" What he had just passed through was an unattended perception turned reality, created by printing a lie on a sign.

There was no scientific facility and there was no danger, if you didn't count Lucky. There were just 5,000 acres of rock outcroppings, a few mesas, assorted vegetation, and a bunch of wildlife.

Visible wildlife included deer, rabbits, ground squirrels, and the like. Invisible wildlife included mountain lions, an occasional rattlesnake, and a few other unsavory critters.

Tarr and his brother, Lucky, had erected the fences and gates a couple years ago to discourage casual explorers. The perception of danger kept most honest folks away. Those few over the years who chose to ignore the warnings, suffered for their mistakes in judgment. Nothing fetal; just memorable.

Tarr dropped the Hummer into four-wheel drive as he

dropped down into a shallow ravine. During spring runoff, the ravine often had a couple feet of water flowing through it.

The big desert tan monstrosity of an SUV easily matriculated the topography and abruptly came to a sharp turn in the road. To the left were the dusty tracks of the road leading out of sight.

To the right was a layer of flat, tan-colored rock extending for several hundred yards before ending at a vertical rock wall extending 200 feet straight up. Scattered throughout the rock formation were scrub oak and a seemingly endless number of very large boulders and rock outcroppings.

To any trespasser driving or walking the road, going right did not appear to be an option, the road obviously veered left.

If the dirt road were taken, it soon turned into a narrow box canyon with yet another gate. This one, however, was electrified with a very unfriendly warning.

To date, no one had ventured beyond it. All had turned back.

Tarr abandoned the road at its sharp turn and turned right on to the rock. Because of the rock's color, the dust on the tires left almost no sign of his passing.

Almost immediately he turned behind a large rock outcropping and disappeared from sight. After a few minutes of weaving in, out, and around huge rocks, the Hummer turned behind one last outcropping and stopped facing the sheer rock wall.

Then Tarr did something very unusual; he pressed the button on a garage door opener. The rock opened and he drove in. A Toyota 4Runner was already inside.

Exiting the Hummer and stepping back out into the bright Colorado sun, Tarr opened a rock-colored metal panel and punched in a code to close the door.

You had to love technology.

Chapter 21

Tarr stood looking around the rocky terrain. Finally, shaking his head in disappointment and raising his hands in mock surrender he whispered softly, "Okay, I give up. Where are you?"

Lucky's laugh preceded his appearance three feet to Tarr's left. Tarr whispered because it was a game between the two. Since childhood one would always sneak up on the other. Whispering had always been a sign of respect acknowledging the other's ability to get very close without detection.

Tarr could hold his own with Lucky as a kid, but after Lucky went through Navy Seal training, it had never been close again.

The two brothers were total opposites in physical appearance. Lucky, who looked like his mother, was three years older, eight inches shorter, and about 100 pounds lighter on the bathroom scales. His light sandy hair and blue eyes were in contrast to Tarr's black hair and dark brown eyes.

Most people would never be convinced they were really brothers unless they had seen their parents. Tarr was a spitting image of their father just as Lucky was their mother. The only similarity between the two was their hairstyle. Both wore it cut short in a military fashion.

Lucky had joined the Navy when he finished high school. He had been in the Brown Water Navy during the drug wars in South America, when Tarr was in high school.

Tarr graduated high school and headed off to college. After his first tour in the Navy, Lucky had gone through SEAL training, and then spent another four tours on a SEAL team in the Middle East.

Lucky stayed in the Seal Teams ultimately achieving the rank of Master Chief. He had retired a few years earlier, after 32 years in the Navy.

Even though Lucky had little formal education beyond high school, he was well-read and encountered few subjects where he felt ill-informed. Being an intellectual required no college degrees; it merely required a heavily exercised intellect.

Many a time the two brothers had stayed up late into the night discussing some obscure theory or ambiguous interpretation of current events. Debate was often heated but never angry.

The two brothers were very fond of each other and one would never hurt the other. They were also very protective of each other. Neither relished the idea of being the last Baldridge.

Tarr was staring at his brother who had materialized as if by magic. "So there you are; not bad for an old brown water swabby. Almost got close enough to touch me."

"I was close enough to touch you, but backed off. I was afraid I'd cause a soft professor like you to faint." Lucky was leaning against a rock and brushing dust off the front of his desert camouflage pants.

"Yeah, you were afraid I'd break your nose before I figured out it was just an old frog sneaking around."

Tarr reached over and slapped his brother backhanded on the stomach. It was like slapping one of the boulders, but Tarr never missed a beat. "Getting a little soft aren't we?"

"Not as soft as you. Are you gaining weight?" Lucky puffed out his facial cheeks to simulate fat.

The truth was that neither Baldridge brother was fat or soft. Even though neither ventured into harm's way any longer, both had seen enough evil to know that it was never far away, even in western Colorado. Such knowledge fostered just enough paranoia in the brothers to keep them in good physical condition.

You never knew when evil might require a swift kick in the ass.

Chapter 22

The sun was starting to go down as the brothers rounded the rock outcropping and entered the natural patio in front of the house.

"I see you were expecting me." Tarr was eyeballing the two lounge chairs Lucky had obviously brought out of the house earlier. There was a small cooler conveniently located between the chairs. He knew what was in the cooler without looking.

"You're so predictable; I don't need a watch anymore." Lucky raised the cooler's top, took out two cut crystal glasses and filled each with ice and a double shot of Gentleman Jack whiskey. All had been in the cooler; they always were.

Tarr took the drink from Lucky's extended hand as both eased into the chairs. "Heard the highway gate alarm didn't you? I'm glad your increasing years haven't affected you hearing."

When the gates and fences had been installed earlier, Lucky had also installed an alarm on both gates in addition to numerous motion detectors strategically placed around the 5,000 acres. No one came on the property without Lucky's knowledge.

It wasn't that he or Tarr were greedy with the beautiful scenery; it was just that they wanted to know who would be brave enough or stupid enough to ignore the warnings.

The entire property had a fence around it. Built with only three strands of barbed wire, it wasn't designed to keep out animals nor humans. It was designed, however, to slow people down enough to see one of the warning signs attached to it every 50 feet.

If someone ignored the warnings and proceeded, they were either very stupid or very bad. It was the bad folks that Lucky wanted to know about.

Like Tarr, Lucky also adhered to the theory that just because you're paranoid doesn't mean they're not after you. Since both brothers had made some fairly significant enemies during the course of their earlier careers, erring on the side of caution seemed prudent. Besides, Lucky just liked screwing around with crap like that. Remember Tarr's penthouse?

The brothers clinked glasses. "To the technology of our paranoia." Tarr smiled at his big brother.

Tarr and Lucky spent almost every Saturday night and Sunday together. Each was all the family the other had. They were obviously very comfortable with each other. That couldn't be said of all brothers.

After a few minutes watching the sun sink into the western sky, Tarr refilled his and Lucky's glasses. "I want to bring you up-to-date on what's happening in town."

"You mean about you killing that nice young finance professor you nearly kneecapped awhile back?" Lucky had a Cheshire cat's grin on his face as he spoke.

"Been reading the local paper online again, have we?" Tarr had an equally cynical grin on his face.

Even though the house was extremely isolated physically, it wasn't isolated electronically. There was a computer uplink hidden among the rocks giving Lucky access to databases worldwide. He was well connected and obviously well informed about the murder. Clearly, his thinking was also running along the same lines as Tarr's.

"So, you gonna tell me about it or what" Lucky was still smiling.

Chapter 23

Tarr was watching a small green lizard catching the last rays of sun on the side of a boulder at the edge of the natural stone patio. "There's not really much to tell. When the boy wonder didn't make class for a couple of days, the students finally got around to reporting it. I think they were hoping to get him in trouble with the Dean.

"Since Gibbs skipped class on a fairly regular basis, no one gave it much thought. When he went a couple more days without honoring the students with his presence, Dean Haller told his secretary to call the police.

"Apparently, the cops went over to Gibbs's house, broke in when no one answered the doorbell, and found a very ripe and very dead finance professor. The really weird part is that he was beaten to death."

Lucky was leaning toward Tarr with his forearms resting on his knees. "Yeah, I know about the beating thing, but why? From what you've told me about Gibbs, he hasn't gotten to know anybody well enough to foster that kind of anger. I mean, you've really got to have a ton of rage built up inside to beat somebody to death. Not to mention what it would do to your hands."

Tarr held up his very healthy and unmarked hands for his brother to examine. "See, no marks, no rage. The guy wasn't worth it. To me or anybody else associated with him.

"I guess he could have been poking some jealous guy's wife, but even then, I still don't see the beating."

Lucky was smiling again. "Used your walking stick on him, did you? Whupped him upside the head I bet."

Tarr was extending his right hand toward his brother with a very prominent and easily understood one-finger salute. "Aren't we cute today? You really need to get out more. Maybe I could arrange a date for you with the GJPD detective who dropped by to see me. He seems to have thought of the same thing. Maybe the two of you could discuss your theories over a venti caramel latte."

Lucky was slouching back in his chair as he sipped the Gentleman Jack. His eyes caught those of his brother over the rim of the glass. In a more serious tone he said, "This thing has your name written all over it. The only thing they left out of the news report was your name and address."

"Tell me about it." Tarr was returning his brother's stare. "I was hoping I was just being a bit paranoid, but if you came to the same conclusion and so did the detective, I guess I'm not. The big question then, is why?"

"You bet the question is why?" Lucky had gotten out of his chair and was now pacing. It was his way of thinking. "You know as well as I do that a hit like this took a lot of time, planning, and money. And a very cool professional hitter.

"Hitters like that aren't listed in the yellow pages, plus they are very expensive. You apparently pissed off a well-connected person of financial means. Any names come to mind?"

Chapter 24

"You know, this is going to sound crazy and I wouldn't mention it to anybody else." Tarr was still watching the lizard as it slithered across the rock and out of sight. "I think something goofy is happening on campus."

"What do you mean goofy?"

"Well, it's just a feeling I've had for the last couple of years. The admissions office keeps reporting that our student enrollment is going up. We even have about 2,000 international students." The sun had started to set and Tarr's face took on a pinkish glow from the fading light.

Lucky's face was casting a shadow toward Tarr as he spoke. He spit a piece of ice from his drink in the general direction of his brother. It was apparent to Tarr that his big brother was going into his country boy persona. "That's a good thing, ain't it? Don't you highfalutin professorial types need a steady supply of young bodies with eager minds so you can mold them in your own images?"

Tarr countered by sending a piece of ice into Lucky's lap making him jump to brush it off. "That's right, we live to mold young minds." There was a healthy dose of cynicism in his voice. "That's where it gets goofy!

Even though the student population is supposedly increasing, my class numbers have actually dropped about 10% over the past two years. We've also had two professors leave and neither has been replaced. And the business administration department is part of the biggest department on campus."

"Have you noticed any other anomalies?" Lucky had switched from country boy to intellectual.

"As a matter of fact I have." The sky was taking on the dark shadows of early evening as Tarr answered his brother.

"Those 2,000 foreign students have got to be the poorest attending students on the face of the earth. I bet I didn't see two dozen all semester. And only about half those in business classes.

"The primary reason most foreign students come to this country is to study business. You don't think they come to the greatest business nation on earth to study home economics do you?

"I think I had three in my Principles of Marketing class, and that was it. You'd think that with an out-of-state tuition of $30,000 a year, they'd want to come to class. My big question is: where are they?"

Lucky was scratching numbers in the dirt with his pocket knife. "Wow! My country calculator says that 2,000 foreign students multiplied times $30,000 equals 60 million dollars. "That's a lot of money; maybe it's connected. You know: money —finance professor?

"But it doesn't really make sense why you would be framed for the murder. What do truant international students have to do with you or with the murder?"

It had gotten dark enough so that Tarr was having trouble seeing the arithmetic in the dirt. "I don't know, but I'm willing to bet something. You know the minute someone is killed, the cops look for a crime of passion or greed.

"If the murder had to do with greed, what better way to disguise it than as a crime of passion? And what better person to point the finger at than a big ole marketing professor who got in a heated argument with the victim and terminated the discussion by whacking him with a stick?

"I could be in serious trouble, Lucky. This has professional hit written all over it. A professional killer without connections to the victim is almost impossible to catch."

Lucky stood and dusted the seat of his pants. "And especially if the hitter was hired by somebody with access to 60 million dollars. Let's continue this inside where we can sit on soft leather furniture and eyeball each other."

Chapter 25

Tarr never got tired of coming home. Ever since he was in the 2nd grade and Lucky the 5th, this hole in the cliff had been their home. Although both were afraid of it and their grandfather in the beginning, the young boys had quickly grown to love the isolated location and the man who had built it.

Grandpa had devoted the last part of his life to his two grandsons. On his deathbed, he told them the years with them had been some of the happiest of his life. After their grandmother had died, he bought the land and built the house so he could grieve alone and not have to deal with others. He didn't think he would ever be happy again.

He told them God had a way of screwing with your plans though. Just when he thought he could sink no lower and had decided it was time to retire to his cave house with a couple sticks of lit dynamite, along came these two little sad kids.

They were his blood, sons of a daughter with whom he had lost touch. He was all they had. And they were all he had. God sent them to each other so they could heal their hurting souls.

Well, it had worked and he lived to see them as grown men. When he died, he left them the house and property. He was buried in the rearmost section of the box canyon just down the dirt road.

Lucky opened the heavy metal door leading into the house. As Tarr passed through and closed it, he pushed a button to the right of the door going in. Slowly, another garage door similar to the one where Tarr had parked the Hummer began its descent. It, too, was painted to blend with the cliff face.

The boys were buttoned up for the night, invisible from the outside world. The house had been built with total privacy in mind. Once the metal garage door was lowered, it completely covered the opening to the outside. When open during the day, vast amounts of light streamed in through the two large windows.

Never one to be trapped, even inside a stone fortress, Grandpa had built in an emergency escape route that went underground and came up in a clump of sagebrush. Even if discovered, which was highly unlikely, there was a locked metal hatch on the outside exit and another barring entrance to the house.

The inside of the house was similar to other houses with some decided differences. First was the ceiling. Unlike most houses with drywall nailed to the ceiling and painted, the ceiling of their house had metal mesh secured to it with heavy anchor bolts drilled into the granite. You didn't want a piece of rock separated from the ceiling conking you in the head.

The 3,000 square feet of space was left much like a Manhattan loft. It was just one large space with a kitchen on the opposite end from the opening. The only enclosed room, a bathroom, was built into the corner left of the door.

As is the case with most cave homes, dripping water is often a problem. Being a skilled engineer, Grandpa had designed a system for channeling the water into a cistern he had blasted behind the bathroom.

He had built the bathroom by the front opening so he could run drain pipes underground to ten 50-gallon steel drums he cut and welded together. He then buried them together about 100 feet off west of the house. He chose that direction because of the downward slant of the land. Gravity is a wonderful thing.

He had also concealed three solar panels in a cluster of rocks and run cables underground back to the house. He had blasted a small 20 foot by 20 foot cavern adjacent to the house and then drilled a connecting 5-inch hole from the cavern to the house.

In the cavern were batteries charged by the solar panels and a back-up gas generator. He ran the electrical conduit containing the wire through the hole and carefully caulked around the conduit to create an airtight seal. The design prevented any carbon monoxide from the generator seeping into the house.

The front of the utility cavern was secured with a garage type door similar to those protecting the front door and garage. It too was almost invisible to the casual observer.

The bathroom used an electric pump to provide water for the shower and toilet. Waste flowed through the gravity feed drain to the steel drums. Each was set up like a mini-septic tank. Grandpa had predicted they would last indefinitely with the minimal use of two or three people.

The stove, lights, computer equipment and other appliances were all powered by the solar electricity stored in the batteries. With an average of 300 days of sunshine a year, the backup generator was seldom used other than to test it occasionally. A water filtration system provided drinking water.

Close to the kitchen was a large homemade dining room table. Grandpa had made it out of 2"x6"x12' lumber. By using eight planks screwed together with strips of flatiron on the underside, he had created a 4 foot by 12 foot table.

One end of it was bolted onto a stone ledge about 3 feet off the floor. The other end was supported by a single leg fashioned from the trunk of an aspen tree.

There had been only one chair at the table when they first came. Now there were three, all homemade by grandpa.

The boys had spent endless hours sitting at the table doing homework during their home schooling years.

The end of the table was where Lucky sat the cooler he had brought in.

The "bedrooms" were on one of the side walls. They weren't really bedrooms; they were three chambers blasted and drilled out of the rock.

Each was about seven feet long, a little wider than a twin bed mattress and about five feet high. When the curtain over the opening was closed, it provided a little privacy to the sleeper.

Wiring for the light in each bedroom was handled the same way it was everywhere else in the house. Conduit started at a junction box and snaked along the walls throughout. The bedrooms, like the rest of the house, were well lit at night.

Just as with the dining room chair, there was only one bedroom when the boys first arrived. It took about two months to get the other two carved out.

Once that was done, a mattress was thrown in, lights and curtains hung, and they had a warm place to sleep in the winter and a cool place in the summer.

Because the house was surrounded by hundreds of feet of rock in all directions except forward, the temperature hardly ever deviated from about 70 degrees. For those really cold days, there was a small electric heater that raised the temperature the few degrees required for comfort.

Tarr was looking around the house like he had never seen it before. Grandpa's vision and skill had been amazing. "Remember when we asked grandpa why a cave house? You remember what he said?"

"Yeah, I do." Lucky had sat down on one of two dark brown leather sofas sitting facing each other in the middle of the room. "He said he had seen cave houses in a couple parts of the world and thought they made a lot of sense."

With drilling and controlled blasting you could create any size opening desired. When it was as big a hole as you wanted, you took the blasted out rock and used it to construct the front wall. Because of the nature of solid rock, it required almost no maintenance.

The solar system and a couple of electric pumps were all that required regular upkeep and that was minimal. There was even an abundant food supply, if you weren't opposed to critter cuisine. Lucky seemed to be more partial to City Market.

In one corner of the house was the library with a third brown leather sofa facing it. Grandpa had bought the three leather sofas years ago. He said he didn't want the boys fighting over who got to sit on what.

There was no TV in the house, never had been. There were, however, bookshelves against most of the walls. One area had always been called the library because it also had an antique pecan rolltop desk sitting against the wall. It was Grandma's favorite piece of furniture and the only thing Grandpa had brought with him. Lucky had added two modern oak computer tables to the area.

Chapter 26

Tarr sat at the dining room table and made a salad while Lucky broiled a couple of steaks. All cooking was done in the house. Things like barbeque smoke attracted too much attention. It could be seen for miles up on top of Glade Park. Since everyone thought the area was uninhabited, someone might come looking for a brush fire.

Lucky was bent over with his head half way in the oven as he stuck a fork in one of the steaks to test doneness. Both boys liked their meat red and juicy. "So, what you gonna do about the killing? You ought to be checking the yellow pages for a good lawyer. My guess is this might get a lot worse in a hurry."

Tarr continued to tear the lettuce into bite sized pieces. "You're right. My gut is doing back flips every time I think about it. I still can't figure out who I pissed off enough to cause this."

Lucky had slipped on an oven mitt and was taking the steaks out of the oven. "My first guess would be a jealous husband, but any woman that would go out with you is probably so ugly her husband would send you a thank-you note and pay for a weekend in Vegas."

Tarr had moved the lettuce to one side and was working on a tomato and couple of cucumbers. "You're confusing my love life with yours. I have you know I've been on three dates with the best-looking history professor on campus. To the best of my knowledge, the only husband she has is an ex. And he lives two mountain passes away in Denver.

"The only person I've pissed off enough to make them turn red in the face, other than the now deceased finance professor, was the President of our fine institution."

"You pissed off the guy in the big office overlooking the quad? The guy who bosses everybody around? The guy who signs your paycheck?" Lucky's head was now buried in the refrigerator as he searched for salad dressing. "You must have a burning desire to leave that bird's nest you call home and move back out to God's country."

"That's the great thing about being a tenured, Full Professor. I can say anything to anybody as long as it has some connection, however limited, to my academic position on campus. And you know me, easy-going company man that I am. I always use tact and diplomacy."

"Tact and diplomacy? Your idea of tact is to piss on only one of the guy's shoes. And diplomacy? Isn't that where you negotiate with the guy while you're holding him six inches off the floor with your big paw wrapped around his throat?" Lucky was holding his own hand up in the air to simulate the aforementioned chokehold.

Tarr let out a belly laugh watching his brother do his shadow choking routine with one hand while pretending to pee with the other. "In the President's case, it would be pissing on a thousand dollar, handmade, imported Italian loafer. But I have to admit, he got really torqued over my questioning the academic integrity of new international centers he wanted to start."

Lucky had given up his acting routine and was headed to the table with two plates each containing a really big steak. "What kind of international centers?"

Tarr reached to relieve Lucky of one of the plates. "The kind where we go to some place like Albania and start an entrepreneurship center to help some struggling third world, ex-Eastern Bloc country jumpstart its economy.

"It's all part of the new mission of the college. It started when President Karp showed up several years ago. He's raised a ton of money from anonymous donors to finance the new centers. We must have a dozen of them scattered around

Europe. Who knows what those things cost?

"One thing about the Prez, though; he has really changed TMC with all the new money."

Lucky was drizzling dressing on the salad he had unceremoniously dumped to one side of the plate by the steak. "Good changes?" He didn't look up as he spoke; he was honing in on the steak with a sharp knife.

"I'm not really sure." Tarr was putting a piece of steak into his mouth as he answered. While he chewed, the wheels were turning inside his head.

"Some are good; we've had good raises every year since he got here. Some bad; shared governance of the college has all but disappeared. In most colleges, the faculty shares in making major decisions on campus. Not us; not anymore. It's like everything is so secretive now.

"That's what made the President so mad at me. I pretty much said to him what I just said to you. I told him the decision to add new programs was a faculty decision and that faculty had an obligation to question the academic integrity of off-campus offerings like the new international centers.

"To my knowledge, not a single full-time tenured faculty member has ever been to one of our international centers, much less reviewed the academic qualifications of the professors there.

"And it's not just the international centers. TMC has an online college with at last count about 3,000 students spread across the U.S. All this is in addition to the international students we were talking about earlier."

Lucky was paying a lot of attention to cutting every piece of fat off his steak before he started eating. "Online students, huh? Isn't that the 'in thing' these days?"

Lucky could see in Tarr's face that he was giving a great deal of thought to the conversation. "Yeah, it's the 'in thing' all over the country, especially for private colleges that get no state funding.

"The problem isn't with the online concept; it's with the fact that campus faculty are not involved in the teaching of a single online class. They're all taught by this online faculty that none of us knows and none of us reviewed their academic credentials. As far as we know, they could be inmates in the federal prison system.

"It's really a little strange, if you ask me."

Lucky was washing down a bite of salad and smiling as he looked at his little brother. "Well, it looks like the Prez didn't ask you. Furthermore, it looks like he doesn't want you injecting professorial indignation at not being asked your opinion.

"So, let me get this straight, Thunder Mountain College has about 5,000 traditional on-campus, good ole all-American students. You've got another 3,000 online students. How many international students do you have?"

Tarr was pushing a piece of steak around his plate with his fork as he thought. "I'm not sure; maybe 2,000-3,000, but no one really knows except the registrar. Most of them come through TMC's language school in Biloxi, Mississippi, before they come to the campus. Language school can take a couple of years."

Lucky had gone to the "library" and returned with paper and pencil. "Okay, what's the damage to attend that little Harvard in the desert you call Thunder Mountain College: 20-30 K a year?"

Tarr had finally speared the pursued piece of meat and had it halfway to his mouth. "You're on the money; tuition and fees run about $30,000 a year.

"We're one of the most expensive schools in the country. A lot of students get scholarships, though.

"With a college endowment[1] of several hundred million

---

[1] A college endowment is the amount of money the college has been given by private donors. The money is available for the college to spend for whatever it deems appropriate.

dollars, very few American students pay the full freight. The full tuition is probably only charged to international and online students."

Lucky had been writing on the page and was starting to do a little math.

International Students	2,000 x $30,000=$60,000,000
Online Students (estimated)	3,000 x $30,000=$90,000,000
Traditional Students estimated tuition after scholarships	5,000x$15,000=$75,000,000
Total Tuition	$225,000,000 per year

"My, oh my! Do you know that TMC is bringing in conservatively, $225,000,000 a year in tuition?"

Tarr whistled softly. "No, I've never really taken the time or had the interest to do the math. And that amount doesn't include the 100 million or so a year the Prez raises to fund the international centers. The total has got to be well over 300 million dollars a year. And there could be countless other revenue streams of dollars flowing into the college that we don't know about."

Lucky had his Cheshire cat grin plastered across his sun-weathered face. "I don't really see a connection between the college's finances and a dead finance professor, but that's a lot of money and there's a dead guy whose specialty was money stuff. You thinking what I'm thinking?"

Tarr's grin mimicked that of his brother's. "You bet I am. That much money has the appearance of evil all over it. Maybe we should scratch around it a little and see if a stink drifts out.

You never know where a skunk has his den."

Lucky's grin had been replaced by a concerned look. "Before we start poking a polecat, maybe you ought to cover that big fat rear end of yours a little. It's hanging out already.

"If someone finds out we're digging, their interest in making you disappear might ratchet up a few notches. I don't want to have to break you out of the Mesa County jail."

Tarr pushed his chair back from the table. "You're right. We'd better put together a tactical plan this weekend. We might also need a little backup. Talked to Jack lately?"

Both brothers laughed as Lucky spoke. "This is gonna be a lot of fun."

Chapter 27

Jack was another Glade Park local the boys had known most of their lives. He grew up on a ranch several miles west of them.

After a couple of years raising the brothers, Grandpa realized the two of them needed to be around kids their own age. In those days, Glade Park was very sparsely populated. Jack's family ranch was the only place with other children close enough to visit on a regular basis.

Before too long, the three boys were inseparable. If one showed up behind a rock in the high desert, the other two were never far away.

After high school, Jack joined the army. Just like Lucky, he became a member of the Special Forces. He was in the Green Berets whereas Lucky was a member of the Navy Seals. He did not choose to make the military a career though.

After a couple of combat tours on a Green Beret A-Team, Jack left the service of his country and headed for the beaches of California. That's where his life took a different direction.

Through some contacts he had made in South America, he entered the import business. That, in and of itself, was not all that bad. The real problem was with the imported merchandise of choice, marijuana.

By some accounts, Jack was one of the major distributors on the West Coast in the early 80's. He had the beach house, the expensive foreign cars, and a yacht at Newport Beach.

Life was good! Good, that is, until DEA came a callin' one night when he just happened to have two tons of grass in his warehouse. The house, cars, and boat were all confiscated by the courts and Jack was sentenced to a California mental institution.

It seems Jack had always exhibited bizarre behavior. The

courtroom was no different. Because the Judge held very liberal views on the use of marijuana and because Jack dealt only in marijuana and never narcotics, the judge decided Jack deserved a break.

Since Jack was obviously deranged at some level, the Judge declared him insane. He was sentenced to a California State Mental Institution until such time as he was capable of reentering society.

A year later, Jack was deemed cured and released. He disappeared from California and seemingly from the face of the earth. For eight years, he was not heard from. Many thought he had simply gone abroad and begun life under a different name with the fortune he had stashed in off-shore accounts.

The truth was somewhere in between. He managed to scrape together enough money from a couple of old friends to finance a one-way plane ticket to Africa. There he joined an ex-Green Beret he had served with in the past.

Jack had two basic sets of skills. One was in the import area. He had gotten lucky with the legal system once; he didn't want to push his luck.

Jack's second set of skills was as a soldier. With his superior training, courtesy of Uncle Sam, and the successful application of that training in hot spots around the world, Jack became a mercenary.

After eight years of one hot spot after another, Jack began to think about the future. Soldiering was the only real skill he had. Since he saw his fighting days coming to an end, he decided to get into the management end of things.

Because of the changing nature of the world, Jack thought there might be the need for a different kind of mercenary. His vision allowed him to start and become one of the most successful security consultants in the world.

Through some old contacts still in the Army, Jack recruited a small team of young ex-soldiers. Instead of flying off to fight in third world countries, however, his soldiers became an elite bodyguard team for the Princes of corporate America.

His soldiers were trained to become an invisible part of a corporate executive's entourage. They learned how to dress and which fork to use at dinner. By the end of the 90's, Jack's company, High Desert Security Consulting, had become the number one company in its industry.

Very few people outside of corporate America's elite knew the company even existed. Even fewer knew it was headquartered on Glade Park just a few miles west of the Baldridge place.

Chapter 28

Tarr had a senior marketing class every Monday and Wednesday from 4:30 to 5:45. After finishing what he considered a dynamic lecture (the students reserved the right to disagree), he was putting his notes back into a rather expensive but somewhat tattered attaché case. One of his students lingered while the rest quickly made themselves scarce.

"What's going on, Seth?" Tarr looked up and smiled. Seth was a marketing major who had struggled as a student for a while until he found his way into Tarr's Principles of Marketing class two years earlier. A change of major and a lot of personal attention had brought him to his third class with Dr. Tarr Baldridge.

Seth seemed nervous as he looked at his feet, but would not meet Tarr's gaze. "I heard the police talked to you about Dr. Gibbs's murder. Then I read that stuff in the newspaper the other day. You don't know this and I wouldn't want it to get around, but I've had some experience with the police myself.

"If it weren't for you helping me out, I'd probably be in jail today. It seems like every time I was about to do something stupid that first year I knew you, you'd stop me in the hallway and ask me how things were going. You always got me to thinking about my future. It kept me out of a lot of trouble."

Tarr reached over and lightly slapped Seth on the shoulder. "It wasn't really anything that I did, you have always been one of the good guys; it just took you a little while to sort things out. Now look at you; you've got the second highest average in the class."

Tarr picked up the attaché and took a step toward the door. Seth was still acting uncharacteristically nervous. Tarr stopped and looked back at one of his favorite students. "Don't worry about the police talking to me; it was just routine."

"It looks like more than that to me." Seth shifted his position so he could look at the man who had been so kind to him.

"Based on my experience, I'd say the cops have you in their crosshairs; they just haven't figured out when to pull the trigger. That description of the killer had your name written all over it. They might as well have published your picture under it."

"Well, I can't say I disagree with your learned opinion of the situation, but I'll survive it. The reason I am so sure is because I'm innocent. Don't worry, I'll be o.k."

Tarr started to leave again, but Seth didn't budge. Tarr knew him well enough to know that he still had something on his mind. "O.K., let's have it; what's stuck in that big brain that's bothering you?" Tarr sat down on the edge of the table to take the weight off his bad leg. Standing for long periods of time wasn't as easy as it used to be.

Seth pulled a classroom chair closer and sat down. He didn't think it polite to look down at his friend and professor. "Do you know Kelsie Daggett?"

Tarr thought for a couple of seconds. "Wasn't she in that Principles of Marketing class you first had with me? As I recall, I had to call you down a couple of times for trying to talk to her while I was lecturing.

"I've seen you around campus with her a few times. What's she got to do with this?"

"Well." Seth's face had turned a deep shade of red. "She and I would have been dating for about two months when Gibbs got tagged. It's all really weird, but it's got to be tied together."

Seth had Tarr's attention. The Professor leaned closer. "What do you mean would have been dating?"

"Like I said, Kelsie and I would have been dating for about two months, if she hadn't left school all of a sudden and gone to

California."

"Students do that sometimes." Tarr shrugged.

"Not if they've seniors really into their finance major who just got truly excited about an independent study they were working on for their advisor. Not if they were planning a weekend in Vegas with their boyfriend. Not if she called me the night she supposedly left and told me she had found out something really scary."

"When did she leave?'

"It was about two weeks before the murder. She just disappeared. I got an e-mail from her the night after we last talked saying she needed a break from school and was going to California. Two or three of her other friends that I talked to got the same e-mail.

"It just doesn't make sense for her to leave like that."

"Do you know what Kelsie was working on for her advisor?" Tarr could see that Seth was on the verge of tears.

Seth took a deep breath and held it for a few seconds. "She told me it was an independent study for Dr. Gibbs and that it was very confidential. After making me swear on my mother's life not to repeat it, she told me.

"Did you know she was a finance major and a work-study in the V.P. of Finance's office?"

Tarr didn't like the way this was shaping up. "No, I didn't know any of that. I used to speak to her on the Quad, but I didn't really know her that well. A student usually has to be in a couple of my classes before I learn much about them. What was so confidential about what she was doing for Dr. Gibbs?"

Seth was obviously very hesitant to break his word to Kelsie. "I guess since she split on me, it's o.k. to tell you. She was helping Dr. Gibbs get information on the finances of TMC."

"Why would Gibbs want that?"

"I asked Kelsie why. She said he wanted to understand everything about the college's financial procedures so he could be better prepared than the rest of the faculty."

"Did she say better prepared for what?"

"She thought he wanted to be a Dean or something.'

"But why all the secrecy; why not just walk into the V.P.'s office and ask him?"

Seth seemed to ponder the question as his brow wrinkled. "When I had Gibbs for managerial finance class, he turned out to be one of those professors who thought he knew everything, you know the type. He'd never admit to the class that he didn't know something.

"My best guess is that he would never admit to somebody like the V.P. that there was something about finance he didn't know."

Tarr shifted his weight to a more comfortable position on the desk. "So, Kelsie's independent study was to find information about the college's finances and secretly give it to Gibbs so he could be viewed as some type of expert on college finances?

"I wonder what she found that scared her? Got any ideas?"

"Not really." Seth stood up as a student came through the door and headed for the back of the classroom. It was about time for the next class to start. "But whatever it was, it sure spooked her. I could hear her voice trembling when we talked.

"I've got to go; I've got to be at work before long."

Tarr followed Seth out of the classroom and into the hall. They walked through a double glass doorway and outside. "Seth, one more question; have you told anybody else what you just told me?"

"No sir, Dr. Baldridge, I haven't told anybody."

"Do me a favor, Seth; don't mention this to a soul. I'll check it out and get back to you. Also, if you happen to hear from Kelsie, please let me know."

"You got it, Dr. Baldridge; I won't mention it. But I doubt I'll hear from her. Something deep down tells me I'll never hear from her again. She's so scared of whatever it was she found, she took off for good."

With his shoulders slumped down and sadness etched on his face, Seth turned and started walking toward the parking lot.

Tarr turned and headed back into the building to his office. As he walked, he tried to process what Seth had told him. Something really weird was going on.

Could Gibbs have been killed because of the information Kelsie gave him? Was she really running or was it something else? And why try to pin it on him. There was one thing that Kelsie, Gibbs, and he had in common.

They were all interested in college finances. He had questioned new international centers. Could there be a connection?

Chapter 29

A few days later, it was fall break and Tarr had Monday and Tuesday off. It was now Monday and he was in a downtown Denver high-rise office building reading a travel magazine as he waited for a two o'clock appointment.

After talking to his student Seth on Friday, he decided he should go on the offensive. Something was cooking in the kitchen and he might just get burned if he weren't careful.

After class on Friday, Tarr had called Doni and asked if she would meet him for a drink at *The Sanctuary*. They agreed on 8:30.

Tarr had just settled into a nice quiet corner booth when Doni walked in. After letting her eyes adjust to the dim light, she saw Tarr and walked back.

Extending his hand as she walked up, Tarr gently guided her into the booth until she was seated close to his side.

Tarr knew a couple things about Doni after several dates. First, she was never late and second, she liked whiskey on the rocks just like him. Damn he loved compatibility.

"Thanks for coming." Tarr was admiring his lovely companion. Very few women looked really bad in the low light of a bar. It took, he thought, an exceptional one to look really good. Doni was stunning.

Before he could say anything else the waiter walked up with two drinks balanced on his tray. "Two Gentleman Jacks on the rocks with water backs. Anything else I can do for you, Dr. Baldridge?"

Tarr put a ten on the tray. "Thanks, Bib; that's all we need; keep the change."

"Doni lifted her glass in the traditional salute. "Here's to a guy that obviously hangs out in this bar so much the waiter knows his name. Did you call him Bib; what kind of name is that?"

Tarr couldn't help but grin at his date's irreverence. "First of all, if you survive the tenure process and stay in this town a few years, you won't be able to go anywhere without bumping into a current student, ex-student or some acquaintance thereof.

"In Bib's case, I had his sister in class a couple of years ago. As to his name, I've never had the courage to ask."

Doni took another sip of her drink and stared at Tarr over the top of the glass. "You know everyone on campus is talking about you. Since the article in the paper about Dr. Gibbs's murder, people are saying they always knew there was something secretive about you and some even described you as scary. The consensus on the grapevine is that you did it."

Tarr smiled at Doni and saluted her. "And a good evening to you too, Dr. Rader. Is the gossip train on campus carrying any good news?"

Doni gave Tarr a reciprocal, if cynical smile. "Yes, as a matter of fact it is. Most faculty say they don't blame you. Gibbs wasn't very well liked."

Tarr put his hand over Doni's, "I've got a pretty big favor to ask. I'm not sure whether or not you'll like it."

Doni tried to read Tarr's facial expression as she spoke, "Well, this is kinda like our fourth date; do you want me to come to your place and provide decorating advice? Maybe you want me to see your etchings or something of that nature."

When Tarr did not come back with his usual smart-ass response, Doni quit smiling. "This must really be serious or else you're really messing with me."

Tarr moved his face closer to hers. "It is serious. If the campus grapevine has convicted me of murder, how long do you think it will be before the police try to follow suit? Right now, I'm on the defensive just waiting for something to happen.

"Doni, if I don't move, I could end up in serious trouble. That brings me to the favor.

"I need a good defense attorney and I need him like yesterday. My personal attorney told me there was only one "go to" guy in Colorado for this type of situation. Guess who he suggested?"

Doni laughed out loud. "Now let me get this straight. You need a defense attorney and you want me to do you a favor.

"With ten years of college under my belt, I should be able to figure this out. Hum, I wonder what favor I could possibly do for you?

"Could it possibly have anything to do with my ex-husband, arguably the best defense attorney in the state of Colorado? I wonder if that could be it."

Tarr was smiling, but weakly. "Well, according to my local business attorney, there is no arguably to it; he is the best. Being the best means he is probably very hard to get in to see. I just thought a call from his very beautiful ex-wife might grease the skids a bit."

"Let me make sure I know exactly what the favor is; you want me to call my ex-husband and ask him to schedule an appointment with my current boyfriend? Is that about it?"

Tarr removed his hand from Doni's and put his arm around her pulling her closer. "Well alright, I'm your current boyfriend, huh? You know, I do have a few etchings I'd like for you to see."

A sharp elbow in the ribs put a little distance between the two. "Etchings you say, I knew you hadn't had a date in a while. On our first date, I kept waiting for you to ask me my astrological sign.

"You're such a helpless little thing, though; maybe I'll ask my ex-husband to see my boyfriend. There's nothing weird about that."

Laughing one of his belly laughs, Tarr said, "Now that we're going steady, would you wear my letterman sweater."

Doni was laughing too. "This is serious business, why are we both making a joke of it?"

Tarr took her hand again. "Because, I suspect, we're both scared. You're scared you'll lose your new hunk of a boyfriend to a prison lover; and I'm scared no one in prison will think I'm pretty."

He blocked her sharp elbow this time. "You are dopey, you know. You must be a little concerned or you wouldn't want to see a defense lawyer."

As Tarr held his defensive posture against another attack of the elbow, he said, "I'm not scared because I'm innocent. I'm concerned because I look so guilty."

"Answer me a question; if you didn't care for me so much, would you think I killed Gibbs?"

"Who says I care for you? Maybe I'm waiting for something better to come along?"

"Okay, if you hadn't been wasting your time with me for the past few weeks, would you believe me innocent?"

"Now that's more like it. I'd have to say, probably not. The weight of public opinion is against you."

Tarr took a sip of his Gentleman Jack. "There you go. Convicted before I've had my day in court.

"But seriously, you see my point about doing something instead of hanging around until the police are forced to move on me, don't you?"

"Yes I do; and yes, I will call my ex tonight as soon as I get home. Tarr, we can both joke about this, but we both know this is serious business.

"Now with the serious stuff out of the way, I want to say something. Don't let me give you any ideas, but I do care for you a tiny, tiny bit; not much, just a little. And on a more pragmatic note, it would be hard to start over again after our lengthy one-month relationship."

Tarr was smiling at her humor. "I do know this is serious, and I will make nothing of your profession of deep, deep love for me.

"But seriously, thank you."

Chapter 30

"Dr. Baldridge." Tarr looked up as his name was spoken. Standing in front of him was a very distinguished looking man in an expensively tailored suit. From the look of him, he spent a great deal of time in the gym. Accenting his athletic build was a full head of what was obviously prematurely gray hair.

"Good morning. I'm Kent Latimer."

"Please call me Tarr."

"Won't you come into my office?"

Tarr stood up, retrieved his cane, and followed the $1,200 suit down a short hall and into an elaborately, yet tastefully, decorated office.

"May I offer you a cup of coffee or something else to drink?"

"No, thank you, I'm fine." Tarr spoke as he settled his oversized frame into one of two matching wingback leather chairs facing the desk.

Latimer seemed to be sizing up the man in front of him as he spoke. "Doni tells me you anticipate being charged with murder in the near future. Why don't we start by you telling me what brings you to this conclusion?"

Tarr liked the direct approach from Latimer, no pleasantries, no get to know you talk, just straight to the point. At $250 an hour for consultation and $500 an hour if the case went to trial, direct seemed like a good idea.

"Well, Mr. Latimer."

"Please call me Kent."

"Well, Kent, it all seems to have started several weeks ago over an academic debate involving student learning as a function of professorial teaching."

Fifteen minutes later Tarr summarized the situation as a conclusion to the question. "So, a professor with whom I had an intellectual difference and one I hit with my walking stick is dead. The campus community believes I killed him; the police are no doubt trying to prove I killed him; and, if I didn't know I was innocent, I might even believe I killed him too.

"The deck seems to be stacked against me. My most immediate concern is staying out of jail as I try to figure out what is going on."

Latimer had not interrupted during Tarr's explanation of the situation; he had merely sat leaned back in his chair, with his ten fingers forming a tent in front of him. "It would appear that certain circumstantial evidence points the murder in your direction. I agree, you probably have a serious problem. But why me, why not an attorney in Grand Junction? There must be someone there who is more knowledgeable about the local situation."

Tarr shifted his large frame in the chair and looked Latimer in the eye. "Two reasons I'm sitting in your office: Doni and my personal business attorney. They both say you are the best and before this is over, I may need the best.

"Someone with deep pockets and even deeper connections is going to a lot of trouble to make it look like I killed Gibbs. If I'm going to survive this, I have to stay out of jail."

Latimer smiled. "You're here because my ex-wife recommended me to you, her current boyfriend; a recommendation validated by your own attorney. I guess that makes sense in a kind of twisted, modern day way. So, if I accept you as a client, what do you want me to do, hire a detective to investigate, just wait for your one phone call from jail, or something else?"

Tarr was beginning to like this guy; he could see a glimmer of what must have attracted Doni to him. "I don't need a detective; I've got that aspect of things under control. What I do need is a get out of jail card if needed."

"When Detective Orr comes after me, he'll do it in such a way that I'll be off-guard or he'll come late at night when all nice little attorneys are home in bed. He will want a couple of hours alone to try and break me down."

Latimer had a questioning look on his face. "Are you afraid of Orr or possibly of being locked up over night?"

"No, I'm not worried about Orr. He's a skilled detective, but nothing I can't handle. I'm more concerned about jail. Remember, the people trying to point this my way are well connected. How hard would it be for me to have a little accident while behind bars?"

"I see you've given this some thought." Latimer spoke as he stood up behind his desk and walked around to the front where Tarr was sitting. Taking a seat in the other wingback chair, he continued, "Let me ask you a few more questions.

"First, why don't you want a detective to snoop around a little? It couldn't hurt having a professional in town to ask a few questions?"

Tarr had anticipated the question, which prompted a smile when it was asked. "I have an old friend who owns a security company. He's helping with the investigation." Tarr didn't think it necessary to clutter up things with an explanation of his own background or the fact that Lucky had come to Denver with him and was, at this very time, doing a little snooping around of his own.

"Second question: You talk like you have experience with law enforcement. I thought you were a marketing professor?"

"I am a marketing professor, but prior to that I was with the Federal Trade Commission. Occasionally, I brushed up against a criminal investigation."

"Third question: Did you kill Dr. Gibbs?"

"No, I did not!"

"Do you have any personal knowledge of his killing or the

circumstances thereof?"

"No, I do not!"

"When you struck Dr. Gibbs in the knee with your walking stick, was it intentional?'

Tarr was smiling again. "Yes, it was. He was an obnoxious little twerp who was making what I thought was a physically aggressive move toward me. I had two choices: turn and pop him one or turn and 'accidentally' stop him. I chose the one I thought would cause the least amount of fallout.

"But let me make something clear; he was out of control. I wasn't. To me, the debate was mildly entertaining; to Gibbs, it was obviously very serious.

"What I hadn't counted on, though, was someone using the situation to try and take me out."

Latimer watched Tarr's body language very closely for tell-tale signs he was lying. No attorney got to his level of success without being able to spot a lie. Either Tarr was a very skillful liar or he was telling the truth. "So, any ideas on who the 'someone' is that is trying to take you out?"

"I've got a hunch, but right now that's all it is." Tarr did not see a reason to add further explanation. He did need an answer to his own question, however. "So, are you willing to accept me as a client given what you know at this point?"

Latimer was obviously not uncomfortable with silence; he simple stared at Tarr for what, with most people, would have been an uncomfortable amount of time. "Doni told me you were innocent. For her to call and ask that I see you, says a lot for what she thinks about you. To my knowledge, she hasn't spent much time on relationships since we split the sheets.

"Even though we are divorced and I'm remarried, I still care about her; I want her to be happy.

"Apparently, you are becoming an important part of her life now. If I can help her by helping you, I'm glad to do so."

Tarr breathed a quiet sigh of relief. He could now spend his time concentrating on the murder and not on how to get out of jail at some future date. "So, what should I do if I'm arrested?"

"I know a retired defense attorney in Grand Junction who is not only very skilled, he also knows all the players there. With your concurrence, I want to call and bring him up to speed about your situation. He'll become the point man for any immediate legal needs. If this thing plays out, and it may well just do that, he'll help me with the case.

"I always like a local face sitting at the defense table when I go to trial. It makes a local jury feel better about my client. I'll give him a call and then ask him to call you if he agrees to help. Any other questions at this point?"

Tarr got to his feet with his cane aiding the ascent. "What about your fees or more specifically the retainer you guys usually require?"

"A $25,000 retainer will do for now; just leave a check with my secretary or wire the money next week." Latimer was extending his right hand to shake as he talked.

Tarr gripped the walking cane in his left hand as he stood and shook the lawyer's hand. Doni had been right, she should have asked for alimony.

Chapter 31

Tarr was meeting Lucky at a Cajun restaurant in the downtown area. After dropping Tarr off at the lawyer's office, Lucky met an old friend who worked for the Colorado Commission on Higher Education (CCHE), the state agency responsible for regulation of all colleges and universities in Colorado.

What Lucky was able to discover was that a private college or university in the state of Colorado has very few serious constraints from the state. First of all, colleges like Thunder Mountain are not subject to "open records law."

There are very weak reporting requirements to and approvals from CCHE. State bureaucracy pretty much disappears for a private school. Such schools bear more resemblance to private corporations than they do to public universities.

Controls are limited to those over any other business. Whereas public universities in Colorado have a governing board appointed by the Governor, private universities nominate and control their own boards.

Private four-year Colleges or Universities that operate in Colorado must be authorized under The Degree Authorization Act. One person is responsible at CCHE for administering the act.

There is no conceivable way that one person can validate the integrity of all the private colleges in Colorado. With just a little imagination, all manner of questionable activities are possible.

The restaurant was just off the 16th Street Mall in Denver. Tarr was dropped off in front by a taxi. Lucky was able to park on a side street about three blocks from the restaurant. Tarr was seated at a table for four just beyond the door to the kitchen.

As Lucky walked up to the table, so did a pretty blond waitress carrying a large serving of fried crawfish. He reached and grabbed a couple pieces of the Louisiana delicacy, from the basket, as he took the seat across from Tarr.

Licking his fingers after stuffing the fried crustaceans into his mouth, Lucky reached for some more. "They still fry up the best 'mudbugs' this side of New Orleans."

Tarr quickly grabbed the basket of fried crawfish and held them out of Lucky's reach. "And you still have the manners of a swabby. Don't you know it's not polite to lick your fingers and then reach back into the basket? At least use your other hand. A fork would really be appreciated, but I know you're still in the initial stages of dinnerware mastery."

"Are you going to let me have some more crawfish or am I going to have to shoot you?" Lucky started searching his jacket for a pretend gun that was not there.

"Okay, you can have what's left." Tarr started to hand the basket to Lucky, but quickly dumped more than half the crawfish on his own plate.

Because the restaurant was too public a place to discuss anything confidential, the two brothers spent the next hour eating and poking fun at each other.

As soon as they made it back to the car and had the doors closed, Lucky begin to bring Tarr up-to-date on what he had discovered. Thirty minutes later they were heading west into the foothills of the Rockies on their way home.

As Tarr admired the mountains up ahead, he glanced over at his brother who was concentrating on keeping the car between the lines. "So, a college like Thunder Mountain doesn't have to have much of its iceberg above the waves then? As long as they don't sell stock in their little venture or try to play with the public schools, they can pretty much hide their activities. That's a cute little setup."

Lucky changed to the passing lane and accelerated around a slow-moving truck as it labored up the first serious stretch of highway climbing the mountains. "Yes, it is. Too bad we can't get a look at their tax returns. If we could, then we would know how much money is really involved here.

"To set you up cost a lot of money. I wonder what you did to make somebody that nervous about you."

"I don't know what I did; my only suspect behavior was when I questioned the President about our international programs. He got pretty pissed as I remember. Whatever it was, I'll bet you a month's pay it has to do with TMC.

"And I think I know how to prove it. I believe I know a possible way to get a peek at Thunder Mountain's tax return. There's an old friend at the Federal Trade Commission who owes me a big favor. Maybe it's time I called it in. Clues to what is really going on have to be buried in the return somewhere.

"Given his current position, I bet he could get a copy of a corporation's tax return without too much difficulty. I'll run down his phone number as soon as I get home.

"In the meantime, did you ask Jack to check out my illustrious President? Who knows where dirt is lurking."

Lucky was in the passing lane again, this time trying to get around a Ford 350 pickup pulling what looked to be a 40-foot travel trailer. "I'll call Jack when we get back and get him started. Now, tell me about your girlfriend's ex-husband and how excited he is to help her current boyfriend. Maybe, with a little luck, all three of you will end up together. What is it the French call that?"

Tarr slapped his brother hard on the arm. "Shut up and drive and I might bring you up-to-date on the meeting with my defense attorney.

"But first, has the parade changed?"

As Lucky glanced in the rearview mirror, he smiled.

129

"Nope, not since we left Junction. I bet parking down by the 16th Street Mall was a bitch for them; except for Jack's boys. They knew where we were going and could plan ahead.

"The cop following us probably just double-parked. What's the worst that could happen; get a ticket he isn't going to pay?

"As for our unknown buddies in the Land Rover, they probably got dizzy from circling the area."

Tarr looked at his brother and grinned. "I really feel bad about them. I bet they didn't even get lunch."

Lucky smiled as he caught sight of them in the rearview mirror. "After dropping you off at your lawyer's office, I called Jack and asked him to have a team pick them up, when we get back in town. It'll be interesting to know whose time clock they're punching."

The smile vacated Lucky's face as he swerved around a slow moving semi. "You know they're going to try and follow me after I drop you off. It wouldn't be too hard to turn the tables on them."

"I could snatch them and make them talk before my evening drink. Might even be fun. I wonder how they like rattlesnakes?"

Tarr rearranged his left leg to ease the pressure on his knee. "I thought all you special forces guys just ate snakes raw after skinning them with your teeth; now I find out you play with them too.

"Try to control those violent urges for now, though. I don't want their bosses to know we're on to them. Let's just let them think I'm running scared to my lawyer in Denver and have no idea I'm being followed around. If they believe I'm afraid enough, maybe they'll let down their guard.

"Remember, to them, I'm just a really handsome and intellectually gifted professor with a, yet to be identified, country bumpkin companion of dwarfish appearance. They probably think you're the condo gardener."

Lucky was able to deliver a quick slap to the stomach

before Tarr could cover up. "Dwarfish gardener, huh? Wait until they discover the truth that I'm your rakishly handsome and mentally superior brother.

"Oh, by the way, I've got a news brief. You're not my biological brother, you were adopted. It's rumored your birth parents were an ape and an elephant."

Chapter 32

The parade made it back to Grand Junction at 5:20. After dropping Tarr off at his condo, it took Lucky another 15 minutes to lose his followers. He then headed west and up to Glade Park. It would be interesting to see what Jack could dig up on the college Prez.

Taking the back way up Little Park Road, Lucky began the ascent. Because the climb was over 2,000 feet, there were several places where a driver could stop and observe the vehicles behind. After two stops, Lucky was confident no one was following.

After about 45 minutes of driving, the entrance to Jack's ranch was just ahead. At least it appeared to be.

The entrance looked normal enough; that is, if you didn't know what to look for. There was the drive, fence going in all directions, a sign, a ranch brand on the sign, the gate, and a few cows grazing nearby.

Lucky couldn't possible see all the security measures even if he looked. He knew they were there, though; Jack was way too careful for them not to be.

As Lucky got in sight of the ranch house about a mile off the main road, he encountered another fence. This one had a closed gate with an intercom to the main house.

Lucky had called Jack as soon as he dropped off Tarr and told him he was coming for a visit and what he wanted. As the 4-Runner approached the gate, it swung open as if by magic. Obviously, there was a security camera or two hidden about.

Jack was sitting on the front porch of the old ranch house watching the truck approach.

Slowing his truck to a stop, Lucky glanced over at his old

friend. The two men's eyes locked. As if on cue, both raised their middle fingers to the other in that universal sign of greeting.

In appearance, Jack was a racial anomaly. He wasn't Anglo; that much was evident. He was about 6 feet tall with black hair quickly giving way to gray. He was neither skinny nor fat; he was somewhere in between. His skin was dark, but not in a Hispanic way. It was more like that of a black Asian. Since Jack was adopted, no one really knew what he was.

He himself, didn't care. Lucky had heard Jack say a thousand times, when questioned about his heritage, "I am what I am. "

Lucky knew Jack's looks could be deceiving. He came across as a very sophisticated man, possibly a Professor or other intellectual.

It was a running joke among the three lifelong friends that Jack looked like the Professor and Tarr the mercenary. It was always reinforced by the other two that Lucky looked like a swabby, albeit an ugly one.

Lucky had seen on more than one occasion what Jack could do with his hands and feet. Even though he only looked like a wealthy gym rat with a few show muscles, Lucky knew Jack was the most dangerous man he knew.

Pulling up a chair closer to Jack on the porch, Lucky accepted the beer extended to him.

"So, non-Anglo looking dude, what's going on in the quest for knowledge concerning Tarr's learned colleague?" Lucky took a long pull on the beer bottle.

"Well, even in the short time my guys have been looking, it's obvious there's something funny going on over in intellectualville. The President seems to have been born academically about 10 years ago. If you check the college yearbooks where he purportedly got degrees, you find no reference to him: no name listing, no photo, no listing of activities, nothing."

Jack took a swig of beer and continued. "It's hard, but not impossible to crack university databases, if you've got enough money. You simply find an appropriate transcript, copy it, change the name, and add another graduate.

"Have you ever read where an educational institution audited its list of graduates? Even if they wanted to, can you imagine the amount of human time that would take?"

"So, you think an academic background could be invented, with enough money involved?" Lucky sat his bottle on the floor.

"Yes, I do."

"But wouldn't someone ultimately discover the scam?"

Jacked laughed, "Are you kidding? Once it's in the computer it becomes fact. Pick a big school with a ton of graduates every year and insert your phony.

"If a potential employer or curious academic checked, a clerical person, most likely a student working in the office, would check the computer and verify the graduation dates. The phony academic, going through the traditional request process, could even have a set of the phony transcripts mailed to any potential employer.

"What you can't doctor, however, are the yearbooks; but who'd bother to check that thoroughly?"

"Only we cynical types, right?" Lucky sneered.

The conversation was interrupted by Jack's cell phone. The ring tone was set to a 60's tune, *Barbara Ann*.

Lucky looked toward the beautiful western vista as Jack opened the phone and put it to his ear.

"Jack, yes, .. yes .., then what did they do? You're sure it was the President of the college they reported to? Oh, the Vice President for Finance. Where are they now? Keep following them and let me know where they stop.

"The guys following you and Tarr broke off at Tarr's place; must have been another team there.

"Then they drove directly to the college, parked outside the administration building, and both went in.

"One of my guys followed them in. They went straight to the Vice President of Finance's office. While hanging around looking at financial aid brochures, my man saw the President hurry in.

"And you're going to love this next part. Once my guys picked up your tail, they ran the plates through one of our connections."

"And?" Lucky gestured with his hand for Jack to hurry up.

"And," Jack continued with a knowing look on his face, "The car is registered to Thunder Mountain Security.

"The meeting didn't last long and the four participants piled in a limo and headed back east on I-70. My guys are on them and will let me know something as soon as they do."

"Back to the Prez and VP, Brother Jack. Anything else?"

"If there is, my guys will find it. I'll let you know."

Chapter 33

The day after the trip to Denver, Tarr and Lucky were sitting on Tarr's balcony having a drink and watching the sun go down. Lucky had passed on the information from Jack.

"So," Tarr sighed, "We now have a good idea whose deep pockets are behind my little social dilemma."

"Social dilemma?" Lucky snorted. "It's more like who's behind your rapid descent into criminal justice hell. But you're right, now we can put a face on the evil. We know the who and probably the why—money; lots and lots of money."

"Now that we know who and probably why," Tarr was concentrating on a jet passing high overhead, "We just need to prove it. Therein, son of my mother, lies the rub. When one has enormous amounts of money, one can cover enormous amounts of stink. It's not going to be easy to peel the layers off Thunder Mountain College. Especially, since we don't know how deeply the evil runs in the organization."

"Well, you work there, how deep does it have to go to get away with it?" Lucky stared at Tarr waiting for an answer.

Tarr took his time formulating an answer to Lucky's question. "Probably not really that deep. I don't think any Professors have to be involved. Give them a good salary, academic freedom to teach their classes as they see fit, a good travel budget, and most will be in hog heaven.

"The Deans don't need to be involved. Give them a fat budget, let them run their schools, and they will be satisfied. That goes for the Vice Presidents as well.

"Beyond those, you have other lower level administrators and administrative assistants. Those are all good jobs for this community; I doubt many would say anything even if something seemed a bit out of kilter.

"So, to cut to the chase, you would need a person on the inside of the Thunder Mountain Foundation, specifically the Director, the College President, the Vice President of Finance, and probably the President of the College's governing board and three other board members to control the votes.

"If any other college employee, other than faculty, started asking questions, you simply fire them. Because Professors have tenure, you've got to find another way to deal with them."

"So," Lucky was repeating what Tarr had said while counting on his fingers. "You need just seven people to run a major scam like this. And if a nosey Professor like you asks questions, you frame him for murder.

"But why a college? From what I read, most of them have trouble breaking even. Not exactly the kind of operation to make a bunch of thugs rich."

"Your point is well taken." Tarr added. "But, what if it wasn't about making money; what if it had more to do with laundering money?"

"What do you mean laundering? I know what the term means, but how could you do that at a college? Students pay tuition; the college pays the Professors and other expenses, and hopefully you break even. What's left to launder?" Lucky seemed genuinely perplexed.

"Not, much if you're honest." Tarr quickly added. "But, what if you're not honest? What if you are as crooked as a contortionist snake?"

"Well, you used to be in the money laundering business before you, uh, *broke your knee in that car accident..*" Lucky was pretending to steer a car and then covering his face as if frightened by a wreck. "If someone asked you to create a money laundering scheme using a college, how would you do it?"

"Well, as a matter of fact, I did used to be in that business." Tarr rubbed his knee subconsciously. "So, how would I set up a criminal enterprise laundering illegal money using Thunder Mountain College?

"Well, to launder large amounts of ill-gotten wealth, you need three things. First, you need a business that has a large potential for cash flow and doesn't really deliver a tangible product. That's so you can start to move large amounts of money without anyone questioning its source.

"What better source than a college; especially a college with international branches all across the world? An illegal enterprise could load up a ton of bulk cash; fly it to a country with cooperative customs agents; deposit it in a friendly bank; and you have achieved the first step in money laundering."

"But, how does that involve the college?" Lucky asked.

"Well," Tarr continued, "the college comes into play when you want the money brought back into the U.S. legally. Getting bulk cash out isn't that big a deal; getting it back in clean is."

"O.K., secret agent man," Lucky said, "How does the college help with getting clean money back in?"

Tarr raised a finger into the air to mock a serious statement, "Ah ha, the million dollar question and step two in a money laundering system, layering. You simply need an illusion of legitimate banking transactions.

"With 2,000 international students, you could launder 60 million dollars a year. Remember, each international student must pay $30,000 a year in tuition. That's a lot of clean money coming back into the country."

"That makes sense," Lucky added, "But how do you move it out of the college accounts without suspicion?"

"Integration or step three in money laundering is where the college really pays off." Tarr looked like he was really enjoying lecturing his brother. "To answer your query, I have two words, research grants. Oh yeah, there is another word, consultants. Maybe even another couple, financial investments."

"Shut up with your words already. I get the point." Lucky

protested. "The college could move the clean money into shell corporations all over the country. With the investments alone, you could move the entire amount."

Arching an eyebrow, Tarr stared at his older brother. "And that's not all. We haven't even gotten to the online students yet. Remember, we have about 3,000 of them also paying $30,000 a year in tuition. They are even more important than the international students.

"Online students can launder 90 million dollars a year without arousing any official attention."

"And how does that work, oh sage of illegal money?"

"Well, grasshopper," Tarr continued, "You use Smurfs."

"You mean, like the little blue dudes who live in mushrooms and stuff?" Lucky seemed genuinely amused.

"Yes, as a matter of fact, you look kinda like a Smurf, but I digress. Smurfing means breaking dirty money into amounts of less than $10,000 dollars, purchasing monetary instruments, and then sending said instrument to a legitimate entity such as Thunder Mountain College, where it is applied to a fictitious tuition balance of a fictitious online student. At the end of a year, you have cleaned a ton of money."

"Wow, what a scam. Do you think your scenario is actually plausible?" Lucky looked to Tarr for his response.

"Plausible, you ask. Now that I have worked through it in my mind, I'm sure it could be done. All you'd need at Thunder Mountain College are a few highly placed administrators and a great big ole bunch of fictitious students from abroad and another bunch of online students."

"But how does one prove such allegations?" Lucky asked in his most distinguished voice.

"Well, Professor Frogman," Tarr added in reference to his brother's formal tone, "One would travel abroad and check out TMC's biggest International Center, the one located in Albania.

"Thunder Mountain College has what is purported to be a

center in Albania. According to annual reports to the faculty, we have, at any given time, about 1,500 registered students in the capital city of Tirana.

"If one was to travel there and stake out said center and maybe check it out one night, when no one was around, then ask around town about the TMC Center, maybe one could reach a determination as to the veracity of the college's claim."

"Okay, Dr. 'I can use big words' Baldridge. I assume by your *one* you mean me. Obviously, if you tried to leave the country, a certain police detective Orr might get concerned."

"That's right my most loyal brother, by 'one' I mean one Luckley Baldridge.

"If I try to go myself, Detective Orr would likely try to stop me. Detective Orr by himself isn't a big concern; my bigger concern is that he would need to get the FBI involved to stop me outside his jurisdiction."

"So, is my little brother afraid of the big, bad FBI?"

"Well, it's like if someone were to ask me if I'm afraid of the dark. My answer would be, 'No, I'm not afraid of the dark; but I'm afraid of what's in it sometimes.'

"The FBI is my 'dark' in this situation. I'm not afraid of them per se; but I am afraid of what a determined federal agency, with the Bureau's resources, could uncover regarding my background.

"If certain details of my background were to be exposed, certain college administrators might construe that as lying.

"Lying during the hiring process, of course, would be grounds for dismissal at Thunder Mountain College."

"Not to mention your proclivity for violence, which is, no doubt, well documented in a file somewhere?" Lucky smiled his most evil smile. "As I recall, you killed at least four in the line of duty with those big bare hands of yours. That little file tidbit would have Detective Orr driving nails into your proverbial legal coffin."

"You think?" Tarr's eyes seemed darker than usual as he responded to Lucky.

Lucky got up to leave.

"Where're you going?" Tarr asked.

"First, I going inside and drain the dragon, then I'm going to call an old friend of mine who just happens to be stationed in Denver. With any luck, maybe he can get me on a military flight out of Peterson Air Base tomorrow to Europe. If that's the case, I need to go home, pack, dust off my passport, and drive back over the mountains."

Tarr looked intrigued. "It never ceases to amaze me what a network of military friends you have. It also never ceases to amaze me that your sense of proportion is so far off."

"Sense of proportion?" Lucky turned to look at Tarr.

"Yeah, sense of proportion" Tarr emphasized. When you refer to a stunted earthworm as a dragon, you have a sense of proportion problem."

"Ah, my poor under hung brother has penis envy. Such a sad state of affairs." Lucky turned to leave with a smile on his face.

With a serious tone in his voice, Tarr looked at his brother. "Be careful, Lucky; these guys play for keeps."

With an equally serious tone, Lucky pointed his finger at Tarr. "That goes double for you little brother. Watch your back. There's not much people won't do when this kind of money is involved.

"I'll call you from Albania as soon as I have something."

Lucky turned and left the balcony.

Chapter 34

After Lucky left, Tarr decided just sitting around all night would not be a productive use of his time. He knew it was just a matter of time before Detective Orr decided to bring him in for formal questioning. There was a better than average chance when Orr came after him, he would come with a murder warrant.

Being proactive seemed a better course of action than just waiting for the hammer to fall. Maybe if he made the bad guys nervous, they would make a mistake. One he could capitalize on.

Since a big unknown was why the guys who followed him to Denver went to Aspen upon their return, maybe a drive to Aspen was in order.

After a quick call to Jack to get the specifics of the Aspen destination, Tarr prepared for a trip to Aspen. Since he wanted to appear clumsy in the sleuthing business, he couldn't have the bad guys discover that he had cover. He asked Jack to pull his cover for the trip. Even though Jack didn't like the idea, he knew it made sense.

Without Jack's men covering his back, Tarr decided he had better even the odds a bit. From the secret compartment Lucky had built under his bed, he took two handguns.

The first was one of his primary weapons of choice these days when he felt the need for more protection than his stick could provide. It was a rather large five-shot revolver called a Taurus Judge. It shot either 45 caliber long Colt rounds or three-inch 410 shotgun shells, or a combination of both.

Because of his large size, Tarr had always been able to carry the large handgun comfortably in a shoulder holster on his left side. Typically, he loaded it with three 00 buckshot rounds followed by two 45 hollow-point rounds. The only thing on two legs it might have trouble stopping was a gorilla. It would, however, ruin even a gorilla's day.

The second handgun was an S&W 22 Kit Gun. It was a much lighter 22 caliber handgun with pinpoint accuracy, when in the right hands. Tarr knew he could hit accurately anything under 50 yards. The Kit Gun, which held eight 22 mini-mag hollow-points, was carried in a belt holster on the back of his right hip.

The only thing left to do was head downstairs, fire up the Hummer, pick up his tail, and hit the road.

Chapter 35

Monument Towers was less than five minutes from Interstate 70. Tarr drove slowly toward I-70 so the tail wouldn't lose him. Jack's men had said the bad guys were not very good at the surveillance business. Apparently, their specialty was a tad bit more hands on, perhaps like murder.

Aspen was a couple of hours east and south of Grand Junction. The drive would follow I-70 east for about 100 miles and then south on Highway 82 for another 20 or so miles.

About 50 miles east of Grand Junction, Tarr pulled off the Interstate at the east Rifle exit. Rifle was a small town with a full array of fast food joints.

Tarr turned right from the exit and drove about a mile to the local Burger King. It was time to identify the tail. It would be a lot easier here than later on. Before he turned right, though, he sat at the stop sign long enough to see two other vehicles exit.

One vehicle was a Dodge Charger, the other a VW convertible. His money was on the Charger, especially after applying his highly tuned surveillance skills to the vehicles' occupants.

The VW was driven by a blond girl maybe 17 or 18 years old. The Charger had two guys in it that screamed "bad guys."

Yep, it was probably the Charger.

Tarr kept an eye on the Hummer's rearview mirror as he headed toward the Burger King. He saw no other vehicles exit from the ramp.

Almost immediately, Tarr entered a roundabout. He exited south, the VW followed him, and the Charger went completely around and back in the direction of I-70.

The guys in the Charger obviously knew the area; the only

way for Tarr to get back to the Interstate was to reverse his path from the Burger King.

As Tarr pulled into a parking space in the restaurant's parking lot, the VW pulled into another just right of him. Just to make sure the blond was not a cleverly disguised tail, he decided to sit and watch her go in.

About that time a teenage boy pulled in after her. Seeing the girl, he walked over and spoke to her. They then giggled as they walked into the restaurant together.

So much for the VW. Tarr knew the Charger would pick him up again at the Interstate.

After a quick burger and draining the dragon (no one was around to challenge his sense of proportion), Tarr hit the road.

The Charger was waiting just past the roundabout. As he passed, he could see them pretending to read a roadmap. Jack's guys were right; these clowns weren't very good.

Just to have a little fun, Tarr exited at the next scenic pull off. He watched the Charger drive on by. After a short stroll to unkink his knee, he got the Hummer back on the Interstate.

Much to Tarr's lack of surprise, the Charger was just down the road from the pull off. One guy was squatting by a rear tire pretending to check the air pressure.

Tarr knew he had to be careful; he might accidently lose these guys. In their defense, though, they thought Tarr was just some absent-minded professor with no ability to detect a tail. At least Tarr hoped that was what they believed. It would make the evening's activities easier.

Chapter 36

Aspen was just ahead. What a great town, if you had the money to enjoy it. The running joke was that the billionaires had run the millionaires out of town. The millionaires had relocated to Telluride.

Joke or no joke, Aspen could be a very expensive town. To own real estate in the little mountain town took some serious dough.

People who owned the showplace properties in and around town were some of the wealthiest people in the world. A single family residence had recently sold for forty million dollars.

Tarr knew the average second home in Aspen was occupied, on average, about two weeks out of each year. What a waste of beautiful real estate.

The evening's destination lay just outside town about a 15-minute drive east. Tarr and his companions in the Charger passed through town and continued east toward Independence Pass.

Frequently checking his rearview mirror, Tarr assured himself his surveillance team was still there. He didn't want to lose them; as a matter of fact he intended to make their acquaintance later in the evening.

The goal for this evening's trip was to let the bad guys know he was aware of their presence. He also wanted them to think he was inept in his feeble attempts to check them out.

Tarr slowed and began searching for a small paved road, which according to Jack's men, was marked by a very large sign saying it was private and violators would be prosecuted to the full extent of the law.

The lights of the Hummer picked up the road and sign just

ahead. Tarr slowed the vehicle and turned on the road. The road reached a small cul-de-sac almost immediately.

Making a hard left out of the cul-de-sac, Tarr encountered a very sturdy gate. Its positioning and purpose didn't escape his attention. Security was obviously a very important consideration here.

A guard dressed as one might expect a guard to be dressed looked at him through the window of a gate/guard house. Referring to a clipboard, the guard walked out of the structure and up to the driver's side window.

Smiling at Tarr, the very courteous and professional looking guard glanced at the clipboard again. "May I help you, sir?"

Smiling back, Tarr replied, "I'm here for the dinner party. Sorry I'm late, but I've never been here before. It took a little longer than I thought."

"I'm sorry sir; there is no dinner party here tonight. You must be at the wrong address."

"Are you sure, I followed the directions to the letter," Tarr replied, using his most surprised expression.

"Here they are right here," Tarr extended the directions he had written down from his conversation with Jack.

The guard took the directions from Tarr's extended hand. "Well, sir, you're right. The directions lead you here, but there is no dinner party. The owners aren't currently in residence."

Tarr had detected the presence of someone else just to the right of the guardhouse and carefully concealed in the trees. No doubt, the place was guarded by more than a single guy in a monkey suit.

His body was also setting off the alarm codes. It's funny how old habits die hard. His instinct to danger had saved him on more than one occasion in his old profession.

Even though his instinct was yelling and telling him to get out of there, Tarr didn't think they'd kill him right here, right now. There was really no reason to; they had set him up perfectly for the murder in Junction.

"You sure they didn't sneak in when you weren't on duty?" Tarr said in a teasing voice.

"Yes sir, I'm sure. Please back up and turn around; you're on private property and need to leave." The guard was losing some of his polished charm.

"If I'm at the wrong place, then who lives here?" Tarr figured he had nothing to lose with the question.

"Sir, that is private information; now please leave or I will be forced to call the Sherriff's Office."

"Sure you will," thought Tarr. "You're about as likely to do that as I am to get into this place tonight."

If this were the kind of place Tarr thought it was, they didn't want any attention from law enforcement.

"Okay, okay; don't pop a blood vessel, I'll leave; but I'm going to tell the Chamber of Commerce about your rude behavior. You're not a very good ambassador for Aspen." Tarr smiled to himself as he put the Hummer in reverse. Let them figure this out.

As soon as Tarr backed away from the gate, the guard hurried into the guard house and placed a call on the direct line to the house.

"Hey boss, something just happened here at the gate." It took the guard a couple of minutes to relay the details of the incident including answering several questions.

"I'll deal with it," came the boss's response. "In the meantime, stay alert. This sounds a little strange. I'm sending three more boys down to back up you and Joey."

Closing the connection with the gate, the boss dialed another number. "Hey, it's Billy at the ranch; we might have a problem."

The Old Man in Denver seemed more confused than mad. "You're sure it was that professor from the college?"

"Well, it sure sounds like the guy. I pulled some time last

week following him around. He left town that day in one of those big Hummers, just like the one that showed up tonight. And the boy on the gate described the driver as a really big guy."

"Let's find out for sure," the voice from Denver said. "Call the guys covering him and find out where they are. If it was him, have the guys following him give him a little scare. I don't want him killed; I just want to know what he's doing snooping around the ranch."

As the Old Man hung up he murmured to himself, "How in the world does he know about the ranch? I'm going to kill those idiots in Grand Junction."

Chapter 37

Tarr headed west back toward Aspen. As he was approaching the city limits, he glanced in the rearview mirror to see if his tail had picked him back up. The Charger was closing on him at a high rate of speed.

The Charger was really eating up the distance between the two vehicles. Just up ahead, a county road intersected the road Tarr was on. He hit the brakes and made the turn without the big Hummer going into a slide.

Being a much better cornering vehicle, the Charger negotiated the turn without losing much ground on Tarr.

With a smile on his face, Tarr glanced at the Charger as its front bumper came alongside his rear bumper. As the Charger pulled even with the Hummer, the passenger pointed to the side of the road and mouthed the words, pull over.

Obviously, the folks at the ranch had decided to unravel the mystery of his appearance this evening. The tail had been chosen to get the information.

Tarr fully intended to comply with the goons demand, just not exactly the way they figured. The Professor was about to teach the two thugs a lesson in forcing a vehicle off the road.

After gesturing for Tarr to pull over, the Charger kept pace with the Hummer in an attempt at intimidation.

Tarr was about to show the two in the car exactly how intimidated he really was. Tarr put a little pressure on the Hummers brakes. His vehicle started to fall back. Before the Charger knew what was happening, the Hummer's front bumper was already behind the car. Tarr continued to brake.

The car passenger began to gesture wildly back toward Tarr. The driver immediately hit the brakes. When the Charger started to break, Tarr accelerated the Hummer.

As the Hummer's front bumper passed the rear bumper of the Charger, Tarr turned into the car.

In response to the collision, the Charger hit the brakes even harder causing its rear end into a small slide. The slide was greatly exaggerated by the Hummer's nudge. The large crash bumper of the Hummer was now pressed firmly against the passenger's side of the Charger as the two vehicles continued down the road. The fear on the passenger's face no doubt reflected the attitudes of both thugs in the Charger.

Tarr accelerated the hummer; the Charger continued its sideways trip up the road; then Tarr tapped his brakes. As the Hummer slowed, the Charger began to spin toward the left hand road ditch.

With dirt flying and tires screeching, the Charger hit the ditch. Its momentum caused the car to flip as a front tire caught the edge of the ditch.

The Hummer slid to a stop as Tarr watched the Charger land on its top. Somehow it had flipped into the ditch, caught another tire, flipped out of the ditch back toward the road, landed on its top and slid about 50 feet.

Tarr drove closer to the wrecked Charger keeping his vehicle lights on the car. He switched the headlights to high beam. Anyone crawling out of the wreck would be blinded by the lights.

Tarr opened the driver's door and got out, careful to keep the Hummer's heavy door between him and the Charger.

Slowly, a body began to wiggle out of the car via the missing rear windshield. Moaning, emanating from the passenger area of the wreck, filled the cool mountain air. Both thugs had apparently survived the wild ride.

Tarr watched as the driver worked himself out of the car and stumbled to an upright standing position. As the injured man attempted to balance himself, he drew a large black handgun from a shoulder holster.

Before the handgun could be pointed his way, Tarr shot the man in his right knee. As his knee buckled from the shotgun shell blast, the man fell to the pavement. The handgun was no longer in his possession. It lay about a foot away from his right hand.

The thug moved to try and retrieve the gun. Tarr shot the gun with a second blast from his own gun. The large black handgun was rendered useless by the charge of 00 buckshot.

No shooter other than a television super hero would try to shoot a man in the knee or shoot a gun away from another's hand. No shooter, that is, other than one who had a shotgun.

Shooting a target the size of a knee or handgun with a single projectile from another handgun was not a guaranteed hit. Most competent shooters would simply aim their weapon at the middle of the target's chest and blast away.

Now, if the shooter possessed a handgun capable of launching multiple projectiles with a single shot, he could take a chance on a smaller target. Tarr's Judge could do just that with its 410 shotgun shell capability.

Shading his eyes as much as possible with a hand, the thug lay in the roadway staring into the bright light.

"Who are you guys and what do you want with me" Tarr was staring down at the injured man. "Have I done something to offend you?"

"No, man; it was just a mistake. You're not who we thought you were."

Tarr sniffed the air as the smell of gasoline whiffed his way. "Just who is it you thought I was? There couldn't be too many men my size riding around in a Hummer."

"We thought you were this big SOB who's been messing around with my buddy's wife. We didn't know what kind of vehicle he drove. Ask my buddy in the car; he'll tell you."

"Speaking of your buddy in the car, it looks like he's back in the world of the living. He's crawling out the window behind you."

"How 'bout you help us?" the thug pleaded after glancing back at his friend, who had made it out of the car except for one foot.

"How about you tell me who you are first, then I might help. On second thought, crawl over to your friend and help him yourself. You've still got one good leg and two good arms. When you finish, toss me both your wallets."

"Are you crazy or something? I'm in pain here."

Tarr's voice took on a menacing tone. "Do what I say or I'll just shoot both of you and come get them myself."

"Okay, okay; don't cut loose with that shotgun again. I'll get the wallets." The wounded man began to pull himself toward his partner.

Tarr smiled to himself. The guy thought he had a shotgun. No reason to tell him the truth. Once the word got around about this, the deception might work to his advantage.

The driver managed to drag himself to a position where he could help his friend fully extricate himself from the car.

Tarr kept a close watch on the two men. There was probably at least one other handgun on the car's passenger, not to mention any backup weapons carried by the two.

Tarr raised his voice as the driver reached into the passenger's pocket, who was once again unconscious. "If I see anything other than a wallet come out of that pocket, you're dead."

The driver stopped his movement immediately. "I'm just getting his wallet."

"You'd better be really careful," Tarr shouted.

"I will, I will, don't get excited with that scattergun." The driver had the passenger's wallet in his right hand. With the left, he was moving very slowly and in as full a view as possible toward his left hip pocket. "I'm getting my wallet now, don't shoot me again."

"I won't shoot you again unless you have a terminal attack of stupid."

The driver now held both wallets in his right hand holding them above his head so Tarr could see them. "What do you want me to do now?"

"I want you to throw the wallets one at a time to me. It's only about 10 feet. If you throw them short so that I have to step into the light, I'm going to shoot your other knee. Do you understand me?"

Tarr could almost smell the man's fear. Since Tarr had shot him once already, there was probably little doubt in the thug's mind that it would happen again.

With great deliberation, the driver tossed the first wallet. It landed a few inches in front of the Hummer's open driver's side door. Tarr used his foot to drag the wallet behind the door.

The second wallet was thrown even closer to the door. Tarr now had both wallets. "Okay, you can relax; both wallets made it."

With a heavy sigh of relief, the driver slumped all the way to the pavement close to his friend. "Will you help us now?"

"No, I won't," Tarr responded. "Now I want you to tell me why you were following me, the real reason." Without saying another word Tarr sent a load of 00 buckshot into the wrecked car's door about a foot from the driver's head. As buckshot has a tendency to do, it spread out with one pellet impacting the car not more than an inch from the thug's left ear.

The driver flinched with the sound and impact of the buckshot.

"Guess where the next shot is going, if you lie to me again."

The driver knew he had no choice but to tell the maniac with the shotgun the truth. "All I can tell you is what I know."

"Start with why you clowns have been following me and who you work for."

The thug tried to see Tarr behind the glare of the Hummer's lights. Obviously the guy wasn't as dumb as everybody thought. "We've been following you because we were told to follow you."

"By whom? And you had better be believable."

The thug figured he could lie and maybe die or tell the truth and maybe die at the hands of his bosses. Since the bosses weren't here and the shotgun maniac was, he opted for the truth. He could always run from the bosses.

"President Karp ordered us to follow you."

"Well, well." Tarr thought. His hunch seemed to be approaching reality. "Why would the President of Thunder Mountain College want me followed? I didn't think he acknowledged my existence."

"I don't know. We're both security at the college. We do what we're told to do. We're just hired help."

"Did Karp tell you to stop me tonight? And don't lie; you've probably already figured out I know more than you guys thought I did." Tarr figured he could bluff the guy a little at this point.

"I wonder what this guy really knows." Thought the thug. He decided not to take a chance. "No, it was the boss at the ranch; he called and told us to stop you. He wanted to know why you came to the ranch tonight. He said not to kill you; just knock you around some. That's what we were gonna do. Honest, we weren't gonna kill you."

Tarr knew this much was the truth. He would have been surprised if his visit to the ranch had not prompted some sort of response. "What's so special about the ranch?"

"It belongs to the big boss from Denver. We go there sometimes with the President and Vice President from the college. I don't know what they do other than meet. I heard Dr. Manci talking about a weekly disk one time but I don't know what he meant. Honest, that's all I know.

"If they find out I told you this stuff, I'm a dead man and so is my unconscious friend here."

"It's strange how opportunity presents itself sometimes."

Tarr thought. "Maybe this guy could become his ace in the hole.

What's your name?"

"Vick, my name is Tony Vick."

"Okay, Tony, here's what I'm going to do. I'm going to forget this conversation ever happened. I suggest you do the same. Your friend has been unconscious since he tried to crawl from the car. No one knows we even talked.

"I suggest you tell your bosses what happened minus the conversation. There is one catch, though. I want you to find out what is really going on at the ranch. They might allow you to hang out there while your knee heals.

"I don't want you to rat out any of your friends; I just want to know what the ranch is really for. If you can tell me that within the next two weeks, I'll take our conversation to the grave; you have my word on that."

Tony was pondering his current situation. He didn't really have any choice. Besides, most square dudes like this professor would keep their word. "I'll do it. How do I contact you?"

Tarr threw the two wallets back to Tony. "Have you got your cell phone on you?"

"Yeah."

"Enter this number in your directory and label it something innocuous like Mary." Tarr gave him the number. "From now on, keep your phone locked.

"Remember, two weeks. Not a day longer or the deal is off."

"I'll call; don't worry. I'm not keen on the guys finding out about this." Tony knew he had two choices; he could get the information and pass it on or he could kill this professor. He had two weeks to do one or the other.

Chapter 38

Lucky walked out of his hotel in Albania. He had arrived in country last night and settled into an American styled hotel in Tirana.

The trip from home had been long and exhausting. Durres Motorway from the airport seemed to be an endless pothole with an even more endless supply of berserk drivers.

Just the taxi ride in from the airport had taken over an hour; 25 minutes to get into town and another 45 to fight city traffic flowing downtown toward City Central.

Lucky's hotel was right off Skenderbeg Square, a remnant from the Communist years. Tirana International Hotel was a good hotel, but somewhat dated. Even dated, it still had a modern look with a lot of glass showing on the exterior.

Lucky checked in at the front desk and picked up his key to a nice double room on the third floor. The television didn't work well, but who cared; there wasn't anything on in English. The room itself wasn't bad. It was in a great location, clean, and not very expensive.

Following a quick shower he hit the bed. Not home, however, not that bad. After a few hours' sleep to try and overcome the jetlag, Lucky had a big breakfast in the hotel's restaurant.

When you were in town to snoop around, the next meal might be a long time removed. He needed to locate Thunder Mountain's branch campus and stake it out for a day or two to get a feel for its routine. Only then, would he know the best way to proceed.

His first chore however, was to contact someone who spoke the local lingo. His buddy in Denver had gotten him on the military flight to Germany where he caught a flight to Albania. His buddy had done one other thing. He gave Lucky the name and address of a contact in Tirana, the capital of Albania.

The contact was a retired Navy Chief of Albanian extraction who had been sent to the U.S by his parents at an early age to live with relatives.

Back in the day of a heavy-handed dictator with communist backing, many parents wanted a different kind of life for their children. The Chief's parents had managed to smuggle him across the short stretch of Adriatic Sea separating Albania from Italy.

Meeting the young child there, his U.S. relatives took him to America. Telling authorities he was an Italian orphan they were adopting, the relatives had few problems. After all, Italy was in disarray after WW II and orphans without papers were everywhere.

Once in America, the child took the relatives' name, became a naturalized citizen, eventually grew up, and joined the U. S. Navy.

After retiring from the Navy he moved to Albania to take care of his birth mother who refused to immigrate. With the fall of communism in Eastern Europe and the strength of the dollar, he could live very well on a Chief's retirement.

Retired Chief Adri Korabit, AK to his friends, lived two blocks west of Skenderbeg Square. Lucky had made arrangements to meet the Chief at a popular coffee shop on the town square. The meeting time gave him about two hours to find the location and check it out.

The Chief was the friend of a friend, not someone Lucky knew personally. Since no one knew who Lucky was or why he was there, the meeting was probably not fraught with danger.

Lucky never took chances though. He had a description of AK and been told to expect a swarthy, slim man wearing a Yankee's baseball cap.

Before heading for the coffee shop, however, he had a little shopping to do. He wanted to find a clothing store where he could buy two or three changes of clothing. Right now, his clothing would identify him as an American. With the purchases and a quick trip back to the hotel, he would be dressed as a middle-class Albanian.

The coffee shop proved easy to find. It was called Starbucks. Who would have thought it? Lucky spotted AK immediately. He was seated at a table for four in the rear of the shop.

Lucky walked past the table where AK was seated. Ignoring the Chief, he went into the men's room and washed his hands.

Stepping out of the restroom, he scanned his surroundings once again. Nothing seemed out of place. He sat down on AK's right in a chair where he could also see the front door.

"Lucky, I presume." AK extended his hand. "Judging by your precautions, I assume you're not in town to view the sights."

Gripping the Chief's extended hand, Lucky laughed. "You know, seeing a certain sight is exactly why I'm in town. As a matter of fact, I'm so interested in one sight; I might hang around it day and night for a couple of days just so I won't miss anything."

With a questioning look, the Chief suggested they grab some coffee and then talk about what Lucky really wanted in Tirana.

With coffee in hand, the two men returned to their table and again both took positions where they could keep an eye on the front door.

After taking a few minutes to fill the Chief in on Tarr's trouble and to explain the real reason for his trip to Albania, Lucky sat back and took a sip of the strong flavored coffee. "So, you ever hear of Thunder Mountain College's Tirana Branch?"

Returning his coffee cup to the table, the Chief pulled out

his cell phone. "Nope, but that doesn't mean it's not here. I'll use this little handheld electronic marvel and check Tirana's yellow pages.

"Well, lookee here; there's a phone number for the place, but no address. That's kind of funny don't you think?"

Lucky's face now had that Cheshire cat-type grin plastered from ear to ear. "That is kinda funny. You'd think the location would be in big letters so potential students could find them. Does it say anything in the ad?"

Looking down at the diminutive screen, AK squinted. "It says to call for more information about its educational programs."

"That's it?" Lucky looked bewildered.

"Yep, not exactly an award winning promotional piece, is it?" AK hit the phone's speaker function and started punching in the phone number as Lucky scanned the front entrance of the coffee shop.

AK and Lucky listened as the phone started to ring. After five rings an automated message came on the line. "All operators are currently busy; please call at a later time."

Looking at the phone, Lucky asked, "You think there might be access to a reverse phone directory on the Internet?"

"We'll sure find out." AK started poking the phone's small keys in quick succession.

Lucky once again looked around the coffee shop. There were two clerks behind the counter, a couple of young women close to the front door, and an elderly couple just walking in. None of the people looked out of place nor paid any special attention to the two retired guys in the back.

AK was smiling. "I've got the address. It's in one of our more colorful sections of town."

Lucky returned his gaze to AK. "By colorful, I assume you mean a part of town where I'll need an automatic weapon just to keep the local populace at bay."

Smiling, AK said, "And we have a winner; what kind of prizes has our contestant won?"

Smiling back, Lucky answered the question with one of his own. "How about a prize that includes some sort of weapon that goes bang?"

"If you'll consider the prize a loaner, I think I can make that happen. Let's take a walk to my house."

Looking around the coffee shop again, both Lucky and AK pushed away from the table and got to their feet.

Ten minutes later the two middle-aged, ex-Navy Chiefs stepped up on the front porch of a small but well maintained cottage. From the outside, it appeared to be about 1500 square feet with two stories.

There was a postage-stamp size front yard surrounded by a waist-high metal picket fence. Behind the house appeared to be some sort of shed. Everything around the property had a well-maintained appearance.

"Home sweet home." AK made a sweeping gesture with his right hand in the general direction of the house.

Unlocking the front door, AK led the way into the house. "We're here alone so don't worry about what you say. My mother is spending a couple of weeks on the coast with her sister in Durres. She left yesterday, so the house is all mine for a while.

"As a matter of fact, since I'm alone, why don't you bunk here while you're in town? It'll save you a few bucks."

Looking around the front room where they were standing, Lucky extended his hand to AK. "Thank you very much. I think I'll take you up on the offer. It might be less suspicious than the hotel. They might wonder when I'm gone for a couple of days and don't sleep in the room.

"I'll only accept your generosity on one condition; while I'm here all meals and booze are on me."

Grasping Lucky's hand with his own, AK laughed out loud.

"Well, that will take care of any money you save from the hotel room."

Chapter 39

AK and Lucky spent the rest of the day doing what any observer would expect of a tourist visiting a friend. First they went back to the hotel where Lucky packed and checked out. After transferring the minimal luggage back to the house, the two men began a walking tour of the city.

After several hours of visiting a museum, viewing the statues on the square, grabbing a light lunch, and doing some tourist-type shopping, the two men made their way back to AK's house. Upon entering, AK stood on his tiptoes and straightened a picture on the wall.

Lucky watched AK with great curiosity. "I saw you straighten that picture the first time and the second time we came into the house. Now you're doing it again. May I assume you don't suffer from some anal compulsive disorder?"

Looking at Lucky, AK nodded. "You may assume I do not."

Lucky walked over to where the picture hung on the wall. Standing on tiptoes, he studied the artwork on the wall. "Very clever, you'd never notice the pressure switch behind the right corner of the frame, unless you looked very carefully.

"May I also assume the switch turns off some sort of security system?"

"Yes, you may once again assume."

"Well, it is a slick way to disarm a security system; how did you arm it on the way out without my knowing?"

"Well, my overly curious friend, I wouldn't tell just anybody my secret. But since I knew of you and some of your exploits prior to meeting you, I think my secret will be in good hands."

AK walked over to the front door. "The alarm mechanism is in the lock on the doorknob. Most locks require you to turn the key to the left and then back to lock a door from the outside. On my lock, you turn the key right first and then left ...alarm set."

Lucky had walked over to look at the door lock. "Well since we're into secrets. What about the prize we discussed this morning?"

"Oh, you mean the one that goes bang?"

"That would be the one," Lucky replied.

AK walked into the house's rather spacious kitchen and gestured for Lucky to follow. When they were both in the kitchen, AK walked up to what looked like a door to a closet. Opening the door, he pulled the chain on an overhead bare bulb hanging from the ceiling.

Looking over AK's shoulder, Lucky could see a steep staircase disappearing into the dim light below. AK led the way downstairs. At the bottom he flipped a switch that sent an amazing amount of light flooding into the space.

The space was surprisingly large, at least 20 x 20 feet.

"This is a fairly common feature in old Albanian homes. Initially, it was built as a root cellar before the widespread availability of refrigeration. Now most of the spaces are just used for storage.

"I converted it into a shop space after I moved in. It didn't really matter to my mother since the stairs are too steep for her. The only floor she ever uses is the first. The two bedrooms upstairs are also my domain. Mom has a bedroom on the first floor and that's also where the only bathroom is."

Lucky looked around at the shop. There was a small metal lathe, an equally small miniature metal milling machine, numerous other pieces of equipment, and a back wall with a vast array of well-maintained hand tools.

AK walked to the wall of hand tools. It covered the entire

20 feet of the wall. The wall appeared to be five sheets of 4x8 peg board. Lucky couldn't determine exactly how the peg boards were attached to the wall.

AK saw Lucky looking at the wall. "Originally, all the root cellars were just dirt rooms dug out between the stone foundations of the houses. Because they were dirt and below ground level, they stayed cool year round. Once refrigeration became common, many people converted the cellars to rooms by lining them with concrete blocks, putting in a vapor barrier, and adding some sort of rough wood paneling.

"That's basically what I found when I came back home. I modified it by adding lighting, pegboard, and a little extra excavation."

"A little extra excavation, huh?" Lucky had moved closer to the back wall. "Okay, I give up, which pegboard panel is it behind?"

AK took a small screwdriver from a metal peg on the left most panel. He inserted the blade of the screwdriver into the third peg hole from the left and third down from the top. The panel moved forward about a quarter of an inch. If Lucky had not being paying attention, he would not have noticed the movement.

AK pulled the panel open as one would do a heavy door. Behind the panel was additional space about the size of a small closet with the exception of its height. It was only about six feet tall.

Lucky walked closer to the opening. A small light illuminated the opening. Inside was a small safe secured to the floor. Above the safe was a small rack secured to the wall. It held three long guns.

To the right of the safe was a narrow piece of pegboard extending from the floor of the opening to the ceiling. Hanging on pegs were half a dozen handguns.

"Wow, nice piece of work." Lucky looked closely at the

latch mechanism. An electronic switch had been activated when the blade of the screwdriver entered the hole and completed an electronic circuit. Simple, but effective.

"K.I.S.S. works every time." AK made a gesture with his hand toward the handguns. "See anything you like?"

Lucky studied the guns for a second, then reached in and selected a medium-sized, black, boxy-looking handgun. "This should do just fine."

"I see you like Austrian hardware," AK was gesturing toward the Glock handgun Lucky held lightly in his hand.

"I've been partial to Glock 9's since I saw my first one over 20 years ago. This one looks like the latest generation." Lucky turned the gun around in his hand so he could look at the barrel.

"It is." AK reached for the handgun. "See these slits on each side of the slide? Those are compensation slots milled into the slide and barrel to reduce the recoil when the gun is fired. They are a factory option available these days. This baby is real pleasant to shoot."

Lucky took the gun back and tucked it into the small of his back in what many refer to as a Mexican carry. "I hope I don't have to find out." He also slid an extra 15-round magazine into his left front pocket.

Chapter 40

After catching a nap and eating a late supper, Lucky and AK both changed into dark clothing and left the house. This departure, however, was via the back door and down an alley. It never hurt to be careful.

As the pair emerged on a side street two blocks from the house, AK pulled a half pint of whiskey from his pocket. He took a long drink from the bottle and passed it to Lucky.

Lucky looked at the bottle for a second, then he also drank deeply from the bottle. "Let me guess, if we're stopped, we should appear to be a couple of drunken buddies out on the town."

"That's right." AK reached to retrieve the bottle. "Public drunkenness isn't much of a concern in Albania. As long as we keep to ourselves, the police will leave us alone. Also, if we're stopped, you're too drunk to talk. Just grunt and stagger around."

Gesturing up the street, AK led the way into the night.

Three bars and two taxi drives later, the pair of ex-Navy chiefs exited a taxi despite warnings from the driver about "This not being a good section of town."

As the taxi pulled away from the curb, the two men turned away from the bar where they had requested the taxi drop them. AK staggered a bit and managed to turn in a complete circle. "No one's paying us any special attention. Let's move up the street a couple of blocks. The address for the college is in that direction."

The men began to argue about the correct address of a friendly female of their acquaintance as they staggered away from the bar. Several blocks later they stepped into the darkness of a grimy alley.

"It's that building across the street and to your right two buildings." AK shifted slightly so Lucky could get a better view.

After observing the building for a few minutes, Lucky staggered into the street. Looking back at AK, he whispered, "Let's stagger down the street and stop in the appropriate doorway for a drink out of your bottle."

Collapsing in the doorway, the two drunks shared the bottle of whiskey. They sat quietly for the next hour and passed the bottle back and forth between them. Each pretended to drink each time the whiskey came his way.

Gradually the street emptied and the two men were alone. Lucky pulled a small flashlight from his pocket and turned to examine the lock on the door. "Piece of cake," he murmured to AK. "Let's get out of here. I've seen enough for one night."

The two men staggered out of the doorway and into the street. The area was dark and deserted. Functioning streetlights were obviously not a city priority.

Lucky staggered and bumped into AK. "Looks like a good place to get mugged."

AK grunted. "You're just saying that because of those four young men that crossed to our side of the street two blocks up."

Lucky had seen the young thugs at the same time as AK. "You know I got kinda stiff sitting in that doorway. A little exercise might feel good."

AK was smiling in the dark. "Yeah, it might. Try not to kill any of them, though. That'll draw some attention I doubt you want."

The four amateur tough guys were about a half block away. They had spread out and were trying their best to appear menacing.

AK stumbled a couple of steps to his left; Lucky stumbled to his right. The four young men were only a few steps ahead.

AK stumbled again and almost fell onto the pavement. Lucky laughed at him then commenced to almost fall himself.

The two drunks were now about 12 feet apart. Plenty of room for proper exercise.

The drunken antics had spread the four men ahead even further apart.

As the distance between the two groups narrowed to conversation range, the apparent leader took a step ahead of the other three. He was one of the two in the middle and closest to Lucky. "Hey, old men, loan me some money; my mother needs surgery."

Because of the language barrier, the comment was lost on Lucky. His response was to grunt and stumble into the thug closest to him. The thug responded by grabbing Lucky with both hands by the collar. He had obviously seen one too many movies.

AK slurred his speech as he responded in his native language. "We just left your mother in the alley back there and she looked fine; but, then again, we could only see the top of her head. It's probably all that time she spends on her knees."

The head thug took a step in AK's direction. "Real funny, old man; maybe we'll see how good you two are on your knees."

As the other three laughed at their leader's response, Lucky made his move. A quick knee to the groin caused his young advisory great distress. The distress south of the border was quickly forgotten, however, when his nose was broken by an expertly delivered elbow strike.

Before the first thug hit the ground, Lucky moved slightly to his left and pivoted slightly. With a snap of his left leg he broke the next thug's knee cap. The young man immediately fell in agonizing pain evidenced by his screams.

AK had moved as soon as Lucky struck. With his most immediate opponent distracted, he simply struck with the heel of his hand. Three down and one to go.

Both men turned and smiled at the last man standing, the guy with the sick mother.

AK feigned a strike and the young man jumped in fear and actually winced. "Hey, mister, we were just kidding around. Thought we'd have a little fun with you guys; honest, we weren't going to hurt you."

"Well that certainly eases our minds; we were really scared. I thought for a minute you were the gang of thugs who have been mugging people around here. But based on your skill levels, that would be hard to believe. You guys would have trouble mugging us if we were dead drunk. Looks can be deceiving, huh?"

AK turned to Lucky and said in English, "What do you think we should do with this one?"

Affecting a strong southern accent, Lucky replied, "He's sure got a purty mouth, don't he?"

As AK translated the response, the now not so tough young man's eyes jumped in fear. Both men laughed.

AK turned and gave the young thug his meanest stare. "If you ever see one of us again, cross the street, leave town, become invisible. If you don't, I'm going to let my friend over here have you. Understand?

"And one other thing, if we hear about any other gang muggings around here, we're going to come looking for you young men. We won't exercise as much restraint in the future.

"Tonight, you got an education in being tough, you guys are not tough; you're just posers. Pose again and you will die."

Thirty minutes later AK and Lucky were back home having real, non-pretend drinks. Lucky hosted his glass to AK. "Here's to the teams. My buddy told me you were in the Navy, he never told me you were a snake eatin', blood pissin', uglier than real life Seal."

With a sly grin AK said, "Who says I was a Seal; maybe I just grew up in a crappy neighborhood?"

"Crappy neighborhood my ass, I know a Seal when I fight with one. Tell me I'm lying."

"You ain't lying; I just try to keep a low profile. Better to be underestimated, don't you think?"

Lucky lifted his glass again, "Here's to good training, bad whiskey, and questionable women."

Chapter 41

The next day at about 11:00, the two Seals took a taxi directly to the Albanian branch of Thunder Mountain College. After paying the taxi, Lucky turned and looked up at the less than impressive signage dedicated to the college. "Well, it's almost the noon hour. Classes should be in full swing. Let's go inside and see what this place looks like."

AK held the door as Lucky walked into the foyer of the building. It was ringed by half a dozen offices. If the building had been in Denver, it would have been rental space for small accounting firms and second rate lawyers. Since Lucky couldn't read the signs, it could have been much the same here.

Lucky walked to the left to what appeared to be a building directory. "AK, how 'bout checking for the college's office number."

AK walked closer to the wall mounted directory. "It's on the third floor in suite 301. Stairs or elevator?"

Lucky turned and headed toward the stairs visible across the foyer. Wide and sweeping, the staircase had no doubt been a grand statement at one time. "Let's try the stairs."

Climbing to the third level, the pair stopped and scanned the hallway. Turning left, they walked past an open door with an unkempt middle aged man busily typing away at what appeared to be an electronic typewriter. Lucky nudged AK while making a gesture toward the door with his head. "Haven't seen one of those in a while."

AK glanced at the ancient piece of equipment. "Hang around Albania long enough and you'll cease to be surprised. We're still basically a third world country with pockets of modern amenities. Over in Durres, we even have an American type university designed around modern American instructional methods. Some American educated Albanian economist is the president.

"Speaking of American colleges, there's suite 301 at the end of the hall."

Lucky let AK take the lead. The door opened to AK's effort. Both men walked into the suite. Immediately inside was a small unoccupied reception desk. On either side of the desk was an office. The reception room was furnished in a shabby fashion with two old chairs and nothing else.

Someone could be heard moving about one of the offices. The two men made their way to the occupied office. AK took the lead for obvious reasons. "Excuse me, are you associated with the American College?"

The response came from a very attractive young woman. "Yes, I am the College Dean. May I help you?"

"I am interested in American business training. Is that available here?"

The young woman smiled in somewhat of a knowing fashion. She knew something the Old Man did not. "Yes, it is available. Tuition is $30,000 American per year with a year minimum required. Are you still interested?"

There had been no questions about AK's academic background nor had the young woman tried to "sell" the benefits of an American style education. She seemed more interested in running off the two men.

AK smiled back at the woman. "Maybe, where are the classes offered?"

"The classes are offered at different locations around the city. You will receive a list of this year's classes, locations, and schedule once you have paid the tuition." The Dean seemed a bit annoyed at the question. "If you don't have any other questions, I'm really quite busy."

AK continued to smile. "Could I have a brochure on the

program and a list of the professors and their qualifications?"

The question seemed to stump the young woman. "We don't have any information here, it's being reprinted."

"When may I drop by to pick the brochure up?"

The young lady was no longer pleasant. "Leave an address and I'll mail it to you as soon as it is available."

AK was like a birddog on point. He knew she was lying. "How about I drop by later and just pick it up?"

"Yeah, sure. Now if you will excuse me!"

AK and Lucky turned and walked out of the office, through the reception area and into the hallway. AK began to translate the office conversation exchange for Lucky. As he did, both men heard the door being locked behind them.

Lucky did not show any surprise at what the young lady had said. "If all TMC international campuses are like this one, it's hard to believe they recruited 1,500 students with no promotional materials and no attempt to sell the potential students on the college. Maybe we should come back tonight and take a closer look at this place. See if they have any admission records."

On the way out of the office building, the two potential students checked for another entrance. They found one tucked under a rear stairwell close to an elevator. It was obviously designed for deliveries.

After another afternoon of sightseeing (just in case anyone was watching) and an early supper, AK and Lucky returned home for a few hours' sleep. When you were in operational mode, you got sleep whenever you could. Both knew they were about to up the danger ante a bit.

At midnight the two ex-seals were standing in an alley behind the college's office building. They had started earlier by visiting two bars. Just a couple of buddies out for the evening.

Using a small light with a red lens, Lucky examined the lock on the building's back door. "Not much of a lock; it's even easier than the front door. Must not be much worth stealing inside."

AK followed Lucky through the back door. Both immediately spread to each side of the door and crouched close to the floor. After ten minutes of listening and acclimating to the interior darkness, Lucky led the way to the stairwell.

The men stopped at 20 foot intervals and listened. The building was quiet. There didn't appear to be any night owls about.

At the stairs, the two men advanced cautiously. Lucky took the lead, followed at about 10 feet by AK. As Lucky scanned the space above, AK scanned that below. Even though the building appeared empty, it paid to be cautious. Young pup seals got to be old grizzled seals by being cautious.

As Lucky reached the third floor landing, he paused and listened for a full 60 seconds. Again, better cautious than dead.

The two men eased into the third floor hallway. No lights were apparent under any of the doors as they moved to suite 301. Hesitating at the door to the suite, the seals once again paused to listen.

Hearing nothing, Lucky opened the lock with little difficulty. Stepping inside, he motioned for AK to check the office on the left. Lucky relocked the suite door.

Moving to the office on the right, Lucky checked the door; it was locked. AK was motioning from the other office that it was unlocked. Seeing Lucky crossing to his location, he waited.

With AK in the lead, they entered the office. Using the small flashlight Lucky started to work around the office in a systematic fashion. This was the office where they had been earlier in the afternoon.

After a careful examination of the office and its furnishing, the Seals found nothing. Making sure nothing would reveal their examination; the two men withdrew to the second office.

Lucky and AK stopped in front of the second office door. Lucky was examining the door with his light. "Take a look at this lock."

AK moved closer. "That's a real lock, not these tinker toys we opened to get in here. You better make sure it's not wired."

"I'm ahead of you there." Lucky had his light directed to the upper corner of the door facing. "If the person installing the alarm is not good or if he is just lazy, this is where it will show. Look real close; you can see small scratch marks left when the wire was run."

AK sighed, "Now what?"

"Well, where there is an alarm, there's got to be an alarm panel close by. It could be inside the locked room or it could be out here somewhere." Lucky began to look around the reception area. "Let's look out here first."

AK found the panel with little difficulty. "It takes a sneaky guy to think of this and an even sneakier one to find it."

Lucky walked over to where AK was standing. The panel was hidden in plain sight. He smiled at AK. "How did you know to look here?"

"Elementary, Watson. These old buildings were built with solid walls. If you want to run a wire, it has to be run along the wall. If you want to run the wire down a wall inconspicuously, you have no choice other than a corner. If you use the corner, you then plaster over the wire. I just looked for a thick corner. When I didn't see one, I looked for something in a corner that would serve the same purpose."

Both men stood examining a floor to ceiling pole lamp.

AK pointed to the switch on the front of the pole. "Here we have your requisite on/off switch. Now if you run your hand along the side of the pole adjacent to the wall, you'll find a small toggle switch about head high. And if you look a little closer at the lights in the pole, you'll see that one is actually an audible alarm."

Lucky stepped closer to the lamp and ran his hand around behind the pole to the toggle switch. "You're right, I can feel it.

Now for the real question; is it fancied up?"

AK was retracing the wire's route from the lamp to the locked door. "I doubt it; electricity isn't reliable enough to put many bells or whistles on an alarm. That's why mine at home is so simple. I manually arm and disarm it.

"Plus there's one other thing, the audible alarm. This system is designed to scare people off. They're not worried about anyone here but your run-of-the-mill burglar. It would never cross their minds that a professional sneak and peek team might show up."

"You're probably right, but let's not take any chances. You keep an eye out the window while I go inside. If anyone shows up, we'll be gone before they get in the building and up here." Lucky reached around the pole lamp and hit the toggle switch.

Both men held their breath and waited; there was no audible alarm emitted. The only sound in the quiet office was a metallic click as the office door lock disengaged.

Lucky quickly moved to the office door and eased inside. A quick glance revealed only impenetrable darkness. The office had no window. Lucky used his small light to find the wall switch. Before turning on the light, he pulled the door closed.

The small room was flooded with florescent light. Standing against one wall was a large floor safe. To Lucky's right was a modern desktop computer. There was nothing else in the room.

Lucky sat down at the computer and began to examine it. Nothing special; just your basic computer that could be bought at Wal-Mart or Albania's version thereof.

The interesting thing about the computer was that it was on; probably not the smartest thing to do if you were accessing and using sensitive files. Lucky opened the Word and Excel programs.

When Lucky clicked on the "Office" button of Word, he could see which files had been opened and used lately. He could also see if the files were on the computer's hard drive or saved to an external file. Lucky thought he knew the answer. He then examined Excel.

Lucky found several Thunder Mountain files on both Word and Excel. All files had been accessed from an external source using the "D" drive and saved the same way. They were probably using an external hard drive connected through a USB port. That explained why the computer was left on. Nothing of any value was stored on it.

There was no doubt in Lucky's mind that the external storage drive or drives were in the safe. Now all he had to do was find a way to get into the safe.

Turning off the light, Lucky exited the room and moved over to the window. "See anything?"

"Not a thing has moved since you went into the office; find anything?"

"Yeah, I found a big ole safe that needs cracking. It probably has all the records for this little operation secreted away from my prying eyes. My guess is that everything is stored on external computer drives kept inside.

While I keep any eye out the window, why don't you go take a look? There's a light switch on your right as you go in. See if you can figure a way in short of blowing it?"

AK spent several minutes in the room before reappearing. "It's a big mother, that's for sure; but it's also an old mother. I bet it's 50 years old if it's a day."

"Any thoughts on getting inside?"

"Well, it looks like the kind of safe small banks used to use in Albania. It was not a vault, but it was big enough to keep the available cash. Since it wasn't a vault, it was usually placed against a wall visible from the outside through a window.

"At night the bank put a spotlight on it. Anyone walking or driving by could see it from the street. A robber could probably get in, but it would be very visible."

Lucky watched a police car coming up the street. Both men

withdrew from the window slightly. The car cruised by slowly and continued on. Lucky let out a small sigh. "So, do you have anything in your machine shop that can be used to pop open the safe?"

AK was smiling to himself in the darkness. "Well, let's think about this some. We could use C-4 on it. Two problems with that, though; one, it would make a lot of noise and two, it might create enough of a mess to destroy sensitive computer drives."

"Can you get your hands on C-4?"

"Lucky, my friend, this is a third world country with a lot of lingering corruption among the bureaucrats. With enough money I can get anything.

"But I don't have to blow a safe that old. I have a carbide cutter that will go through those two old hinges in a heartbeat. There's only one problem though."

"And what might that problem be?"

"If we use a cutter that sophisticated, people will notice. Those same people might start asking enough questions to lead them back to me."

Lucky certainly didn't want to create a problem for his newest friend. "What if you cut the hinges, we steal the disk, and then we blow the safe with an excessive amount of C-4?"

AK laughed out loud. "Now, thinking like that is what kept you from being a Navy officer."

"So, Mr. AK, third world procurement specialist, can we really get some C-4?"

"Of course Tadpole. There's a small strip-mining operation about 20 miles this side of Durres. We'll just do a little midnight requisition."

Chapter 42

By 2:00 AM, AK and Lucky were back home. They decided to get a few hours' sleep and talk about the safe later.

By 10:00 AM, both men were up, showered, and sitting at the kitchen table drinking coffee. Time to think about a plan for getting into the safe.

Lucky had been thinking about AK's involvement in this whole deal and didn't feel comfortable getting him in any deeper. "I think maybe I should do the rest of what needs to be done alone. There's nothing in this for you. If we screw up, the whole thing could come back on you and your mother. You guys have to live here; I don't."

AK took a thoughtful sip from his coffee mug then set it on the table. "You're right, there appears to be nothing in this for me. And the whole thing could go south and blow back on my mother and me. But, I've been bored stupid since I moved back here; since you've been here, I feel like my old self.

"Yeah, there's some danger involved here, but not much. If we plan this right, there won't be any trails leading anywhere. It'll just look like some amateurs tried to blow the safe and used too much explosive. We can bury the detonator and timer in the C-4 so they'll vaporize with the blast. The only thing we really have to be concerned with is you and your presence in town. Someone might start looking for connections back to Colorado."

Lucky knew what AK meant by being bored. He'd felt the same way since retirement. The past few days had really got the old blood flowing. "If you're serious about continuing and it sounds like you are, I can handle the part about my presence and the Colorado connection.

"My trip here was a bit unorthodox to begin with. I hitched

a military ride from Colorado to Germany. In Germany I caught a flight directly here."

AK looked a little bored. "You really are an old Seal; you already told me all this."

Lucky held up his hand to halt AK's interruption. "I know I did, but I didn't tell you I traveled under one of my passports from the old days. Since most of the stuff we did was off the books, so were the passports. I forgot to turn them in.

"I didn't think it was smart to leave a trail back to my brother; not with the kind of people involved. So, as far as anyone knows, I'm a Canadian.

"I could catch a flight this afternoon back to Germany. Then I could connect to Rome and by tomorrow this time, I could be in Brindisi, Italy. There's a guy I know there with a fast boat that could run me across the straight to Durres. He can probably help me pick up the detonators and any other items we'll need for the safe.

"You could pick me up there in Durres, we can kill a little time in town, drop by for a little midnight shopping at the strip mine, and be at TMC's Tirana campus by 2 AM or so."

Chapter 43

Using the same route, through a couple of bars, as they had before; the two retired Seals arrived at the campus. The cordless carbide cutter and C-4 plus other essentials were concealed under their coats.

Lucky looked at the back door lock and then at AK, "Let's pick the locks like we did before, but on the way out, I'll use the pry bar to make entrance look a little less sophisticated."

AK smiled, "Good idea. The local punks are probably not well schooled in the art of lock picking."

In less than five minutes, the two men were standing in the interior office once again examining the old safe.

Looking at the carbide cutter, Lucky pointed at its cylindrical body. "It's amazing what uses you can find for the egg shell foam lining of a good gun case."

AK patted the foam which had been repurposed as a noise suppressor. It had been wrapped around the body of the grinder and duct taped into place. "Well, it ain't sophisticated, but it will do the job."

Moving toward the door, Lucky looked back at AK. "I'll keep an eye out at the suite's front door, just in case. That is if you don't need me to supervise you. Try not to drop the grinder."

"Try not to trip on your way to the front door; the trip is fraught with obstacles for an old frog whose slack ass is dragging the ground."

Lucky acknowledged the other Seal's comments with the traditional one finger salute.

Moving silently to the front door, Lucky opened it far enough to see any lights in the hallway or hear a more stealthy approach.

Back in the alarm secured office, AK attached a high quality carbide blade to the cutter. With a movement of his thumb, the blade began to spin at a high rate of speed. Satisfied that the noise was sufficiently suppressed, he began work. It took less than 10 minutes to slice through the two hinges.

Turning off the light before opening the inner door, AP whistled just loud enough for Lucky to hear.

"Are you awake out there?" he whispered.

Lucky quietly eased the door closed and locked it. Moving back to the inner office, he and AK closed the door and turned the light on. "Damn, that didn't take long."

AK rubbed the edge of one of the cuts. "Look at this piece of crap. It's made out of some sort of composite metal, stuff we used to call 'Pot Metal'. It looks strong and is heavier than hell, but it has little strength based on any kind of hardness scale.

"In this instance, perception of strength is all this old safe has going for it. It barely eroded my carbide blade."

As AK removed the blade from the body of the cutter, Lucky stepped forward and begin to examine the contents of the safe.

Inside the safe were two external hard drives, each about the size of a paperback novel, but thinner. Holding up the drives, Lucky turned so AK could see, "Bingo, two drives, probably one plus a backup. There's also what looks to be maybe 10 to 15 thousand dollars in cash, no doubt petty cash or bribe money."

Nudging Lucky out of the way, AK took a look. "The only other thing in the safe is this ledger."

Thumbing it open, AK began to examine its contents. "It appears to be a contact list of phone and email contacts. I see several contacts in Colorado and what appears to be several more with a local air freight company."

Reaching for the small ledger, Lucky looked for himself. "Most of the Colorado contacts are at Thunder Mountain

College, with another one located in Aspen and another in Denver. There are also banking contacts and some account numbers both here and in Denver and Grand Junction.

"This should answer a lot of questions once I get it into the right hands. Right now, though, we better set the safe to blow and get out of here."

As AK looked on, Lucky pressed C-4 into the partial hinges left attached to the safe. He and AK then lifted the door back into place. More C-4 was pressed into the spaces around the door. Finally, a timer set for 20 minutes and a detonator were embedded in a baseball sized clump of explosive and molded around the combination lock.

AK looked on smiling. "Gee, I hope we used enough bang, bang."

Lucky smiled in return. "Well, you know what they say, 'If a little will do, a whole bunch should do even better'."

Both men laughed as they looked around to make sure they had left nothing behind.

About 20 minutes later, the two Seals were drinking beer in a bar several blocks from the TMC Campus. Just as they clinked glasses in a toast to "Blowing Shit Up," a muffled boom could be heard in the distance.

Putting their glasses down, both men got up and left the bar.

Chapter 44

Later sitting in AK's kitchen, the two men looked at their ill-gotten gains.

Lucky picked up the money and threw it across the table to AK.

AK looked down at the money. "What's this?"

Lucky extended his hand across the table. "Thank you AK; I know you didn't do this for money, but we had to bring the money with us. Minus the thousand bucks I left in the safe to provide evidence, there's still well over 10 grand left. Keep it for a rainy day."

"What about you, Lucky? Don't you want to keep some of this?"

"Naw AK, there aren't many rainy days in the high deserts of Western Colorado."

Chapter 45

Three days later Tarr was spending Saturday night with Lucky on the "patio" in front of their cliff home.

Upon getting back from Albania, Lucky had called Tarr.

Tarr immediately called his Department's Administrative Assistant and informed her of a family emergency back east necessitating him flying to Boston immediately. He anticipated missing the rest of the week, but would be back in classes on Monday.

Neither he nor Lucky had left their cliff house since. Every waking moment had been spent examining the computer information from the TMC Albania Campus.

Chapter 46

As Tarr and Lucky looked over files and spreadsheets at their house, there was another meeting taking place at the Aspen Ranch.

After hearing about the break-in at the Albania Campus, the Old Man from Denver had ordered an investigation. He wanted to make sure the burglary was really the work of local punks and nothing else.

With more information in hand, Old Man Barberri called a meeting of the TMC contingent. The college President and Vice President had just arrived and were standing in front of the Old Man, Philip (the Barbarian) Barberri.

Looking over the top of his reading glasses, the Old Man sneered at his underlings. "Do you guys believe in coincidences? Well, I don't; never have, never will. And I don't think this Albania thing is one. Tell me what's going on in Grand Junction."

Vice President Manci cleared his throat nervously. "Everything is going according to plan; the girl's disappearance has been accepted as we set it up. No questions at all. The police are all over our patsy professor. He'll probably be arrested anytime now. Our guys followed him to Denver where he talked to a defense lawyer. He obviously feels the same way we do."

The Barbarian was still glaring. "What do we know about this professor; have you checked up on him? Where is he right this minute? What's he doing; who's he talking to about all this?"

President Karp jumped into the conversation. "I had our contacts at the FBI run a background check on him when he first began to question our international programs.

"He's our senior marketing professor. Before TMC, he worked for the Federal Trade Commission. He has a bum knee from a car wreck. Oh, yeah; he is one big son of a bitch, 6'5" or so, probably goes for 250 or 260 pounds."

"Anything else?" The Old Man didn't seem satisfied.

Manci took over the explanation. "Our FBI contact said there wasn't much information in his file about what he really did for the Federal Trade Commission.

"Another interesting thing; Professor Baldridge seems to live beyond his means. He lives in a fancy penthouse and drives a Hummer."

"What about family?" The Old Man seemed to be getting impatient.

"Well," Manci nervously added, "The only family appears to be a brother, one Luckley Baldridge. Brother is retired Navy; spent most of his time at Coronado Island, San Diego. Not sure where he lives, but he has a Grand Junction P.O. Box."

The Barbarian looked over his reading glasses again. "Did you say he spent most of his career at Coronado Island?"

"Yes, sir."

"Do the two of you have any idea what goes on at that island? Any idea at all? You two pretend college men ever hear of the Navy Seals? How about Special Operations? How about some of the best trained fighters in the world?"

Manci looked at Karp. "Back when we did the check, we weren't thinking about much other than the Professor. How dangerous could a gimped up professor be?

"I see your point now, though; it's a different ballgame."

"You bet your dumb ass, it's different." The Barbarian was starting to take on the physical attributes of his nickname. "I want to know exactly what the brother did and I want him followed, in addition to the Professor.

"Now bring me up-to-date on where the Professor is and

what he has been doing."

Apparently, it was Karp's turn on the carpet. He looked with apprehension at the Old Man. "We've had guys on Baldridge since the last time we were here.

"Mostly, he goes to the college and then goes home. We've lost him a couple of times on the weekends. As a matter of fact we haven't been able to find him now for several days. He told the College he had a family emergency and had to fly to Boston.

"We tried tailing his brother a couple of times after he visited Baldridge. We lost him both times.

"One thing, though; it happened the day Baldridge and his brother came back from visiting the lawyer in Denver."

"Spit it out." The Old Man shouted.

"Baldridge showed up at the front gate."

"Yeah, I know." The Old Man was frowning. "The boys called me that night. I decided to shake him up a bit. When the boys tried to run him off the road, he got the better of them. For future reference, a Charger can't push a Hummer off the road.

"Both the guys got banged up pretty good when the car rolled. Tony got the worst of it. His knee had so much gravel rash; it looked like a load of buckshot hit him.

"The Professor just kept going. A little cooler than most professors, don't you think?

"Here's what we're gonna do. We're going to take a break for a couple of hours and have a little dinner. Before we start though, I want one of you to call our FBI contact. I want to know what Baldridge's brother did in the Navy; and second, I want to know if Baldridge really flew to Boston.

"Now get to it. This night is just getting started."

Chapter 47

As Tarr lifted the glass of Jack Daniels, his phone rang. "Hello. Yes, this is the big son-of-a-bitch who ran you off the road."

Tarr talked for a couple of minutes then hung up. He turned to see Lucky watching him. "Remember, I told you about my visit to the Aspen Ranch and my little dust up with the Charger?"

"Yes, I remember, asshole brother of mine. You went off and had fun without me. You owe me one car wreck and a shooting."

Tarr was now sucking on an ice cube as he returned Lucky's stare. "Well, that was my new BFF Tony. He's at the Ranch and was reporting in. Right now, he's still afraid of me. If he ceases to be cooperative, however, you can shoot him in his other knee. Will that make you happy?"

"Oh yes, little brother, that will make me happy. And I won't have to do it with that handgun shotgun monstrosity you used. I'll do it with my Sig 9MM.

"But before you get too depressed about your poor marksmanship, tell me what your new Best Friend Forever had to say."

Chapter 48

The crew was back in the Old Man's study waiting for the Barbarian to speak. "Let's have it; what did our source find out?"

Manci was the first to speak. "There is no record of the Professor flying to Boston either commercial or private. Wherever he is, he didn't fly there, at least not using his own name."

The Old Man looked concerned. "Where was he when the Albanian campus was hit?"

"I checked on that as soon as I heard about the burglary," Karp added. "He was on campus that day teaching his classes, as usual."

The Old Man shifted his glare to Manci. "What about the brother? Any information on him?"

"Well, as it happens, there is quite a bit of information about him. He was a Navy Seal for most of his career. As a matter of fact, he is something of a legend in the Special Operations community. At least, that's what my contact said.

"According to him, a lot of what Navy Chief Baldridge did is still classified. Suffice it to say, he was one of the baddest ass Seals to ever have served.

"Again, according to my source, he can do it all: demolitions, hand-to-hand, sniper, small arms, and heavy weapons.

"When it comes to Seals, the guy was one of the best when he served, if not the best."

"Well, isn't that just wonderful," snarled the Old Man. Two brothers: one a legitimate badass and the other one smart enough to get through all the college bullshit and become a professor. A real academic, I might add; not phonies like you two guys.

"You two guys are real geniuses. Do you know what we have now?"

Both Manci and Karp were busy studying their shoes.

"What we have are two brothers that, when combined, equal a major pain in our collective asses. A pain that, I might add, didn't exist until you decided to get them involved.

"I should have known better than to let you combine a personal problem with business. Now we have to deal with these assholes in a more direct fashion that will, no doubt, bring more heat down on the operation."

Karp was seething. "I'll handle that big-assed professor myself. By this time next week, he will be fertilizing cacti in the Utah desert."

The Old Man was standing and pointing his finger at Karp? "You won't do any such thing. Your personal vendetta against him is what created this problem.

"No, for the time being I want you to continue your job pretending to be a College President and Chamber of Commerce Man of the Year.

"The only other thing I want you to do is call the Enforcer. Tell him I want him on standby and ready to fly to Grand Junction on a moment's notice."

"How long of a standby?" Manci asked.

Practically foaming at the mouth by now, the Old Man merely lowered his voice as he stared through Manci. "As long as it takes to figure a way out of this situation.

"Now get the hell out of here and let me think. I'll let you know what I want you to do. During the interim, keep your heads low and your mouths shut. Do not, and I mean do not, create another problem for me."

Chapter 49

Detective Orr had been summoned to the Chief's office. As he walked through the office door, the Chief looked up and smiled. "So, where are we on the Gibbs's case? The City Council has been on the City Manager's ass demanding to know what's going on.

"You remember the City Manager don't you? The guy who hires and, I might add, fires Police Chiefs. I need to give him something."

Orr smiled back, "Yes, I remember the City Manager who hires and fires Police Chiefs, who coincidentally, hires and fires Police Detectives."

They were both smiling, but each knew the situation held little humor.

Orr looked at his notes before continuing. "Well, as you know, one Dr. Arthur Gibbs, Professor of Finance, at Thunder Mountain College and I might add, a mostly detested Professor of Finance, was beaten to death."

"Mostly, you say?"

"I say mostly, because I'm trying to be kind. So far, I have not found a single employee or student at TMC who has anything good to say about the recently deceased Dr. Gibbs.

"Forensics has pretty much been a bust. Gibbs was beaten to death. The killing blow was one hell of a shot to the nose, which broke the decedent's nose and drove said nose bone into the brain.

"The one physical anomaly existing was a complete lack of defensive wounds on the corpse. You would think that even an academic wimp like Gibbs would have raised his arms in defense of such a horrendous beating."

The Chief was jotting down notes, "Any physical evidence at the scene?"

Orr glanced back down at his notes. "There were no signs of forced entry, possibly indicating that Gibbs knew his killer.

"The bedroom where he was killed was not disturbed. It was almost like Gibbs got out of bed, went and stood in a corner, and without resistance, allowed someone to beat him to death.

"To the casual observer, the murder seems to be a crime of passion perpetuated by one big strong extremely pissed off individual."

The Chief looked up with a raised eyebrow, "As opposed to the casual observer, what does an exceedingly competent homicide detective think?"

Pausing to take a postponing breath, Orr responded. "In the humble, yet well informed opinion of your most handsome homicide detective, it would seem possible that the scene was staged."

The Chief smiled, "Anything else lead you to this conclusion? And by the way, you are the ugliest homicide detective I have on the force."

Orr smiled back, "I resemble that remark, since I am your only homicide detective. Be that as it may, there was a tire track left on the grass. It matched the kind of tires put on most Hummers or possibly large trucks, say an F350.

"A nocturnal, excessively urinating senior citizen who lives across the street from the murder location, told me he heard a vehicle during the early morning of the murder, around 5 AM. He said it was either a large SUV or pickup truck. His aging eyesight precluded exact identification."

"How does that observation impact your conclusion?"

"It's just too convenient."

"How so?'

Detective Orr wrinkled his forehead, "Did you read the front-page newspaper headline the day after the murder?"

"Yeah, I read it. What does it have to do with your learned opinion?"

"Well, I only have one suspect in the case and that article did everything to describe him except publish his name. He had a physical altercation with Gibbs, he drives a Hummer, and he's big enough to carry your desk around on his back."

The Chief's interest had been peaked, "If some 25-year-old cub reporter for the paper put together enough evidence to get the story by the paper's editorial board and lawyer, why aren't you moving on it?"

The grin was back on the Detective's face. "I am, but not in the way you think. I'll explain, but let me tell you about the suspect first.

"He is one Dr. Tarr Baldridge, senior Marketing Professor at TMC. A couple of weeks prior to the murder, he and Gibbs got into a heated argument concerning some obscure theory of interest only to eggheads.

"According to witnesses I interviewed, Baldridge was not angry. As a matter of fact, as he turned to walk away after the argument, he wished Dr. Gibbs a good weekend.

"Gibbs, however, was extremely agitated and grabbed Baldridge by the shoulder, subsequently causing Baldridge to abruptly spin around.

"A sidebar is needed at this point before I continue the story. Like I said earlier, Baldridge is a sizeable specimen, probably weighting a conservative 250 pounds. Said pounds are housed on a 6'5 or better frame. Baldridge walks aided by a very substantial walking stick, which has been a necessity since a car wreck some years ago. You get the picture yet? He is one big son-of-a-bitch who carries an extremely stout stick.

"Back to the altercation. As Gibbs grabbed Baldridge's shoulder, Baldridge spun around in a startled fashion. Because of poor balance, he led with the stick, which according to Baldridge, accidently struck Gibbs in the knee.

"Baldridge professed accident; Gibbs declared on purpose. Baldridge apologized, smiled, and walked away. Gibbs angrily stomped away and proceeded to hobble around for the next few days feigning serious injury."

Orr continued, "So, can you see why Baldridge is a suspect?"

The Chief nodded in agreement, while waiting for Orr to continue.

"As you no doubt surmised, I immediately went to interview Dr. Baldridge. As we shook hands, I sneaked a peek at his hands, especially the right. Not a mark on it. It was what you would expect from a guy who makes his living talking and not physically working.

"Although it seemed strong, the right hand was unmarked. The coroner said it was his opinion that the blows to Gibbs's body had been delivered by the murder's right hand.

"In addition to the aforementioned, his ride of preference just happens to be a big ole Hummer."

The Chief was nodding his head, "I see what you mean. But back to my original question, why aren't you moving on it? It being the evidence."

The Detective still had his grin fired up, "Because after interviewing him, my gut says he's not our guy. Even though he's not our guy, there's something about him I can't get my finger on.

"Baldridge was not intimidated by me at all. This guy was smoother than owl shit on ice. If I paused trying to make him uncomfortable enough to want to fill the dead air with conversation, the asshole just sat there maintaining eye contact and smiling."

The Chief was hanging on Orr's words, "So, you're not going to arrest him then?"

"I didn't say that."

"But, if you don't think him guilty, why bring him in?"

Orr was frowning, obviously in a more serious mood, "This murder was a professional hit set up to make Professor Baldridge look guilty.

Someone went to a lot of time and money to make him look guilty. Let's make them think they were successful and see what crawls out of the woodwork."

The Chief rose from his Chair in the universal sign that the meeting was over, "Sounds like a plan to me; keep me plugged in."

Chapter 50

It was a beautiful day in Grand Junction, Colorado. A small thunderstorm had passed through the valley the night before. It left the air crystal clear and clean.

There was not a cloud in the sky. The sky was a color blue only possible in the altitude of a state like Colorado. Truly, a beautiful day.

Dr. Baldridge was teaching an eight o'clock Marketing class. He was reciting two of his favorite Marketing mantras. *"A LIE TOLD 2,000 TIMES BECOMES THE TRUTH and PERCEPTION LEFT UNATTENDED BECOMES REALITY."*

The door from the classroom into the hallway was open. Standing just outside the room listening was Detective Orr and two uniformed Grand Junction Police officers.

Detective Orr stepped into the classroom followed by the two officers. Detective Orr extended his hand to Tarr. "Dr. Baldridge, you're under arrest for the murder of Arthur Gibbs. *You have the right to remain silent. Anything you say can and will be used against you in a court of law. You have the right to speak to an attorney. If you cannot afford an attorney, one will be appointed to you. Do you understand these rights as they have been read to you?"*

Tarr, who had turned to look at Detective Orr, turned back to his class with a smile on his face. "This should convince you that the mantras are alive and well. We'll continue this discussion at the next class meeting. Class dismissed.

"If any of you are into sadomasochism, feel free to stay and see me handcuffed."

"Do you understand these rights?" Detective Orr had to raise his voice above the clamor of the students.

Tarr was again facing Detective Orr. He appeared completely relaxed and was smiling. "No, I don't, could you email me a copy with margin notes?"

"Okay smart-ass; put your hands behind your back. Cuff him up, guys."

Tarr made no effort to put his hands behind his back. "If you cuff my hands behind my back, I won't be able to use my walking stick; if I can't use my walking stick, I won't be able to walk. If I can't walk, you guys will have to carry me. Obviously, your plan to arrest me is flawed. Do you really want to carry me?" Tarr was once again smiling, although the smile had morphed into more of a smirk.

"Shut up, Baldridge." Orr could hear students snickering behind him. He also noticed that none of the students had left. This was proving too entertaining to miss.

A student chimed in. "They have wheelchairs at the Mall. I can be back with one in a couple of hours." The rest of the students howled with laughter.

Tarr, sensing that his smart-mouthed students were getting a little too involved, raised his voice. "Why don't you just walk me out; what am I going to do, run?"

Orr grunted. "Yeah, right. I guess that will have to do."

Pointing at one of the officers, Orr said, "Cuff yourself to his non-stick-using wrist." Pointing to the other officer he said, "Clear a path. I'll bring up the rear."

The first officer seemed hesitant as he carried out his order to cuff himself to Tarr. It was probably a clear invitation for Baldridge to jerk his shoulder out of its socket.

Fifteen minutes later, Tarr was sitting handcuffed to a table in an interrogation room at the Grand Junction police station.

Chapter 51

News of Tarr's arrest quickly began to spread across campus. Within 10 minutes, it reached the President's office.

Karp immediately picked up his desk phone and dialed Manci's extension. Looking at the phone display, Karp knew who was calling. "What's up, Dan?"

Karp responded with excitement in his voice. "The police just arrested Baldridge. Did it in the classroom, right in front of the students. I bet the prick was so scared he crapped his pants. He's probably begging for his mommy about now."

"Don't count on it." Manci shot back with concern in his voice. "Remember, he had a couple of our best guys crying for their mommies on the road awhile back.

"I'll call the Old Man and bring him up to date. In the meantime, call the Enforcer and get him headed this way. That's probably going to be the Old Man's call.

"And another thing, Baldridge's brother has to live around here somewhere. Put our lawyer on it; I want every real estate record in the county checked, if that's what it takes.

"That's probably where Baldridge was when he disappeared. We'll need that location for the Enforcer.

"And one last thing. Call our man in the District Attorney's office. I want to know how strong the arrest warrant is. If it's just a ruse to sweat out a confession, we need to know."

Chapter 52

Tarr's one phone call after being arrested was to his brother, Lucky. The call was part of Tarr and Lucky's tactical plan for dealing with the whole situation involving Tarr's arrest.

"Hey, bro; it's me. Guess what happened?"

"Hey back, little brother. I'm guessing your oversized ass is occupying a chair at the local police station. Right?"

"That's right, the good ole boy Detective plucked me right out of a Marketing class about one hour ago. It's time for us to implement our ARREST PROTOCOL."

"I'm on it little brother."

Lucky immediately made three phone calls. The first went to Kent Latimer, Tarr's high-priced attorney. The secretary put him right through. "Mr. Latimer, Tarr's been arrested."

"Okay, Lucky, it's time to see if they really have any evidence connecting Tarr to the murder. I'll call my associate in Grand Junction, Jim Mangrum. After practicing law there for almost 40 years, he has friends everywhere.

"As a matter of fact, when I talked to him about helping on the case, he said he had a judge friend who would look at any arrest to make sure it was legitimate and not simply an over-eager police officer.

"I'll get him on this right away. He'll be at the police station within the hour.

"Tell Tarr to hang in there; we're on this."

Lucky hung up the phone and made the second call. "Hi Doni, it's Lucky. Tarr has been arrested for murdering *Gibbs*. He said to tell you he'd call as soon as he could."

"Thanks Lucky, I just heard. Let me know what I can do." Doni nervously hung up the phone. Tarr had told her he would probably be arrested, but she had talked herself into not believing it. He also said he and Lucky had a plan. She hoped it was a good plan.

Chapter 53

Tarr was fairly sure that his arrest was just a fishing expedition on the part of Detective Orr. To show Tarr how serious they were, the police had put him in an interrogation room and handcuffed him to the table (just like on TV).

This was not the first time Tarr had been handcuffed. When he was a young agent for the Federal Trade Commission, over-eagerness and naivety had landed him handcuffed on the floor of a dingy Detroit warehouse.

Luckily for Tarr, the money launderers had been as naïve as him and weren't into murder. They left him in the warehouse and escaped. His colleagues found him a day later.

After that embarrassing screw-up, Tarr vowed to never be handcuffed again without knowing how to get loose. Within a month, he had learned to pick the cuffs open using several commonly available items.

Prior to his arrest, he had distributed a handout to his students. The paperclip securing the handouts was now in his shirt pocket.

Getting the paperclip from his pocket was no problem with his hands cuffed in front of him to a bar attached to the table. It took Tarr almost 10 seconds to pick the locks. Unobserved!

Unlike what is depicted on all TV crime shows, your average police interrogation room in a small town does not have a camera recording every action or a two-way mirror. If a confession or interrogation needs to be taped, a camera and tripod are brought into the room.

As a matter of fact, there was a camera on a tripod already in the room. Limping over to the recorder, Tarr removed the tape and, using the paper clip, ripped the tape. Tarr didn't like being taped.

Just to irritate Orr, Tarr hid the handcuffs under the camera recorder's bottom panel. He then sat back down and relaxed, with his hands out of sight under the table.

Tarr had hardly had time to settle in when the door opened and Orr strolled in. "How does it feel hotshot, to be handcuffed to an interrogation table? Any smart-assed remarks now?"

Before Tarr could respond, the door opened again and one of his attorneys, Jim Mangrum, quickly walked in. "Tarr, you don't have to say a thing.

Detective Orr, what's this all about? Why did you arrest my client? Unless you are filing formal charges against him, we're out of here."

None of this surprised Orr, he merely stared at Tarr without even looking at Mangrum. "I arrested him because he is the only one in the county with a motive to kill Arthur Gibbs. Plus, there's something really strange about him; he's too cool about the whole situation. He is sitting there pretending not to have a care in the world. Kinda like a really seasoned criminal."

About then, Tarr raised both hands above his head in an exaggerated yawn.

"What the hell?" Orr yelled as he jumped up knocking over his chair in the process. "How did you get out of your cuffs? I put them on you myself."

Orr walked around the table; his intent to recuff Tarr. "Where are the cuffs? What did you do with them?

Stand up, jerk!" A quick pat down of Tarr revealed no cuffs. Orr then spun around as he looked for the missing cuffs.

Tarr was using his hands to feign ignorance. "I don't remember any cuffs, maybe you're in early dementia.

"Forget the cuffs and I'll answer your questions. I have nothing to hide." Tarr stifled a laugh, trying to hide it behind his left hand.

"You're real funny, Baldridge; let's see how funny you are

after about 36 hours in a holding cell with drunks and meth heads puking on you."

Mangrum leaned toward Orr. "My client is being cooperative; he's offered to answer your questions. Against my advice, I might add.

"There will be no holding cell involved. You have three choices: release my client, charge him, or take him up on his generous offer.

"I might add, however, if you choose option two and charge Dr. Baldridge, Judge Busby is on my speed dial. I have already briefed him about the situation and discussed this harassment.

"Just one more point, I am not primary counsel to Dr. Baldridge; Kent Latimer is. He has no doubt contacted the local District Attorney by this time. You did consult the DA prior to this; didn't you?"

"Shit! I can see you were prepared for this little rendezvous, huh Baldridge?" Orr had assumed a posture of resignation as he spoke.

Tarr's tone took on a more serious tone. "After the murder headline in the newspaper, what would you have done? The suspect's description had everything except my name and mug shot.

"I decided retaining the best defense lawyer in the state might not be a bad idea."

Mangrum interrupted. "May I assume you have chosen option three, Detective Orr?"

"Yes," responded an obviously pissed off, but resigned Detective. "Do you mind if I tape this?"

Tarr replied in the affirmative.

Orr reached around and hit the on/record button on his recorder. He had done this so many times, it never occurred to him to double check it.

"Now, Dr. Baldridge, have you been read your Miranda rights and do you understand them?"

"I'm sorry, Detective, that query contains two questions, but I think I can decipher your intent.

"Yes and no. I was read my rights, but I don't understand them. Now you have another set of options.

"One, I get up and leave or two, I answer your questions off the record."

Orr reached behind himself once again and hit the off button.

Mangrum smiled, Orr frowned and the questioning started.

"Did you kill Gibbs?"

"No, but I think you already know that. I made a phone call to a friend in the Denver District Attorney's office after my first meeting with you. She said you were the best homicide detective in the department when you retired. She also said you were a good guy. The vote is still pending regarding your good guy status.

"Another reason I think you don't believe I did it is that you picked me up without a warrant. That told me immediately you didn't have any evidence or you would have used it."

Orr was intensely studying Tarr's face. "Why is it that you know so much about police procedure? If I didn't know better, I'd think you were a cop at some point."

Tarr's Cheshire cat's grin magically appeared. "I watch a lot of *Criminal Intent* on television. It's very informative."

Orr raised his voice as he stood up. "Cut the crap, Baldridge."

Tarr looked into the reddening face of the Detective. "I will if you will. I'll even start.

"I won't confirm that I have law enforcement experience; but I won't deny it either."

Mangrum gave Tarr a somewhat startled look but kept quiet.

"Your turn, Detective."

Orr sat down and let out the breath he had seemed to be

holding. "I'll take that as a yes on the law enforcement experience. I'll treat the answer as classified information, since it probably is."

Tarr nodded in response to the Detective.

Orr continued. "May I assume you were a federal investigator?"

Tarr nodded once again.

"May I assume you are currently investigating this case?"

Tarr merely smiled in response.

"You know who did it; don't you? If you didn't, you wouldn't be so friggin' cocky."

Yet another smile from across the table accompanied by a question. "Why did you bring me in? I think I know, but I'd like to be sure."

Orr assumed Tarr's brief retorts. "Why?"

"I think you believe I was set up and you just wanted to shake the bushes to see what fell out.

"Well, has anything fallen out?"

"No, not so far; but it's still early. How about you; what have you learned?"

Tarr was concentrating very hard while reading Orr. "Detective, I think my friend in the Denver DA's office was right about you; I've never known her to be wrong about a person. I think you are probably a good guy and a good detective.

"But I don't think you can solve this case without my help. It has nothing to do with your skills; it's just that it would never have been solved by you, me or anybody else except for one thing.

"That one thing involves a very specific skill set that I acquired in my previous and much classified career. Obviously, someone has a big bone to pick with me and saw the murder as a convenient way to pick that bone.

"There was no way they viewed me as anything other than a big obnoxious Business Professor."

Orr's interest had, no doubt, been peaked. "What are you saying? Do you know who did this?"

"Of course I do and so do you. It was a professional hit."

Orr was getting excited about now. "I agree it was a professional hit; the bigger question is who ordered it?"

Tarr nodded in agreement. "Even if we knew who ordered it, the even bigger question is why? And why involve me?"

"You know who ordered it." Orr stared at Tarr.

"Within certain parameters, Detective, yes I do; but proving it is still out of reach."

"Are you going to tell me or not, Baldridge?"

"Not yet, but I promise you I will. You are going to be indispensable in sorting out the players in this little drama.

"Are you going to be around the rest of the week?"

"Yeah, since I don't know what you seem to know, I'll still be trying to solve Gibbs's murder."

"If I call and give you some information and ask you to show up with a SWAT team at a certain location, will you do that, Detective Orr?"

"I tell you what, Baldridge; I don't know you very well, but my instinct tells me to trust you. So yes, if you give me a good reason, I'll show up with SWAT."

"There's a good chance, Detective, it might be in a neighboring county. Can you handle that?"

Tarr didn't really think he would need a SWAT team, but it never hurt to have one in reserve.

"Yes, Professor, I believe I can. Just one last question, where are my handcuffs?"

"Try the camera recorder's bottom panel. You might also want to check your recorder; there might be a problem."

"Asshole," was the last thing Tarr heard as he and his attorney exited the interrogation room. He knew the next few days would be very dangerous and unpredictable. Maybe, though, he would have some fun.

KILLER TUITION

If Tarr let himself accept the truth, he'd admit that this whole thing really had the old juices flowing. He didn't realize how much he had missed being in the game.

Chapter 54

Jim Mangrum turned to face Tarr as soon as they were outside the Police Station. "Well, that was, without a doubt, the most unusual interrogation I've ever sat in on.

"I couldn't tell if Orr wanted to hug you or kill you when we were leaving."

"Sorry to spring everything on you like that, Jim. There are a lot of things about my past that I prefer to keep in the past. Nothing illegal or horror inducing; just things that might upset the gentle natures of my intellectual colleagues."

"That's okay, Tarr, I've a few of those things myself; I imagine most people do.

"I'll call Latimer when I get back to the office and fill him in. I don't think you will have much more to worry about from Orr. Even though he obviously doesn't like it very much, he seems to have accepted your help and involvement in his murder case."

"Thanks, Jim. Can you give me a ride back to campus? I need to take care of a little college business, then get my car."

"No problem, Tarr. But please be very, very careful. This isn't a game. Even though it is evident you have done this type of thing before, it was quite a few years ago and you were no doubt younger. You probably weren't anchored by a walking stick in those days either."

"Whenever I'm paying as much per hour for advice as I am for yours, Mr. Attorney, I have a strong tendency to take it. But please don't worry, I have some very skilled people watching my back and helping with this."

"Okay, I'll take your word for it, Tarr. Where do you want dropped on campus?"

"The Library will work just fine."

As Jim continued to drive, Tarr sent a text message. "Can you meet me on the second floor of the Library in ten minutes? I'll be in one of the small study rooms in the back."

Within seconds, Tarr's phone beeped with an incoming text. "See you there."

Chapter 55

Opening the car door as soon as Jim stopped the car, Tarr hurriedly got out while throwing a quick, "Thank you," over his shoulder.

He made it inside the Library and upstairs to a study room without attracting any attention. The reason for his stealthy trip had nothing to do with skill; it was manifested by the fact there were few students around after about three o'clock in the afternoon. His stay at Police Headquarters had been a long one.

Doni rushed into the study room a few minutes later. After being careful to move the sign on the door to "Occupied," she closed the door, checking to make sure it was locked.

After giving Tarr a long hug, she flashed him her most mischievous smile. "So, how's your day been going, Dr. Baldridge? Anything interesting happen? Been to any exciting locales; meet any new people?"

"I have to say, Dr. Rader, my day has been absolutely loaded with interest. Nothing I haven't experienced before, however."

Pausing for a response, Tarr noticed a surprised look fill Doni's face. "Nothing you haven't experienced before; exactly what does that mean?"

As Tarr's expression took on a serious note, Doni sat down by him and took his hand in hers. A serious face replaced the mischievous. Tarr managed to eke out a timid smile.

"Doni, before I start talking, I need to tell you how important you have become to me. I hope what I'm about to say won't change your opinion of me."

Doni did not speak, letting her silence express the uncertainty she was feeling.

"Do you remember our first date at *The Sanctuary* and my story you asked me to tell. Well, there was a bit of fiction woven carefully into the truth. I think you knew that by your expression a couple of times."

"I did, Tarr, but I chalked it up to typical male embellishment. Was it something different?"

Tarr's timid smile was slowly being replaced by the real thing. More like reverse embellishment. I'll start talking and you stop me when you have a question."

"Okay, Mr. Man of Mystery, you have my undivided attention."

"My sin of lying to you is one more of omission as opposed to commission. First of all, everything I told you about my brother and me, our growing up, living in the cliff house and so forth are all true. My widower status, education, and working 10 years for the Federal Trade Commission, are also true.

"Now, for the fiction. I never really told you what I did at the Federal Trade Commission. If anyone ever asks, I give a very general answer like working in constraint of trade, unfair pricing, unfair advertising, etc. I say I was primarily an office drone doing research and expert testifying. All this is a lie.

"What I really spent the ten years doing was undercover investigations. I was a federal law enforcement officer. My specialty was money laundering. For much of my career, I was kind of on loan to the FBI.

"During the course of my undercover work, I helped put a lot of very nasty people in jail, including numerous Mafia and drug cartel types. I have also killed people in the line of duty.

"One night during my tenth year, I found myself alone in a very dark alley, with a very unpleasant young man from Uruguay. My cover had been blown and he was seeking to terminate my contract with his cartel.

"His preference for contract termination was a very wicked folding knife with a six-inch blade. While I was busy negotiating my side of the deal, he showed a serious lack of agreement by inserting the blade of the aforementioned knife through my knee."

Doni cringed as she visualized Tarr's telling of his story. She did not speak, however, opting rather for silence so Tarr could continue.

"Taking umbrage at the young man's crude behavior, I reciprocated by pulling the knife from my knee as I fell in the inky darkness. Not seeing what I had done, he reached down and grabbed me by the collar; no doubt intending to rework my pretty face.

"He was rewarded by having six-inches of sharp stainless steel plunged into his left temple. The fight and my undercover career ended that night, with me laying on my back bleeding and groaning in a urine- and vomit-soaked back alley.

"That, Dr. Rader, explains the walking stick."

Doni no doubt was stunned but not lacking words. "You are a scary man. Truly a time when life was stranger than fiction. What happened to your Federal Trade Commission career after that?"

Tarr had a strange look on his face, seeming to see the past in his mind, as he continued to speak. "I was offered full disability retirement. No one at the FTC knew me outside a select few and because of the perceived danger to my life if I surfaced, the powers that be decided to keep my record in a top secret classified, *need to know only*, file.

"A while later I showed up to interview at TMC, car wreck story and walking stick in hand."

"That's one hell of a story, Tarr. Anyone looking in your black eyes knows something dark is behind them, but no one could ever imagine this."

Reaching up to put her arms around Tarr, Doni hugged him as tightly as she could. "Tarr, I'm so sorry you had to relive the horror of that night. I'm sorry you are having to endure this hideous mess."

"Does this mean you still like me? I'll take your hug and comments as a yes."

"Wait a minute buster, you're still not off the hook. What does this story have to do with the murder of Dr. Gibbs and you being dragged from the classroom in handcuffs?"

"First of all, there was no dragging or handcuffs involved in my classroom. It is all connected, though."

Tarr told Doni how.

Then he suggested she go home, pack a bag, drive to the airport immediately and catch a flight out of town. San Francisco might be nice.

"I don't see why I should have to leave," she protested.

"You need to leave, Doni, because the whole campus knows we have been seeing each other. That includes the President and Vice President. We can't take the chance they will try to get to me through you."

"Doni shrugged her shoulders in a physical display of acceptance." Alright, I'll go, but you had better be careful. And I expect to receive a phone call the minute this thing is over."

Tarr was visibly relieved. "Good, now let me tell you what you need to do right now, when we walk out of the library.

"Before I left the Police Department, I called a friend of mine who is involved in all this. He sent two of his best men to escort you home, to the airport and then accompany you on the plane to Salt Lake City. At Salt Lake City, they will put you on a charter flight.

"The charter flight will take you to San Francisco where you will be met by one of his female agents who will drive you to a hotel in Napa Valley. She will stay with you until this is over."

"All your expenses are covered. I'll call you as soon as this is over."

"Listen, Tarr Baldridge, the only reason I'm willing to go

along with your James Bondesque plan is because of what you told me. I know I am in danger, but I am also aware of the danger to you. Promise me you'll be careful."

Tarr held up his right hand as if to take an oath. "I'll be as careful as *a whore in a confessional.*"

"And one other thing, Tarr Baldridge; you aren't young anymore and this isn't a game."

"Yes, Dr. Rader," Tarr whispered as they walked outside.

Chapter 56

As soon as Tarr got off the elevator in the Business Building, he ran into the Dean's secretary. "Dr. Baldridge, Dean Haller wants you to report to his office as soon as possible.

"I was on my way to your office to put a note on your desk, since you haven't returned my calls to your office or home. I was afraid you were not answering any calls because of what happened this morning.

"The Dean said it was very important. He seemed very upset about something. It would probably be best if you went right now."

"Yes *mam*, thank you *mam*; I'll report right away, *mam*." Tarr heard the secretary whisper, "Smart ass" as he turned to walk away.

The Dean, Randy Haller, was pacing his office like an expectant father in a maternity ward. As Tarr walked through the door to his private office, the Dean practically leapt at him. "Damn, Baldridge, where the hell have you been?"

"And a hearty hello to you too, Randy. By the way, why are you called Randy? I've been meaning to ask. Doesn't randy mean lustful and/or lecherous?"

"Cut the shit, Baldridge; this is serious. In all my years in the Academy, I've never had one of my professors jerked out of a classroom and hauled off to jail in handcuffs."

"Well, that's not exactly what happened." Tarr tried to interject.

"Shut up, Baldridge, and just listen." The Dean was now red in the face and perspiring. "I got a call from President Karp telling me in his words, 'Send that smart-assed, son-of-a-bitch home, when he gets back to campus. And tell him not to come back until I tell him to come back."

I don't know what your problem is with the President, but it must be a doozy, judging by his tone. But look, Tarr, you and I have always been friends; there is no way I think you killed Gibbs. That is absolutely ridiculous.

"I'm sorry I'm an asshole today; the President made me jumpy. He made it sound like I'd be fired if I didn't run you off posthaste. I'm sorry."

"Randy, I appreciate your vote of confidence, given the untenable situation this arrest has created for you. If it makes you feel any better, the police released me without charging me with Gibbs's murder.

"Obviously, they are just fishing; they don't have any more of an idea who did it than you do. I will leave campus, though, just as instructed. I suggest you call the President and tell him you kicked my ass and sent me scurrying off.

"I will not be going home, however; I will go into seclusion where the press nor anyone else will be able to find me. I'll get in touch with your office when I think it is appropriate. I assume you have made arrangements to cover my classes."

"Thanks for your understanding, Tarr." The Dean seemed to be regaining his usual unflappable composure. "I hope all this is sorted out soon. I know your students will miss you."

Tarr turned and walked out of the office. He needed to head for that seclusion he had mentioned. There was a cliff house with his name on it just waiting for him to come and seclude.

He had to get up to the Glade Park Ranch and their cliff house without a tail, though. Well, an hour spent losing a tail didn't seem all that unreasonable given the stakes of this very dangerous game in which he was now involved.

With that in mind, Tarr spent the next 50 or so minutes totally frustrating those who were attempting to follow him.

Chapter 57

The first thing Tarr did after arriving at the Cliff House was fill Lucky in on the happenings of the morning. Just when he was finished bringing Lucky up-to-date, his cell phone rang.

It was his favorite BFF snitch, Tony Vick, who was currently very well ensconced in the Aspen Ranch, while nursing a very badly mangled knee, thanks to one Dr. Tarr Baldridge, aka: the bad-assed professor.

"Hey, Tony, how's the knee?"

"Screw you and the horse you rode in on, Professor."

Tarr laughed as Tony took a calming breath. Obviously, making the call was stressful, to say the least.

"I've got some hot news for you, Professor Bad-ass. I heard some of the boys talking about the Old Man ordering in some guy called the Enforcer. The boys were laughing and setting up a pool on how many days you have left above ground.

"All I could figure out is your name is the only one on the Enforcer's hit parade. This guy has been around for a while. I first heard of him six or seven years ago.

"The way I hear it, the guy has never missed. He's also real good at making accidents happen or making the hit look like somebody else did the thing. Know what I mean; sound familiar to you?"

"Yeah, Tony, the Enforcer's modus operandi sounds very familiar. One more question, Tony?

"How many guns are usually at the ranch?"

"Listen, Professor, I can't go on being your snitch forever. They catch me and I'll end up sleeping with the fishes."

"Answer this one last question and I'm done with you, Okay?"

"Okay, Professor, but then I'm done for good, no more phone calls. Right?"

"Right, Tony, no more calls."

"Most nights, there are three on the front gate; then there's a second gate farther in toward the house with two more. The main house has two more, except when the Old Man's here that jumps to six. Then the little house has four more guns plus some mousy little guy who probably carries a pocket calculator instead of a piece.

"That makes it 11 unless the Old Man's here, then it jumps to 16. It's not always the same, though. These numbers can change by three or four; there's really no way of knowing. Now I'm done with you, right?"

"That's right, Tony, you're done. Thanks for the info. Now, to return the favor, I suggest you have a severe attack of pain in your knee. So severe, you think you need to go home to Chicago and see a specialist. Leave tomorrow and don't come back. Understand?"

"I understand, but you better understand, too. These guys around here are the real deal, no street thugs or wannabes. They're all made guys. Whatever you're thinking about doing will probably get you dead. But better you than me."

Tony hung up.

Tarr took the next few minutes filling Lucky in on Tony's call.

Things were starting to get interesting.

Chapter 58

As Tarr was filling in Lucky on the phone call with Tony, the alarm for the front gate sounded. Lucky picked up his phone and punched in a number. "Yo, that you asshole?"

"No," the voice replied, "It's the Avon Lady. I've been told you have a desperate need for my products."

Lucky hung up.

Looking on, Tarr smiled. "Jack?"

"The one and only," Lucky replied.

Jack showed up a few minutes later. Lucky and Tarr met him on their "Patio," with chairs and a cooler. They all took the time to pour themselves a drink.

Jack held up his glass to Tarr. "Here's to you, convict. Make any new girlfriends on the inside; or are you the girl? I can't remember."

Holding his drink up, Tarr said, "You know you're the only girl for me, Jack."

"Speaking of girls, Tarr, I am happy to report that your Miss Doni is safely and soundly entrenched at a very nice little Napa Valley Inn."

"Thanks, Jack, I can't tell you how good that makes me feel. Now I can concentrate, with you ugly mutts, on saving my ass and, at the same time, solving that little money laundering problem at TMC."

Lucky spoke as soon as Tarr broke for a breath. "Tarr, I asked Jack to see what background he could uncover on the President and VP of your very profitable little college.

"Jack, would you tell Tarr what you told me. I haven't gotten around to filling him in."

"And guess what else I've found for my favorite Baldridge

brothers? Not much.

"To recap for you, Tarr, these guys' academic records go back about ten years. It's as if they sprung from the womb fully grown and educated.

"Since any second-rate hacker can penetrate a large university's student database, it would be less than challenging to add a fictional student and a solid academic record. My guess is that's the story on both guys.

"I easily found evidence of college records and degrees by having my guy hack in to the schools they say they attended. But try going back and finding high school records or any evidence of their existences in their hometowns and you get zilch, nada, nothing.

"After I talked to you, Lucky, I web searched both of them and again, nothing. No news clippings, no published research, nothing.

"Whenever I come across this type of thing in my security business, nine out of ten times it means the people of interest were invented.

"Since college and university administrative jobs don't require any type of security clearance, the cover identities, correspondingly, don't have to be very deep. I mean, who checks this type of stuff? I'll tell you who, nobody."

Tarr, listened very intently. "What you are saying makes sense to me, too, based on my experience with the Federal Trade Commission.

"But, for a sophisticated scam like this, more people have to be involved. At least four more."

Lucky and Jack looked at Tarr with questioning eyes. Jack spoke up first. "How do you figure that, Tarr?"

"Well guys, forged credentials will only get you so far; you still have to get the jobs. To become a President and a Vice President at TMC, both successful candidates for the jobs have to be approved by a majority of the College's Board of Trustees.

There are seven appointed board members. Therefore, four members can control the board."

Lucky appeared a bit confused. "So, to make this work, you need four of the board members to be involved. Tarr, didn't you say appointed board members? How does someone or some group arrange that?"

"Simple, older brother: money. Since TMC is a private institution, board appointments are usually associated in some way with donations to the TMC Development Foundation. The more money you donate to the Foundation, the more say you have in board members. Current board members select new board members who are retiring. Over a period of a few years, control could take place."

"Wow," Jack enthusiastically injected, "This is a well-thought-out and well-funded bunch, whoever they are. Any ideas, Tarr?"

"Yeah, but it's more than an idea. Remember my little drive to Aspen where I had to rough up some guys following me who tried to run me off the road. You may also remember I turned one of the guys.

"Not long before you got here, he called to warn me that a professional assassin called the Enforcer was coming to kill me. When I asked him about the number of bodies guarding the Aspen Ranch, he warned me that they were all made guys.

"So, after years of college where I finally tuned my deductive reasoning skills, I have deduced that we are dealing with some arm of the Mafia."

Jack laughed but quickly assumed a more solemn tone. "Damn, Jack. If we are dealing with a major Mafia money laundering operation in Colorado, we're dealing with a not-so-gentle man by the name of Philip Barberri. Affectionately referred to as the *Barbarian* by Mafia insiders.

"My security company has brushed up against this bunch a couple of times. They should be taken very seriously. Screw with them and you simply disappear, never to be seen or heard from again.

"Boys, we better think this through very thoroughly. And at the end of the day, when all is said and done, someone else's fingerprints need to be on this thing, not ours."

Tarr's Cheshire grin had once again magically appeared. "I couldn't agree more, Jack. How do you two feel about the local Grand Junction Police getting all the credit?

"Now, to accomplish this, we need just two small things. First, we need to break into the Aspen Ranch and steal all of TMC's illicit financial records. And second, we need to lure the hired professional hitter here to our little neck of the woods and make him disappear forever.

"Oh yeah, I forgot a couple of other things. We need to steal a ton of money and make it look like Karp and Manci did it. We also need to make both of them disappear.

"And Jack, I need all the information you can get about a professional assassin called the Enforcer. Mostly, I'd like to know if he prefers to kill from a distance or up close and personal. An email address would also help.

"Any questions?"

"Oh, is that all?" Lucky said with his most sarcastic expression.

"Yeah, sounds easy enough to me." Jack said in an equally sarcastic fashion.

Tarr laughed. "Jack, you know I was kidding about the email address, right?"

Chapter 59

The Old Man was fuming as he waited for his Grand Junction crew to clear gate security and arrive at the big house.

What a mess. It never ceased to amaze him how one amateur could ruin an operation that took years to set up and was just now reaching its potential.

The whole thing had been his idea. One Sunday morning several years ago, he was reading the newspaper and happened upon an article about the University of Denver's foundation. What a gold mine!

He had one of his lawyers look into how college foundations worked and what it took to set one up. After he learned how little oversight college foundations required, he knew he had stumbled on a unique opportunity for hiding and moving money.

The only thing he needed was to find a small private college in an isolated area. A couple of weeks later his people found Thunder Mountain College in Grand Junction, Colorado. Since he was already well entrenched in Colorado, he figured it was a very doable concept.

He really liked TMC because it was small, yet well respected. The one aspect of the college he really liked was that, because it was small, TMC's Board of Trustees also functioned as the Foundation Board.

With only one board controlling everything at the college, he knew that within one or two years he could get enough of his own appointees on the board to have a majority vote.

After that, he would have the board fire the President and one or two other key administrators and replace them with his own men.

With a few donations to TMC and appropriately applied

pressure to four board members, it had taken two years to get total control of the College Board and another two to get the money laundering mechanism in place. It had been fully operational for only two years, but what a great two years. So far, about 200 million dollars a year had been laundered and they were growing double digits this current year.

Currently, money was flowing in from every Mafia family in the country. Hell, it was so successful, Barberri had to ration the amounts he could take from the various families around the country.

Because the total laundering process was controlled by the family, it was foolproof. Because it was foolproof, he could charge a premium fee of 10% for his laundering services.

Forty million in profits so far and this year was growing.

What made the whole thing even better was that tuition and fees from the real students paid all the expenses of running the college. His was the first Mafia-controlled college, but not for long. There were already several other families looking at doing the same thing.

Who would ever have thought Higher Education could be so profitable?

Thinking about all the money and prestige brought to his operation had cooled him off a bit. He wasn't nearly as mad.

That quickly changed, however, when President Karp and Vice President Manci walked through the door. They refused to make eye contact until he spoke. "How did you two idiots let things get so screwed up?

You assured me it was all under control. You were going to frame that professor. How did that work out for you?

Both men were now looking at the Old Man. In the Mafia hierarchy, VP Manci was the senior man and President Karp was, in reality, number two on campus. Manci spoke up. "Not so well. We underestimated Professor Baldridge as well as Detective Orr.

Baldridge went off and hired the best criminal defense lawyer in Colorado. The guy hasn't lost a case in ten years. Who would think a college professor could afford a lawyer like that?"

Karp anxiously added a comment. "And what about that Detective? We have since discovered he retired from the Denver Police Department where he was their best homicide guy."

"Let me tell you college boys something. I don't really give a crap what you know now. Why didn't you know all this before?

"What I want to know now is what you intend to do. One lousy amateur finance professor started this whole thing just because he was curious. Now everything is getting way too visible.

"Do I need to remind you that we have run about 400 million dollars through your little college not counting this year? We don't want publicity. We, meaning me, want this whole thing to disappear. How do we do that?"

Manci hurriedly offered a plan. "I think we can solve the whole thing with Dr. Tarr Baldridge's suicide. The accompanying note will express his regret for taking Dr. Gibbs's life.

"The college will then start a scholarship fund for deserving TMC finance students. We'll all express our shock and regret. The whole thing will be old news in a couple of weeks."

The Old Man shot a stare at President Karp. "What do you think, Dan? Can we spin this thing in the press to our advantage and make it go away?"

"Absolutely, sir. We'll low-key the whole thing. We won't do any press conferences out of respect for Dr. Gibbs's. He would not want a great deal of publicity out of concern for his students and his desire that their learning process not be interrupted. That was the way he conducted himself while alive; we will honor him the same way in death."

Manci could not stifle a belly laugh. "That's the biggest pile of BS I've ever heard. It's so outrageous, it has to work."

"Okay, guys, tell me how you plan to do it. I don't think the

Professor will kill himself on demand, much less getting him to write the suicide note."

Manci was obviously the thinker between him and Karp. "The note will be easy; we banned Professor Baldridge from campus, so we have complete access to his office computer. We'll compose something appropriately sorrowful.

"As far as the suicide itself, we've got the Enforcer standing by just waiting for our call. We'll leave that in his most capable hands.

"The last piece of information we need should be available to me tomorrow. We've had trouble finding out where the Professor has been staying. We've been watching his girlfriend's place, but he hasn't shown. As a matter of fact, she's gone. Flew out of town and hasn't come back."

"Hey, numbnuts," the Old Man barked. "Does her disappearance bother anybody other than me? Sounds like the Professor has rat-holed her somewhere until all this gets resolved. That makes things a little more complicated, don't you think?

"If he's that scared, then he is going to be hyper-vigilant. If he's cautious, then his brother won't be far away. You remember his brother, don't you? The frigging Navy Seal."

"We're on it," Manci said in a not so confident voice. "By tomorrow this time we'll know where the brother lives. We'll stake the place out until Baldridge shows."

"That sounds solid enough," the Old Man said in a questioning voice, "But we need a backup plan. You're the Professor's boss aren't you? How about calling him first thing in the morning and have him come in immediately for an important meeting?"

"I can do that. I've already got his cell phone number from one of his friends in the Marketing Department. We've been trying to track it, but Baldridge is smart enough to disable the GPS function.

"I'll call him on the way back to Grand Junction."

"Good, Greg." The Old Man had calmed down quite a bit. Make sure you have at least three cars on him when he leaves. You should also be able to get a tracker on his car.

"Don't let the sun go down tomorrow without knowing where he has been hiding out. Do you understand what I'm saying, Greg?"

Greg's blood ran cold under the Barbarian's dark stare. "Yes, sir; I understand. We'll get the job done."

Chapter 60

Tarr, Lucky, and Jack were in the midst of bouncing plans off each other. Tarr had informed them that his attempt to get TMC tax returns had been a bust. It seems the buddy he had been counting on was out of country for a month.

As the three men digested that piece of disappointment, Tarr's cellphone rang.

"Hello."

"Dr. Baldridge, this is Dan Karp. I am calling because I think we need to sit down and talk about the whole Gibbs's matter. I'd like your take on what is really going on and how the situation is impacting TMC's public image. Does 10:00 tomorrow morning, in my office, work for you?"

"Yes, Dr. Karp, 10:00 in your office works for me. And thank you for the call. I've been extremely worried about all this and especially how it's affecting my job.

"I really love my job at TMC and am concerned all this could result in my termination. I really need this job and don't want to lose it. Thank you for giving me this chance to explain my side of things."

Chapter 61

Karp closed his phone and smiled at Manci sitting beside him in the car. "He'll be there tomorrow morning. And guess what? The sucker is running scared. Sounds like a big blubbering loser. 'I love my job; I don't want to lose it; thanks for letting me explain; blah, blah, blah.' Maybe, I'll go ahead and fire him tomorrow. Who knows; it might make an already depressed person kill himself."

They both laughed uncontrollably.

Chapter 62

Jack looked on while Tarr talked to President Karp. Tarr hung up and turned to face the two with a huge grin on his face.

Lucky couldn't contain himself. "Why didn't you put Karp on Facetime so you could post a picture kissing his ass?"

Jack couldn't stay quiet. "If you keep sucking up to him when you meet, he might want to get a room. What's up with your routine?"

"Well, guys, this could well be the solution to one of our problems. While I'm meeting with the Prez tomorrow morning, I'll be a long way from my vehicle. My guess is they'll put a tracker on it. They will also have plenty of time to get a couple of cars in place to follow me.

"Now, all we need to do is decide where we want me to be when the Enforcer shows up to do his thing."

Chapter 63

As President Karp and Vice President Manci were having a good laugh while rolling down the highway, the Baldridge boys and Jack were having an equally good laugh back at the cliff house.

Everything was starting to move into place.

Chapter 64

Tarr arrived a few minutes before 10:00 and parked his Hummer on the top level of the parking garage. There was hardly ever much traffic on the top of the structure. He wanted to make sure the boys attaching the tracking device to his vehicle weren't disturbed.

Dressing in his best suit, Tarr wanted the President to think he was trying to make a good impression.

Passing from the foyer into the office, he was immediately greeted by a very attractive young woman in her mid-twenties. Tarr expected nothing less.

"Hello, Dr. Baldridge, Dr. Karp will be right with you; he's just finishing up a long-distance conference call. It's running a little longer than he expected. I'll stick my head in the door and let him know you are here."

"Of course he is," thought Tarr. "He's probably playing Internet poker until he thinks I've sweated enough."

Fifteen minutes later, Karp came rushing out of his office complaining about long-winded colleagues, while at the same time, extending his hand.

Tarr slowly stood up taking most of his weight on his walking stick. "Good morning, Dr. Karp, thank you so much for meeting with me. I can't tell you how much I appreciate you taking valuable time out of your hectic schedule."

Tarr hoped he was being sufficiently subservient.

"You're welcome, Dr. Baldridge, please come in and sit down. I'd like to start by asking you to recap the last few weeks starting with the time of Dr. Gibbs's tragic death.

"But before you start, I have to be honest with you. I'm getting considerable pressure from four of my board members to terminate your employment at TMC. It is their collective belief that your association with the murder of Dr. Gibbs and your subsequent arrest for his murder are causing irreparable damage to the public image of the institution.

"Also, it didn't help that you were dragged from your classroom handcuffed, kicking and screaming."

"If it matters, I wasn't handcuffed, kicking or screaming."

"Well, be that as it may, I need you to say something to me that I can carry back to the aforementioned trustees and convince them of your innocence. Do you understand what I'm saying?

"Dr. Baldridge, not only your career, but your entire way of life is on the line here. Please defend yourself!"

"Dr. Karp." Tarr was looking at his hands as he fidgeted in the chair. He wanted to convey the image of a frightened and defeated man. "I don't really know what to say.

"First of all, I'd like to assure you that I had absolutely nothing to do with the murder of Dr. Arthur Gibbs. Even though we were not close friends, we definitely were not enemies. The minor altercation we had in the faculty dining room was most certainly not serious enough to murder somebody over.

"For goodness sake, I'm an academic and respected member of the Academy. We academics don't kill people; we try to help them. Teaching is a helping profession.

"I know all the evidence points to me; I can't explain that. I couldn't explain it to Detective Orr, who is convinced I murdered Gibbs and I can't explain it to you.

"I would think an honored academic such as yourself could review the evidence and see it is all circumstantial. There is not one bit of empirical substantiation supporting the thesis of my guilt.

"That's the reason I'm not in jail right now. That, and a very expensive lawyer who has some influence with the local District Attorney's Office. I'm lucky just to be sitting here today."

"Is that all you have to say in your defense, Dr. Baldridge?"

"Well, I guess that is all, Dr. Karp. I'm so depressed by all this I don't know what to do. Isn't there some way you can help me?"

"I'll do my best, Dr. Baldridge, but don't get your hopes up. If I were you, I might start thinking about another line of business."

As Tarr walked out of the Presidential Suite, he couldn't help but smile to himself. Karp was the one that would need another line of business."

As soon as Tarr left his office, Karp quickly picked up his phone and punched in a quick series of numbers. "Baldridge is on his way back to his car. Is everything set? Good, keep me updated. I want to know as soon as possible if the information from the lawyer and the tracker both end up being the same place."

Chapter 65

The previous night at the cliff house, Jack had some of his contacts discreetly inquire about the Enforcer. They told Jack the Enforcer was a professional hit man for hire. 'Big revelation there.'

Mostly, though, he was known as an enforcer for the Mob, thus the name. Word on the street was the Enforcer had been around for ten or so years and had a reputation for never failing to deliver on a contract.

No one knew where he lived or what he looked like. And not just any clown could contact him. Apparently, there was a cutout between the clients and the Enforcer himself.

The most important piece of information received, however, was the Enforcer's preferred mode of operation. It seems he was a close-in killer. A real hands-on kind of guy.

That was good news. If Tarr and the boys were dealing with a long-range sniper, things would be a lot more complicated. Whereas you could control the environment for a close-in hit, you could not for a long-range sniper shot.

Tarr was thinking about this as he walked back to the parking garage. Time to put phase one of their plan into motion.

Chapter 66

Just as Karp was finishing his phone call about Tarr, he received another one on his cell. As he put the phone to his ear, he heard no greeting only, "I'm here, do you have a location and timeline?"

The voice was low pitched, calm, and somewhat intimidating. "We've got a tracker on the target's car and should have a location soon.

"Two teams are running a very loose tail so as not to spook him. But I can tell you one thing, he's scared. He just left my office after practically begging me not to fire him. What a disappointment; I thought he had a bigger set than that."

The low voice spoke again. "Please describe the person in question. Start with physical attributes."

"Sure. He's probably 6'5" and weighs about 250/260. He's a Marketing Professor, unmarried, lives alone, and has a brother living locally. The brother is a retired Navy Seal. They don't live together, like I said, but they may be together now. The target has not been staying home for a few days.

"We think they are up on Glade Park, the mountainous area immediately west of town. He and his brother own some sort of ranch up there."

The voice was back, although somewhat more concerned in tone. "A Navy Seal in the mix doubles my usual fee. You Okay with that?"

"Yes, I am and expected something of that nature."

The voice continued. "Does the subject have any military or law enforcement experience?"

"No, he's just a big 50-year-old softie who teaches Marketing. Before coming here, he worked for the Federal

Trade Commission. Probably wouldn't know a gun from a hair dryer."

"What about the timeline? How long do I have to get set up?"

Manci hesitated knowing the Enforcer wasn't going to like the answer. "Twenty-four hours and it has to look like a suicide.

"I know this is a hurry up job, but it is very important to our friend in Denver. If you accept the job with these two conditions, I'll triple your usual fee. Will you do it?"

The voice on the other end of the line was silent. Finally the Enforcer spoke. "I will accept the contract.

"Now as to what I need. Get me photos of the subject and his brother. Also, I need their vehicles' descriptions and license plate numbers.

"Text those things to me when you send the location. Send them to the number I'm calling from. It's a burn phone. I will only use it 12 hours before ditching.

"I assume you've figured some way to generate the suicide note. Leave it at the desk of the La Quinta hotel in the name of Bill Parsons. Do that immediately. I'll swing by later and pick it up.

"I'll check into a motel down the street and get a few hours' sleep.

"If at all possible, I also need the GPS coordinates of the location. It's not like I can stop a neighbor and ask for directions.

"When you find the Professor, leave at least one guy to watch him. I'll need that guy's phone number when you call me with the GPS information. You can tell him I'll make initial contact when I'm in place.

"It's imperative that your guy have eyes on the Professor until I am in place. The guy must stay until I call him and tell him to leave. Not one minute before.

"If I don't get GPS coordinates, I'll need a guide. And just so you won't be surprised, the guide must be disposable. You get my meaning? No one sees my face and walks away.

"Wire the money to my account as soon as we disconnect."

The phone was disconnected.

Karp immediately dialed the Old Man in Denver. A few minutes later he disconnected. He was satisfied the Old Man understood and agreed with what was about to happen.

Chapter 67

Jack had come up with an idea for dealing with an assassin who liked to work in close. Give the assassin an isolated location visible from the highway. A place that could be kept under observation with a good pair of strong binoculars.

Add to the location a very depressed and anxiety-ridden man who was trying to find courage from a whiskey bottle. Who could resist sneaking up on a passed out drunk?

Jack even knew the perfect location. When Jack had decided to move his security operation back to his homestead on Glade Park, he wanted more land. Besides, land in those days was cheap and readily available.

One piece in particular he bought was several miles from his old ranch. It wasn't in a good location really, because it wasn't contiguous to his other land. It was, however, in the perfect location for a cliff house.

Ever since Jack was a child and spent so much time with Tarr and Lucky in their house, he said that one day he would own his own cliff house. Well, this particular 35-acre piece of land contained a cliff face perfect for such a dwelling.

Jack had not gotten around to building his dream house yet, but he had maintained the small 800 square foot log vacation cabin on the site. The cabin set at the base of the very cliff where he intended to carve out his own cliff house.

The cabin was what Jack considered a cookie cutter mountain cabin. It had one level, one bedroom, one bath, and a porch that ran completely across the front. The entire porch was visible from the two-lane highway.

The security company often put up some city slicker client there who wanted an authentic mountain experience. It never ceased to amaze Jack how such a small accommodation could influence a multi-million dollar contract. To each his own he guessed.

Chapter 68

After leaving the President's office, Tarr swung by a local pancake house and had a leisurely breakfast. He then went to another part of town and hit an ATM machine. He was going to run his mob tails all over town.

Tarr did not want to head to the cabin until about four o'clock. He wanted the men following him to be nice and tired first. Sitting in a car all day and pissing in bottles took its toll. Before the festivities planned this evening, he wanted fatigue to have settled in.

A tired Mafia crew would be much easier to deal with. Dirty, hungry and pissed off would be even better. Tarr didn't think the Grand Junction operation had enough Mafia soldiers to provide relief.

One car, maybe two, was back there somewhere with probably two men per car. Boy were they going to be in for a long stay.

After the ATM, Tarr drove to a large liquor store. If the tail was close, and he figured they were since he was not trying to lose them, he wanted them to observe him buying a couple of fifths of Jack Daniels. Leaving the liquor store, Tarr then drove to City Market, a large grocery store chain started years ago by a couple of entrepreneurial brothers.

Taking his time in the grocery store, Tarr stopped at a Starbucks inside the store and had a cup of coffee. He then wandered the isles buying non-perishable food, the kind of stuff a man would buy if he were going to stay put for a while.

Loading everything into the back of the Hummer, Tarr then drove back east on a major thoroughfare until intersecting the street where his apartment was located.

Pulling into the underground garage, Tarr waved at the building's garage attendant. He got out of his vehicle and carefully looked around, in his most accurate portrayal of true paranoia.

While waiting for the elevator, he continued his act. Tarr hurried into the elevator as soon as it arrived and its doors opened. He smiled to himself as he inserted his security key and punched the button for the penthouses.

Chapter 69

Dr. Karp's private phone rang. He had been waiting for several hours for a report from his crew tailing Baldridge. By the incoming number he knew it was them. "What's going on; I've been waiting for you guys?"

The soldier on the line sounded frustrated. "We followed him like you told us to. First, he went and had breakfast, then to an ATM, then to a liquor store, then to a grocery store, and finally home over on Horizon Drive.

"Us and the guys in the other car tag teamed him so we could stay close but not make him suspicious. Looks like he is stocking up on booze and junk food for the long haul. Wherever this prick is going, he's planning on staying a while.

"He's upstairs now doing who knows what. We're parked where we can see the parking garage exit. Harry and Joe are parked so they can watch the front door. What do you want us to do?"

"I want you to stay put, that's what I want you to do. You lose him again and all our asses will end up covered by desert sand and cactus. I'm sending over a GPS unit to you, so keep an eye out for one of the boys.

"I assume at least one of the four of you can use it. The only way we're gonna get our out-of-town friend to Baldridge is with GPS coordinates. We found the County Clerk's record of his brother's house up on Glade Park, but it's just plot numbers and crap like that. His mailing address is some dinky store up there.

"As soon as you find out where he's been hiding, send me the GPS stuff. And I want at least one of you four with eyes on the house or whatever he is staying in. There aren't that many roads up there. If you lose him, you guys might as well just shoot each other. Don't come back here."

"But Boss, we ain't eaten all day and once we get up to Glade Park, there ain't nothing there except rocks and sand plus a few scrub trees. What we gonna do."

Karp said in exasperation, "I'll send some food and water with the GPS. Just don't lose Baldridge!"

Chapter 70

The elevator stopped facing the foyer of the two penthouses. Tarr carefully peered out to make sure there were no surprises. He didn't expect any, but expectations like that could get you killed.

Cautiously, Tarr stepped into the foyer and quickly to his door. He quickly glanced at the opposite penthouse door to ensure it was securely closed. It was.

The big man was in his apartment in a heartbeat. His two-phase security system had not been tampered with.

Double checking the entire apartment, Tarr felt secure in the fact that his home was left alone. He had dropped by to get a few things and change clothes.

The first order of business was his bed. Concealed within the confines of the bed's frame was something called a bed vault. The bed vault was a gun safe.

Tarr accessed the safe and took out two handguns. The first was a Glock 9 MM with a 17 round magazine in its grip. With a round loaded in the chamber, the gun held 18 rounds of the nastiest Hornady ammunition available. Tarr put the Glock plus a shoulder holster and six additional 17 round magazines on the nightstand.

The second gun was a five shot North American Arms Black Widow single action revolver, in 22 Magnum. This is the deadliest small gun on the market. He put it on the night stand as well.

Tarr then changed into clothing more appropriate for the desert. He strapped on his shoulder holster with the Glock. He then slipped on a medium weight jacket. The Black Widow went in his front pants pocket.

By 3:30 Tarr was exiting the elevator and walking to his Hummer. He felt a lot more comfortable with the Glock under his arm and the Black Widow in his pocket.

Tarr took his usual precautions leaving town. He was sure they were following him, but he had yet to sight them as he had before. If he made it too easy, they would get suspicious.

It took Tarr almost an hour before he got to Jack's cookie-cutter cabin. He had spent almost 30 minutes driving around town in a classic evasive maneuver. Without a tracker, the followers would not be able to keep up.

After a few more evading maneuvers in town, Tarr worked his way over to the southwestern part of town. From there, he drove up the back side of the Colorado National Monument on a local strip of asphalt called Little Park Road.

The road meandered north and west climbing the monument to the Glade Park area. As Tarr reached the end of Little Park Road, he turned west on the intersecting highway.

Before long the cabin came into view on the south side of the highway maybe 150 yards off the road. The cabin's drive was merely a two-lane track running through the high desert area of scrub brush, rock, cacti, and occasionally large boulders.

There were no other houses within view. A person on Jack's property could see literally for miles. The two cars following Tarr had their surveillance work cut out for them.

Chapter 71

Tarr didn't bother to signal his turn. He made a hard left turn off the two-lane blacktopped road and headed toward the cabin. Instead of parking out front like most people would, he kept going around the house and to the back. He figured that was what a nervous person would do. After all, he was supposed to be afraid.

As Tarr walked up to the back of the cabin, he noticed the door was ajar. Walking into the kitchen, he could see Jack peeking through the front window.

"So, peeping Jack, what do you see?"

"What I see, you poor scared professor, is one car, with two occupants slowing as they pass on the road. They're moving on down the road. Wait, wait for it. Yes, we have car number two also occupied by two. It didn't slow down. They're obviously talking to each other.

"Now, if they are really following you, one car will come back by, but not the second. They will need to stop and strategize a bit, but their options are really limited to one. They have to cover your escaping both directions.

"They also need to get eyes on. That means putting somebody in that scrub brush about 20 yards east of the drive; it's the only thing with any cover for a half mile in either direction. Otherwise, they have to get a set of eyes high on the bluff behind the cabin. Probably not an option. I'd hate to be the poor sucker they elect for scrub brush duty."

Tarr had walked over and was standing at the window by Jack. "Sounds like you've been here a few times. How many of your boys are outside?"

"Two snipers on the bluff out back and rear cover for them

a hundred yards back. I figured if you, Lucky, me, and two young tough bucks outside can't handle one guy, maybe we three old guys ought to check out assisted living."

There was the sound of a vehicle pulling up to the front of the cabin. Lucky soon came sauntering through the front door. "What's up boys? Where's the tail?"

Jack spoke up. "There are four soldiers in two cars. They just went past. There're down the road a piece we imagine trying to figure out what to do."

Tarr took a second to scan the road again. "We figure they will dump one guy by the clump of scrub brush just east of the drive. With a good powerful pair of binoculars, he can keep an eye on the cabin. The rest will no doubt find a place down the road to get the cars out of sight."

Chapter 72

"Why do I have to be the one hiding in a bunch of bushes on the side of the road? I'm not exactly dressed for this Daniel Boone crap."

An older looking soldier, no doubt in charge of the little group frowned at the guy speaking. "You're the youngest one of us and in the best shape. Besides, I picked you so shut up and get ready. With any luck, you won't have to spend the night."

The other two soldiers laughed. One of them piped up. "Think of it as camping. You know the rough kind of camping, no food or water, no tent and no fire. Real rugged western kind of camping. You're gonna love it."

"Bite me, you jerks."

"Okay, you three, cut out the crap. This is how it's gonna go. Joe you drive your car; Steve you hide low in the front passenger seat. Stop the car between the bushes and the cabin. Open your car door and get out. Leave the door open. Joe you walk around and stoop down by the passenger side rear tire like you are checking something.

"Steve, you stay low and crawl out of the car and into the bushes. Make sure you get behind those bushes.

"Joe you stand up, kind of shake your head in disgust, then come back around and get back in the car. Drive off very slowly like you have some sort of car problem. Find a place on down the road toward town and get off the road. Make sure you can see the road, though.

"Steve, you settle in with your phone and binoculars.

"We'll find a place around here and get the car off the road and out of sight. Harry, you're with me. I want you to call in the GPS coordinates right now.

"Steve, make sure and call if you see anything and I mean anything at all. Any questions?

:Oh, and Steve, take your coat. If we're out here all night, it'll get cold."

Steve grunted in protest. "What do you mean we? I'm the only one out in the open. The rest of you guys will be sitting in a car, all nice and warm."

Chapter 73

As Lucky and Tarr took a moment to look around the cabin, Jack kept an eye out front. "Hey boys, guess what? A car just stopped in front of the scrub brush. Looks like he has some kind of tire trouble. Poor guy, hope he can make it back to town."

All three old friends smiled, in what most people would consider, a very evil fashion.

Tarr was truly impressed with the cabin. "Jack, this is really nice. I hope blood blends in."

Lucky laughed. "We'll try to create a spray pattern that looks like contemporary art."

"You two guys are so funny. Maybe you should take your act on the road."

"Speaking of the road, have you spotted the second car?"

"Not yet, my guess is they're down the road a ways, in anticipation of a westerly escape."

Tarr was trying to move the sofa to a position against the wall. Lucky was looking on in amusement. "What you doing little brother?"

"I think we might want to rearrange the furniture so we can funnel the hitter to the place where we can take him without excess danger to my precious body."

Jack had turned briefly from the window. "That's what you call that mountain of a body, precious? Hell, your head's big enough to be on Mt. Rushmore. As for your body, Lucky and I will just get behind you. We'll be safe for sure."

Jack picked up a handheld radio. "Okay, boys, watch is to you. Let me know when you get movement."

Lucky was looking on. "How many shooters?"

Jack responded. "Two of my best snipers on the bluff.

They've got the cabin area and road covered for a thousand yards in each direction. I've also got back door cover for them".

Lucky was studying every area of the cabin. "Alright, guys, now seriously, how are we going to take this guy once he gets inside? Jack, it's your real estate, what do you suggest?"

It took the next 30 minutes to agree on an approach.

Lucky got to his feet from the table where the three had been sitting. "Time for us to wander out on the porch. I'll stay for a while then make my exit.

"With me gone, the crew outside will report that Tarr is alone. As soon as it gets dark, I'll come back via the bluff. Jack, please make sure your boys on the bluff's back door remember I'm coming. It's hard enough rappelling down that bluff when I'm healthy; I definitely don't want to do it with a bullet in my butt."

"You got it, good buddy; just make sure the bad guys think you're gone for the night after you leave.

"Now, it's time you two get going on the big scene."

Chapter 74

As Lucky, Jack and Tarr prepared to present their theatrics, Steve, the designated bush surveillance guy, was making his first report from his bushy hideout. "It's me, Steve." A truck is parked in front of the house. Looks like the brother's. I remember seeing him in it that time we trailed the Professor to Denver and back."

"Okay, Steve, keep me posted."

Chapter 75

Jack extended what looked like a bottle of Jack Daniels whiskey to Tarr. "Okay Professor, let's see how convincing a drunk you can be."

Tarr took the bottle from Jack's outstretched hand. "Nothing like tea in a Jack bottle to smooth out the nerves.

"How's our friend in the scrub brush doing? I assume your boys have eyes on him. It wouldn't take much of a rifle shot to hit me from there. Me sitting on the porch getting drunk makes for a very inviting shot."

"Oh Professor, you have so little faith. I just checked with my guys. They have reported that our friend out there is the only thing in sight for a thousand yards in each direction. Even as we speak, one of the boys has our friend's head centered in his scope. My other guy is on constant scan mode in both directions.

"The stupid prick out in the scrub brush might as well be wearing a sign. He's dressed in a white shirt; not exactly desert camouflage. His discipline is even worse than his clothing; he's already smoked two cigarettes.

"He does have what appears to be a really nice big pair of binoculars, maybe even with night vision. He's keeping them directed at the cabin.

"He's a real amateur in the desert, though; my boys report he hasn't done a visual recon of any of the terrain around. He's obviously a city boy with a really nice pair of binoculars.

"We could take him at any time. Keep that in mind. It may be something we can use."

With the Jack bottle in one hand and his walking stick in the other, Tarr had a little trouble opening the door. As he got the door open, he felt Jack nudge him.

"Don't forget your prop." Jack was pointing to a double-barreled shotgun leaning just to the left of the door.

"Oh yeah." Tarr tucked the bottle under his left arm and grabbed the gun with the left hand. "Anything else, Mother?"

"Just make sure you drink the whole bottle of 'booze' before you come in. You'll need to stay outside a couple of hours."

Tarr stepped out into full view of the watcher. He stumbled on his way to an intended chair. He put the bottle on a table just right of the chair. The shotgun went against the doorframe before he sat down.

A couple minutes later, Lucky joined him. All three of them thought it might be better if both brothers were seen on the porch drinking.

Within the hour, Tarr and Lucky each had several drinks while taking in the scenery and watching the sun start to drop from the sky.

Chapter 76

The sun was now rapidly falling from the sky. The entire western atmosphere had taken on an orange-pinkish hue. Lucky got up slowly like maybe he had over-indulged a bit. "Time for me to make my grand exit, little brother. You and Jack watch your asses; I'll be back in a couple hours."

Lucky made his way slowly toward the truck. Fumbling with his keys a bit, he opened the truck door and pulled himself up and behind the wheel. He slowly drove away.

Tarr watched his brother's performance from the porch. He himself needed to spend more time with the Jack bottle before heading into the cabin.

Chapter 77

The phone was ringing in the west car. "Hey, it's me, Steve. The Navy Seal and Professor have been hitting the bottle pretty heavy for about an hour. The brother just got in his truck and left. Looks like he might be headed back to town."

"Okay, good job. Keep your eyes open. It'll be dark before long. Make sure you use the night vision on the binoculars after the sun goes down."

The crew boss disconnected but immediately punched in another number. "Joe, it's me. The brother has just now left the cabin. He'll be by you any minute now. Follow him and let me know what he's up to."

Chapter 78

Tarr continued to sit on the porch, kept company by Jack Daniels. He was drinking straight from the bottle by now. Every once in a while, he would jump up like he had heard something. He would look around nervously and then sit back down.

It was time to up the theatrical antics. Tarr got sluggishly to his feet and stumbled to the edge of the cabin's porch. Hugging a support beam with one arm, he unzipped his pants with the other. Actually urinating didn't take any acting. A half bottle of tea made that part easy.

Tarr had leaned the shotgun against the doorframe when he first came outside. Now, as he slumped back into the chair, he jerked his head around toward the gun, as if he just now remembered it. He made a motion with his hand toward the gun as if saying, "Forget it; it's too much trouble to get back up."

Another hour on the porch and Tarr tossed the empty booze bottle off the porch and in the general direction of the road. As he tried to get out of the chair, he stumbled and fell on the floor. Dragging his stick with him, he managed to reach one of the two support beams holding up the porch's roof. With considerable effort, be managed to pull himself up.

After holding on to the beam for a few minutes, he managed to get his walking stick pointed toward the front door. With what he hoped the watcher would think was drunken stupor, he managed to get to the door.

As Tarr entered the front door, he turned, with what appeared an afterthought, and grabbed the shotgun by its barrel. Dragging the gun on the floor, he managed to get inside and close the door.

Chapter 79

Lucky picked up a tail down the road east of the cabin. "Try to stay with me," he said in the rapidly approaching darkness of his truck.

It took Lucky about an hour to drive across the Glade Park area and down the mountain to the small town of Fruita. Hopefully, his tail was still with him.

Just inside the city limits, Lucky turned into an upscale residential neighborhood. He turned into a driveway almost immediately.

As Lucky got out of his truck, the porch light came on in front of the house. The door opened and a woman greeted Lucky with a very passionate hug. He returned the hug and quickly, the two of them were inside and the front light turned off.

A half hour later, all the lights were turned off except for what Lucky's tail thought was probably the bedroom. It too was soon turned off.

Lucky was obviously in for the night.

Chapter 80

"Hey, Boss, It's me, Joe. I followed the brother to Fruita where he met up with a hot little number at her house. From what I saw, I'd bet a hundred bucks he's in for the night. Anything going on at the cabin?"

"Steve just checked in. The Professor sat on the front porch for a couple of hours with a shotgun and a fifth of booze. The fool drank the whole fifth. I'd say he's scared out of his mind. Hell, we could just drive to the house right now and cap his ass.

"I called Karp and told him, but he said no; wait for the Enforcer to handle it. So we wait. Get back up here as soon as you can."

Chapter 81

The Enforcer had gotten a couple of hours' sleep. After picking up the suicide note, he called President Karp. "What's going on? You guys find the Professor?"

"Yeah, we found him. My boys have been watching him for several hours. He's in an isolated cabin up on Glade Park. That's the mountainous area just west of town, remember? Right now he is alone and very drunk.

"One of the boys has the cabin in sight. Baldridge sat on the front porch for a couple of hours with a shotgun and a bottle of booze for company. He must be pretty well shaken; he drank the whole bottle straight.

"I've got guys up and down the road on both sides of the property. Then there's the one I mentioned out front a hundred yards or so from the house. Not many people live up there full time, so there's not much traffic.

"The land up there is really flat, just a high desert. There are small bluffs scattered around and big rocks sitting everywhere. We could only get one guy in close before dark. He's hiding in a bunch of bushes just off the road."

The Enforcer did not like to work like this. Usually, he'd stalk the target for a couple of weeks getting a feel for the guy. Tonight, he had to do a job based on second-hand information. Risky, very risky. But then again, they were paying a sizable bonus for the risk inherent in a hurry up job. He'd just have to make it work.

"Okay Karp, tell me about the Navy Seal brother, where is he?"

"He was there earlier, but left. He's shacked up over in Fruita for the night. One of my guys followed him and hung around until he was sure what was going on. Even if he finishes up and decides to head back to his brother, we'll know. Remember, I've got guys on both ends of the road; he's got to pass them."

The conversation went quite for a few seconds while the Enforcer processed what he had been told. "Alright, it sounds like your boys have the place locked down pretty good. Here's what I want you to do.

"Text me instructions on how to get from downtown Grand Junction to the general location of the Professor. Send me the general locations of your guys as they relate to the cabin. Send me the GPS coordinates for the cabin. Also, I need to know the exact location of the guy out front of the cabin.

"Since the Professor is drunk, it sounds like the sooner I do this the better. Tell your boys I'll be there as soon as possible. I'm driving a black Jeep Wrangler. Tell them to just let me pass, no signal, no nothing.

"Tell the guy out front that I will be rolling in without lights. Since I don't know the terrain, I'll have to get to the cabin by going up the driveway. Shouldn't be much of a problem with the guy probably passed out by now. Your guy should see me moving in. I'll park about a quarter mile east of the drive. Make sure your guy doesn't get jumpy and doesn't interfere in any way.

"Make sure you send me the phone number of the guy out front. I'll call him right before I enter the cabin to make sure everything is quiet. Communicate with him my intentions. I won't speak when I call; I'll just listen for his all clear.

"You got all this?"

Karp had been taking careful notes. The last thing he needed was to screw up and have the Enforcer come a calling. "Yes, I've got everything.

"You'll have everything you need within 10 minutes."

Chapter 82

By the time the Enforcer was starting his drive up to the Glade Park area, Lucky was driving an old jeep up to the general area where the sniper's rear guard was hiding. Using a handheld radio Jack had given him, he checked in with the guard.

"Lucky's in the area, where are you?"

"I'm about 25 yards to your east. Everything is still quiet, sir. I'd leave the Jeep here; any closer and your lights might show over the bluff."

"That's an affirmative. Lucky moving out."

About the time the Enforcer passed the guys waiting east on the road, Lucky was sneaking in the back door of the cabin. But not before whistling to those inside.

Chapter 83

Jack and Tarr were both on high alert in the cabin, with one watching front and the other back. They both heard the whistle. Jack was covering the back door and was first to respond in a musical voice. "Who's there?"

Lucky responded in the same type voice. "It's the killer, may I come in?"

Tarr had moved more to the center of the room. "You two are real cute. Are you having fun?"

"Actually, this is kind of fun, little brother. It gets pretty boring up here sometimes. Nothing like a little murder in the air to get your juices flowing."

Jack was on the radio. "Well, if it's fun you want, we better put on our party hats. Sniper one just reported movement on the road about a quarter mile east. He says it's a dark vehicle driving with no lights. He says there is one person exiting the vehicle and moving this direction on foot.

"Sniper one, let me know when the guy's at the driveway."

Lucky was at the cabin's bar. "We better hurry. Tarr, over here. I need to make you smell like a drunk."

Tarr stepped to Lucky's side. "How you want to do this?" Tarr flinched when Lucky threw a full glass of whiskey on his chest. The liquid was now running down the front of his pants.

Jack had moved to a position just inside the bathroom door. Tarr let his large frame down on an oversized sofa. He partially covered himself with a decorative blanket kept on the sofa. Lucky was crouched behind the bar.

Jack had his radio to his ear. "Sniper two, how's our boy in the scrub brush?"

The radio against his ear emitted a whisper. "Still there; no movement."

Sniper one was back. "Subject is at the top of the drive and cautiously moving your direction. Instructions?"

Jack whispered into the radio. "We've got it from here. If for some reason though, the subject exits after you hear gunfire inside, take him. Otherwise, wait for my call. All radios on silent now." Jack hit the off button.

Jack spoke just loud enough for Lucky and Tarr to hear. "Here he comes. Tarr make sure the top of your body armor is covered by your shirt. Lucky, you have the Kel-Tec; remember our locations. Tarr, if things go south, you and I hit the floor while Lucky corrects the situation."

The Kel-Tec shotgun was their ace in the hole. It was a modern short-barreled gun that currently had 14 rounds of 12-gauge misery distributed between two loading tubes with round number 15 in the chamber. One loading tube held 7 rounds of double ought buckshot and the other held 7 rounds of 12-gauge slugs. A slug in the chamber completed the load. The shooter had the advantage with such a gun of selecting which tube to shoot.

Lucky decided to go with the slugs first, since it was likely the killer would be wearing body armor. Even though the slug would not penetrate the armor, it would however, knock the killer off his feet.

Tarr and Jack were each armed also. If possible, though, they wanted to take the killer alive; he would be a good source of information for Detective Orr.

The three men calmed their breathing and waited. All three had been in more of these situations than they could remember.

Everything now depended on good planning and fate.

Chapter 84

The Enforcer had about as much confidence as a mouse in a rattlesnake den. There were just too many unknown variables. The biggest was probably this God-forsaken terrain. There was a reason he was a close-in killer. He was a city guy. In a city, you could get next to a target with little difficulty.

Out here in the desert, the target could see you coming. He didn't like that, even if the target was drunk and asleep. The fact was, the target might not be as drunk as the watcher thought.

This Baldridge guy was one big sucker. Different people handled alcohol in different ways. Because of his size, the Professor could come out of the drunken stupor much quicker.

Another big concern was the shotgun. Drunk or sober a man could still kill you with such a gun. Because a shotgun shell holds numerous pellets that all came out the barrel at the same time, the shooter doesn't have to be as accurate.

A 12-gauge double ought buckshot round contains 15 pellets, each 33 caliber. A person can be killed by one pellet. Now imagine 15 of them forming a ten inch or so circular pattern.

The bottom line is that even a drunk that misses the perfect point of aim can still kill you. Dead is dead.

The enforcer was traveling with his usual fanny pack of tools. He had on his night vision glasses and gloves. His lock pick gun was at the ready as was his 357 magnum handgun, a weapon using extremely high velocity ammunition.

Tonight though, a couple of additions were added. To his usual dark shirt he added a Kevlar collar capable of defeating small caliber ammo and stopping a garrote. Over the shirt and collar, he wore combat level body armor.

His philosophy was simple. When information is scarce increase precautions wherever feasible.

The Enforcer also carried a small frame 38 caliber handgun. It was the Professor's gun of choice for suicide.

Making his way to the side of the cabin with no problem, the Enforcer carefully moved to the rear and stopped for a moment to observe. Thank goodness there was no dog.

He listened for any out of the ordinary sound. He smiled to himself. What in the hell was an out of the ordinary sound out here in the middle of nowhere?

The Enforcer carefully took out his cellphone and punched in the number of the man out front in the bushes. He did not speak. A voice came over the phone. "All clear."

"Well," he thought, "Nothing ventured, nothing gained; play hard or go home; to the aggressor go the spoils; whatever. It was do or die."

He silently inserted the lock pick into the door's mechanism. As usual, the lock opened without difficulty. Waiting a few seconds, he eased the door open wide enough to get through.

With his night vision, he could make out the layout of the room. Against the east wall was a large sofa where an even larger man was breathing heavily. There was the very distinctive smell of alcohol in the room. What a sloppy drunk!

At a slight angle and across the room appeared to be some sort of bar. To his immediate right was a partially closed door revealing a sink. Probably a bathroom.

The Enforcer took a calming breath. Maybe this would be an easy payday after all. He stepped past the bathroom door and toward the sofa.

Suddenly, something of moderate force struck him in the back of the neck. Without hesitation, he spun and fired. His mind recorded a reassuring thud before he was struck in the back with the force of a jack hammer.

As his mind registered the sound of the shotgun, the

Enforcer was flung by its force toward the man on the sofa. Muscle memory had caused him to hold on to his handgun. Fate had positioned him face down on the man he had come to kill. His first thought was to complete the job.

The Enforcer brought the gun up and toward the man's head. Squeeze the trigger, don't jerk it. Why would he remember that in the second it took him to align the gun barrel?

The extremely sharp crack of a high velocity bullet filled the room. The smell of burnt gun powder assaulted the nostrils. Ears were ringing from the explosive sound.

Chapter 85

Tarr, Jack and Lucky had waited patiently. They all knew the killer wouldn't run up to the cabin and kick in the back door. He would be patient; he would take his time. He would look and listen. Only when he was satisfied everything was normal, would he enter.

Jack was closest to the door and probably first to hear the door ease open. Lucky and Tarr would have heard it a fraction of a second later.

Jack held his breath. He could feel the killer looking in his direction. He sensed more than heard the killer move toward the sofa. It was time.

What Jack held in his hand looked like a gun and it was, sort of. It was a Taser capable of shooting two barb tipped wires 35 feet. Once the barbs connect with skin, a massive electrical shock would be delivered which was capable of temporarily disabling the person shot.

A Taser was the perfect weapon if you wanted the subject alive. To be effective, however, the barbs needed to embed in skin.

Jack had anticipated body armor so he had aimed at the neck from a distance of less than ten feet. What he did not anticipate was a Kevlar collar. The barbs struck the back of the neck and bounced off.

In the time it took Jack's mind to register what had happened, the Enforcer had spun and sent a round dead center into Jack's chest. Jack stepped back from the blow and fell.

Before the Enforcer could shoot again, Lucky had sent a 12 gauge slug into his back just below the shoulders. The force propelled the killer onto the sofa.

Lucky watched in horror as the Enforcer brought his handgun up to Tarr's head. Before Lucky could get a clean shot at the killer, a single shot rang out in the cabin.

As the Enforcer had landed on top of him, Tarr had brought up his own gun, the small high velocity 22 magnum called the Black Widow. It was held in his right hand and shielded on his chest by his left hand.

As the Enforcer was raising his gun, so was Tarr. Tarr's trip was shorter; he shot the Enforcer under the chin and straight up through the brain. He then used both hands to push the killer off him and to the floor.

"Clear." was the best sound Lucky and Jack had heard in a long time.

Tarr raised his voice again. "You guys alright?"

Lucky shouted, "Clear," followed by Jack's "Hit, but Okay."

Since Lucky was the only one on his feet, he was the first to shine a small flashlight on the Enforcer. "He's down for good."

He found Jack not far away. Tarr was now on his feet and moving to Jack. "Where are you hit?"

"Mostly in my pride. How could I miss a shot that close? The sucker was really fast. He spun and shot me before I could react to the miss. I took the round on the ceramic plate over my heart."

Tarr turned to the dead man on the floor. "Lucky, let's put that light on him again. Shine it on the back of his neck.

"Look, Jack. The barbs marked his collar in the perfect spot, but they didn't penetrate."

Jack was rubbing the collar material between his fingers. "I think I know why. The asshole was wearing a Kevlar collar. I've heard about them, but never seen one. Next time, I'll aim for the ass."

Lucky turned the Enforcer over on his back. "Look at that exit wound on the top of his head. What did you shoot him with?"

Tarr held up the mini revolver. "My Black Widow in 22 magnum. Those new red tipped self-defense rounds really take care of business. I only had time to jam it under his chin and pull the trigger."

"Well, little brother, I'll never make fun of your itsy bitsy gun again. As a matter of fact, I'm going to get one myself."

Jack was the first to bring the conversation back to the situation. "What do we do now? We don't have a witness for Detective Orr. Do you guys know how long we'll be hung up explaining a dead body to the Sheriff's office?"

Tarr looked back down at the body. "Too long. We still have another little thing to do regarding the Aspen Ranch."

They all pondered the situation for a minute before Jack spoke up. "You know these guys we have been dealing with are a bunch of screw-ups. Present dead company excluded. Why don't we turn this in to another screw up? It'll give us some breathing room."

"What do you have in mind?"

"What if the killer and our friend out front accidentally shot each other? We could stage it to look like an accident. There's only one hard part. We have to kill the guy out front."

Tarr was frowning. "Isn't there another way?"

Lucky was deep in thought. "Hey Jack, how many guys you ever see take a 30 caliber slug in the shoulder and not pass out?"

Jack was smiling like he had figured the thing out. "That would be none. There's not one guy in a thousand that can take that kind of pain and not faint."

Tarr was watching the other two. "Oh, I see. We have one dead and one wounded. We could even drug the wounded guy with morphine so he doesn't remember much of anything."

Lucky was now thinking. "Jack, can one of your guys put a 308 round through our watcher's shoulder?"

"Hell, Lucky, I can do that at the range we're talking about and so can you. Either one of my boys on the bluff can put it through either eye. Which shoulder you think?"

Lucky was now in a full belly laugh. "Whichever best presents itself. Are your boys using sound suppressors?"

Jack turned his radio back on. "The 308 is suppressed. I'll make the call."

Tarr put a hand on Jack's shoulder. "What about our shots? Didn't the guy out front hear them?"

Jack turned to look at Tarr. "Probably not. First of all, this cabin has twice as much insulation as most. I beefed it up to make sure my citified guests don't get cold. That much insulation keeps most sound inside.

"Second, the guy out front is more than 100 yards away. If any shot was heard, it was the higher velocity 22 magnum. But most significant here is that a shot was probably expected.

"Before I make the call, though, check the guy's pockets and pack. Lucky immediately did just that. "Nothing unusual here, except this suicide note written by you."

Lucky passed the note to Tarr, who examined it with a small shielded flashlight.   "Damn, I should have been a creative writing professor. Great style admitting my guilt in the murder. My inner turmoil was just more than I could handle."

The other two men laughed. Jack then made a call.

Within one minute, Jack was answering his radio. He looked down at the dead assassin as he spoke. "Our killer here was a very bad boy. He shot the man out front through the shoulder."

Lucky was busy wrapping the killer in the blanket that Tarr had used on the sofa. "Jack, where's your combat first aid bag?"

"In the bedroom."

Lucky hoisted the killer up on his shoulder in a fireman's carry. "Grab a couple shots of morphine and catch up with Tarr and me on the drive." He turned and headed out the front door, with Tarr in close pursuit.

A few minutes later the trio of men had dropped the dead killer on the ground close to the clump of scrub brush. Lucky cautiously approached.

Jack was on the radio. "Sniper one says he's about ten yards due east of you, Lucky."

Lucky moved forward still in a cautious mode. "Here he is, out cold. Tarr, check the wound to make sure he'll live. I'll position the body so it looks like an accidental shooting. Since he only shot once in the house the unfired rounds in his gun will be right."

Tarr bent down to check the wounded man. "Great shot. Went just high enough to break the collar bone. It passed through, so nobody will suspect it didn't come from the killer's gun."

Jack quickly administered a dose and a half of morphine into the back of the right leg of wounded man. "No one will notice the injection prick back there."

Jack and Tarr walked over to where Lucky was positioning the body. Lucky looked up at Tarr. "We need for you to kill him again. You know we have to cover up the small entry wound made by the 22 magnum."

Tarr held up the wounded man's gun. "I know, but it's harder than it looks. I have to back off a couple of feet so there are no powder burns and then shoot as close as possible through the original wound channel.

"You guys get ready to move out. I think I'll shoot twice so there is a big wound."

Lucky was looking at Tarr's walking stick. "On second thought little brother, we don't know how long the other bad guys will wait before coming here to check things out.

"You're not exactly an Olympic sprinter these days. You go ahead back to the cabin. When you are close, Jack and I will deal with this."

Tarr gave his big brother the one finger salute and started

toward the cabin.

Lucky double-checked the position of the body making sure the killer's gun was close to his shooting hand. Before shooting the dead man again, he rolled up the blanket they had used to transport him. Handing it to Jack, he motioned toward the cabin with a movement of his head.

Once Jack started back, Lucky stepped away from the body. In his shooting hand, he held the unconscious man's gun. In his off hand, he held his own handgun. There had to be three shots, one toward the wounded man and two in return fire into the Enforcer's head.

Lucky held his own gun in the air and fired once. He quickly fired two shots from the wounded man's gun into the corpse: one under the chin and a second into the face. Placing his own gun back in the holster on his hip, he quickly moved to the wounded man and dropped the other gun. He then took off jogging toward the cabin.

Chapter 86

The two soldiers on the west end of the road were standing by the car smoking, when they heard the three shots. Harry's head jerked to attention. "Hey Boss, you hear those shots?"

The Boss's phone started ringing. He picked it up. "Yeah, we heard it too, Joe. I don't know what it was. I'll give Steve a call."

The Boss let Steve's phone ring several times. When it wasn't answered, he knew something was wrong. Steve usually had the phone in his hand.

The Boss listened for another five minutes. No more shots or noise of any kind. "Load up, Harry, we're going back and check on Steve. This just doesn't feel right."

The Boss steered the car back to the road and turned east. Since the sky was full of stars and the moon was out, the Boss drove with just the parking lights on until they were about a half mile from the cabin.

As they closed in on Steve's hiding place, they stopped the car and continued on foot. If the Professor was as drunk as had been reported, there shouldn't be any problems. If they had problems, they'd deal with them.

"Harry, the bushes are just up the road. Let's move into the desert and come up on them from the side opposite the road."

The Boss and Harry moved slowly and carefully. As they got closer, they could hear a low level groan. "Help me, help me."

"Be careful, Harry. We don't know who that is. You work around and come in from the desert side of the bushes. I'll keep going this way and come in from the west. If anything kinky goes down, we'll know who's where."

They had only been separated a couple of minutes when Harry said he saw somebody on the ground. As the boss moved forward, he could see a second body.

"Harry, there's another body over here. This one isn't moving. Let me get a light on him. He's dead; took one through the head."

"Hey Boss, Steve's over here. He took one high in the shoulder. He must have moaned before; he's out again though."

"Let Steve lay there and come over here."

Harry took another look at Steve, then moved off toward the Boss's voice.

As Harry walked up, the Boss put the light on the corpse's face. "You know this guy, Harry? I've never seen him before."

"Beats me, Boss. You know people always look different when they got a couple holes in their head, but I ain't never seen him either.

"And look at the way he's dressed. Looks like some kind of ninja all in black. What's with the sissy fanny pack?"

The Boss had knelt down by the body. First he looked at the man's face more closely, then at the way he was dressed and finally at the fanny pack. He then moved the light to the surrounding ground.

Reaching a little to one side, the Boss picked up a small five-shot revolver. "Here's his piece. There's a lock pick gun in the pack along with some gloves and a note.

"Get a little closer, Harry and hold your light on this note; I wanna see what it says.

"Holy shit; this is a suicide note for the Professor. You know what that means? This has got to be the hit man. Unfreaking believable! Steve killed the Enforcer."

Harry was looking back into the darkness that enveloped Steve a few yards away. "Steve killed the Enforcer! Why'd he do that? You think the Enforcer got the Professor before Steve got him?"

The Boss was looking across the road at the darkened cabin. "I don't know; I hope so; but there's no way to know. I do know one thing, though. We have to sanitize this place.

"First thing, help me get this body closer to the road. Then we'll check on Steve. You said he took one high on the shoulder, right?"

"That's right, Boss."

"Let's get him closer to the road too."

Most people don't realize how heavy a dead man is or, for that matter, how heavy a wounded man is who is passed out. It took the two mob soldiers almost ten minutes to move the two men closer to the road.

"Okay, Harry, go get the car. Drive back slowly with your lights off. When you get to this spot, stop and pop the trunk. We'll throw in the stiff, get Steve in the back seat and then drive slowly away.

"We don't want to make a lot of noise, just in case the Professor is still breathing. If he is still alive, he's probably snoring away. Steve said he drank a whole bottle of booze."

A very nerve-wracking 20 minutes later, the Boss and Steve pulled their car into the area where Joe was parked.

"Joe, I want you and Steve to get the body out of the trunk. Here, take my phone and take a half dozen shots of the stiff's face using different angles. Bring me his fanny pack plus anything else you find on his body.

"Then one of you take his keys and go get his Jeep. It's not too far back down the road. Remember, be quiet and don't use the lights."

"What are you going to do, Boss?"

"I'm taking Steve and dropping him off at our very friendly and highly paid Doctor back down the mountain on Little Park Road. He'll earn his money tonight. Then I'm going to see Karp.

"You guys, I want you to find a place around here and bury that body. And make sure it won't be found or dug up by a coyote.

"Then I want one of you down the road west of the cabin. The other one stays here. I want to know as soon as possible if the Professor is still alive.

"You guys got that?"

"Yes, sir."

"The Boss waited until the body was moved from his car and he had all the Enforcer's stuff. Remember, call me as soon as you see something about the Professor. And don't screw this up!"

Chapter 87

The Boss didn't have real far to go. Little Park Road was on his way back into town. The Boss pulled into the Doctor's gravel drive. The house set off the road on what looked to be seven or eight acres.

Being a compulsive gambler, the Doctor had come to Karp's attention a couple of years ago, when a Doctor who could keep his mouth shut was needed for a little emergency with one of his men.

The Doctor's wife had long since left and taken the kids. Considering the isolated nature of his home, he was the perfect guy. The more he worked for the Mob, the quicker he paid off his gambling debt.

Picking up his cell phone, the boss dialed the Doc's number. A sleepy voice finally answered. "Hello."

"Hey Doc, I'm in your drive with one of our men. He's been shot. Open your garage door."

In less than a minute, the garage began to rise. The Doc was standing inside with just a tee shirt and boxer shorts on.

The Boss pulled the car in. He quickly got out of the car and opened a rear door. "Give me a hand, Doc. He's out cold."

The Doctor did not say a thing. There wasn't really much to say. He would do what needed to be done and never say a thing to anybody about it.

They took Steve by the feet and under the arms and struggled with him into the house and down the basement steps. After the last Mob emergency, the Doctor had set up a very rudimentary clinical room in the basement.

The clinical room had a deadbolt lock on it. No one needed to see what was concealed behind the door. The Doctor had to shift Steve's weight to use the key in his left hand. Finally getting the door open, they carried Steve in and put him on a sheet-draped table.

It had taken the Doctor several weeks to set up the room. Since most of the drugs needed for such a setup were controlled, the Mob had stepped up and supplied them through their own sources.

The Doctor did a quick examination of the wound before setting up a drip in his arm to administer necessary drugs. "It looks like it went in and out without a lot of damage. It will be painful, but he should make it just fine.

"I'll get the wound cleaned up and taken care of. I'll keep him sedated through tomorrow night. You should be able to move him day after tomorrow."

"Thanks, Doc. Someone will check in with you." The Boss turned and headed back upstairs and to his car.

Before leaving, he made a call. "Dr. Karp, it's me, Prinelli. I need to see you. Something really weird happened up on Glade Park tonight. It involves our visiting friend who was helping us with that job. I believe it is a very serious complication."

Karp's interest was piqued immediately. "Be at my house in 15 minutes. Come in the back way."

Karp disconnected and immediately placed a call to Greg Manci, the VP of Finance on campus. To all outward appearances, Dr. Karp was in charge of the college and Manci was an underling. Within the Mob structure however, Manci was the headman and Karp followed instruction.

"Greg, we've got some sort of problem with our friend from out of town. Prinelli is on his way to my house now. He said it was serious. You might want to sit in on this."

"I'll be right over."

The line went dead.

Chapter 88

Manci and Karp had just finished making drinks when Prinelli knocked on the rear door. Karp set his drink down and made his way across the expensively decorated family room. He always thought that was a curious descriptor for the room, since he had no family.

As Karp opened the door, he could see that his under boss was distressed. He offered Prinelli a drink, which the Mafia soldier eagerly accepted.

Karp and Manci waited patiently while their soldier took a big gulp from the drink glass. "I don't know what's going on, but here it is. We did everything you guys wanted us to do.

"We followed the Professor to where he was hiding. We sent the GPS location back, then I figured a way to get Steve in a bunch of bushes across the road from the cabin. I then had a car about half a mile down the road in each direction.

"I had the brother followed after he showed up, then left. We made sure that the Professor was in for the night and alone. Plus that, he was really drunk.

"We waited and watched for hours. The Enforcer finally showed up and called Steve to make sure nothing had changed. He then called again to make sure things were still quiet.

"Steve called me each time after the Enforcer called him. We assumed after the last call that the Enforcer was about to enter the cabin.

"The next thing I knew, we heard three shots. They sounded like they came from the area where Steve was. Harry and I got there as quickly as we could and still be quiet.

"Then it got real hinky; we found a dead guy all dressed up in black like a ninja. He had been shot a couple of times in the head. We searched him and found a lock pick gun, a few other things, and the Professor's suicide note.

"Not ten yards away, we found Steve. He had taken a round high in his shoulder. He was passed out, so we couldn't talk to him."

Manci was getting more concerned by the minute. "Whoa, you found the suicide note and a lock pick gun?"

He turned a blistering glare toward Karp. "These idiots killed the Enforcer, and it sounds like they killed him before he got to the Professor. How could that happen?"

Even though perplexed, Karp couldn't help but smile.

"What's so damn funny?" Manci shouted. "How are we going to explain this to the Old Man? He's gonna skewer our asses and burn us at the stake."

Karp was thinking. "Maybe not. The high and mighty Enforcer got taken out in a gun fight by one of our most inexperienced shooters."

"But why?" Manci was so upset he had trouble getting the words out without stammering.

Manci may have been the boss, but Karp was President for a reason. He was smooth under pressure and thought well on his feet. "I think I know why.

In one of my conversations with the Enforcer, he said he had never been seen and intended for it to stay that way. He said that if he had to talk to one of our guys face-to-face, it should be one that wasn't that important to us. His inference was that he would kill anybody who saw his face.

He must have thought Steve got too close a look at him."

Looking over at Prinelli, Karp asked, "Do you think Steve could have seen the Enforcer's face?"

"Well, it's possible; I gave him our binoculars and they are very powerful. They also are night vision.

"Since you can break a leg in the desert at night, my guess is that the Enforcer would have had to stalk down the paved road, then go up the drive to the cabin. We know the Professor drank a fifth of booze, so it wouldn't have been much of a risk.

"If he went in that way, he would have passed within 20 yards of Steve. If Steve saw him coming and followed him using the binoculars, he would have had a good enough view to maybe recognize him again.

"I bet the Enforcer picked up a flash off the binoculars and knew one of us had a clear view of him. He then went on up to the cabin to throw Steve off with the final call. He then took a chance and circled away from the cabin, through the desert and back to Steve's location.

"After we found the body, we found his gun. It had been fired."

Manci's breathing had started to return to normal as he spoke. "So then, the Enforcer was sneaking up on Steve and Steve must have heard him.

"The Enforcer knows he has been busted, so he takes a snap shot at Steve and catches him in the shoulder.

"Steve responds instinctively and double taps the Enforcer."

Karp was shaking his head in disbelief. "So that young-assed kid gets lucky and puts two through the Enforcer's head. Talking about a couple of once in a lifetime shots!

"By the way, did you take care of the body?"

"Yeah, I told the boys to bury it in the desert. We did take a bunch of photos of him, though. Let me know if you need them. I've also got the stuff we took off him.

"That reminds me of Steve. He's at the Doc's house. He'll be alright, but will need to be at the Doc's place a couple of days."

Karp nodded his head in agreement with Prinelli's actions. "That sounds good; just double check with the boys that they buried him deep enough. We don't want that body resurfacing.

"Hang on to the Enforcer's stuff and the photos. I'll let you know about them later."

Manci decided it was time to take charge of the conversation and try to deal with the real issue. "You know, all this shit would be funny, except for one thing. That bothersome Professor is still alive. Right now, he's snoring away peacefully in the cabin and sleeping off the booze he drank.

"We, meanwhile, are up and awake trying to figure out how to tell the Old Man what happened and, more importantly, what didn't happen.

"Prinelli, I want to know about the Professor. I assume he is still alive, but I want to know for sure.

"Greg, meet me in my office no later than nine. I will call the Old Man no later than 9:30. We need to put our heads together before then."

Manci rose from his seat signifying an end to the meeting.

Chapter 89

The Old Man was not happy. "Are you two screw-ups sure Steve killed the Enforcer. That all sounds a little too convenient. I mean really; an inexperienced shooter like Steve gets shot in the shoulder, then has enough guts and skill, to not only return fire, but to return it like an Olympic marksman?

"I don't believe in that kind of luck. As a matter of fact, I don't believe in luck at all.

"And what's up with the Professor and his Seal Team brother. It seems a little strange that the Professor gets so scared, he runs off to a secluded cabin and gets drunk.

"Plus, he's so afraid, but his brother doesn't stay to protect him; he runs off to score a little from his girlfriend?

"If the Professor is so scared, why not take his brother and hole up in his penthouse? That place has the best security in Grand Junction. We'd have had to wait him out.

"No, this whole thing sounds a little too fishy to me. It sounds like a well-coordinated plan to pull the Enforcer out into unknown territory on short notice; isolate him; kill him; and then make it look like some dumb kid killed him.

"This is what I want done over there. Dig up the body; take it to the Doc and have it examined. I also want the Doc's opinion about what kind of round went through Steve's shoulder.

"I've shot plenty of guns in my time and one thing you always have to remember is that the muzzle velocity of a short-barreled handgun is reduced significantly by the barrel length. The round out of a snub-nosed revolver hardly ever exits the body.

"The through and through shoulder shot sounds like something with more power than a belly gun.

"I want to know something by this time tomorrow morning." The phone went dead.

Chapter 90

The two college administrators sat silent for a few seconds, still staring at the speaker phone on Manci's desk. Manci looked up with an obviously pained expression. "He's right you know; we may have been suckered. You've been around Baldridge quite a bit; does he seem like he would scare easily?"

"Now that you ask, the answer is, 'No'. That guy is really starting to piss me off, again. But how could he know we would send somebody after him? It doesn't really make any sense. If he knows something, why not just go to the cops?"

"I don't know either, but we need to get on with what the Old Man wants. Call Prinelli and tell him what to do."

Chapter 91

It had taken Jack and the Baldridge brothers the better part of a day to get the cabin cleaned up and back to guest readiness. Most people have never had to deal with copious amounts of blood on their living room floor, much less splattered brain matter.

Well, guess what? It takes a lot of elbow grease and generous applications of certain chemicals to remove the physical and smelly evidence left behind after a person is shot in the head.

The one redeeming fact in the whole situation was that the hole in the Enforcer's head was relatively small as gunshot wounds go.

Lucky was helping Jack move the furniture back into place. "Little Brother, what we gonna do now? Our little theatrical illusion with the body isn't going to confuse the Italian boys for too long."

Jack looked over at Tarr. "He's right, you know. By tomorrow, they will have started to rethink the whole situation. And if they have access to a doctor with gunshot wound experience, our ruse will be up. They'll know that we know they're after you. They'll also start to get really curious as to why you haven't ratted them out to the cops."

Tarr had been relaxing in a large oversized leather chair watching his brother and friend. "The way I figure it, when you're a crook, you think the only reason someone does or doesn't do something is money.

"Since I'm, by their standards, just a college professor living on a fixed income, they're probably wondering what I want. And how to find out."

"And how to kill you in the process." Jack added to the speculation."

"To our benefit, though, we know they need for the killing to look like a suicide." Lucky added as he sipped on his third cup of coffee in the last hour. "They still need to blame the Gibbs's murder on you. They can't afford the kind of heat that a second murdered professor would bring. The whole thing has to appear as a murder suicide."

Jack's face was wrinkled with concern. "Yeah, they need a suicide, but they have to figure we saw the suicide note on the assassin's body. That makes it more complicated."

Tarr was nodding his head in agreement. "It is getting complicated, but they don't know about our 'Jack in the Hole'.

"If they figured out we killed the assassin and shot the soldier, they probably give most of the credit to you, Lucky. By now they know everything about me and also about you being a Seal. Since they probably don't know about my unsavory pre-college life, they think you are doing all the heavy lifting on this thing.

"In their deviously linear minds, they have a bunch of soldiers who have to deal with only one real threat. They will, no doubt, respect your skills, but they will have faith in their superior numbers. They just have to lure us to the right place.

"As long as we keep you a secret, Jack, we have an edge."

"I agree." Jack nodded. "But right now, we need some sleep. We can't stay up 48 hours like we could in our thirties.

"To do that, we need to deal with our shadows out on the road. Tarr, why don't you two guys head back to your apartment in town? That should pull both tail cars after you. I'll head back to my place. Let's touch base no later than noon tomorrow. I'll call you and we'll discuss our next move."

"Sounds like a plan." Tarr was smiling at Lucky. "But just in case they haven't figured things out, you need to ride on the floorboard. We'll swing by the house in Fruita. Why don't you call ahead and ask your friend to have the garage empty and the door open. We'll stay a few minutes, then leave in separate vehicles heading back to my place."

The two Baldridge brothers got up and left. Jack would be heading out once he saw the trail car pass. A quick call after that would yield a ride in less than five minutes.

Chapter 92

At exactly 9:30 the next morning, the Old Man's phone in Denver was ringing. "Okay, Manci, let's have it. What's the deal on the Professor and his brother? Did we get them or not?

"Dan had the boys stay on the cabin after they buried our friend. There was no action until late the next day. The Professor finally left and went to the house in Fruita where we saw his brother dropped off the night of the shootings.

"He stayed for a few minutes, then he and his brother got in their vehicles and headed back to the Professor's place in Junction. Our boys say they are both still there."

The Old Man's voice sounded like it could freeze water. His tone was as menacing as the two administrators had ever heard

"What did the Doc say?"

"Well, sir, you were right; nothing was as it seemed the night of the shoot-out. First of all, the Enforcer was shot, not two times, but three.

"The first round was small and shot at close range, almost a contact wound. It was a 22 caliber, but judging from the damage, most likely a 22 magnum.

"Shots two and three were fired close to the wound channel made by the 22. It's very likely they were fired in an attempt to hide the 22. Pretty smart move actually, but not smart enough. They were just a little off.

"The shot that hit Steve was probably not from a handgun. The Doc did a tour in Iraq back in the day and said, if he were forced to guess, he'd guess a 308 rifle caliber. Just like snipers use.

"Doc also said the angle of the wound suggested the shot

originated 80 to 100 feet higher than where we found Steve.

"Sir, Baldridge obviously suckered us in. His brother could have easily made that shot. All he had to do was to sneak away from the girlfriend's house, use another vehicle he had stashed and somehow get up on the bluff behind the cabin.

"Someone with his skill and knowledge of the local terrain could easily avoid the stakeouts on the highway.

"How do you want us to handle this?"

"Well, boys, when you messed with the Professor, you seemed to have awakened a sleeping bear. One thing, though; I can't figure his angle. What is he trying to do?

"Is there any way he could have sniffed out what's going on at the College?"

Manci quickly spoke up. "He's a bright guy like most Professors are; that's for sure. Bright's not enough, though. He would have had to see our records. And as we all know, there is only one complete set.

"Once we update the records at the Ranch each week, we destroy any associated records on campus. Everything here is set up to look legit and support our publically published stuff.

"The only other records were kept at the Albanian office and that can't be a problem. They were all destroyed in the recent burglary attempt. So, unless the Ranch has been burglarized, we're in the clear."

The Old Man spoke very softly and deliberately. "What if the burglary and explosion in Albania was not the work of amateurs using too much C4?

"Wasn't your original beef with the Professor because he questioned the international campuses?"

Karp cleared his throat. "We can account for Baldridge's time during the burglary. There's no way he could have been there."

The slow, deliberate voice came over the phone again. "But what about the brother?"

Silence filled the dead air in Manci's office.

The voice continued. "He would have the know-how and experience to make an explosion look like whatever he wanted it to look like. Breaking into an old building like that would be child's play for a Seal."

"But what does he want?" Karp was asking this time. "Since he doesn't seem to want the police involved, it's something else. I'd guess money. He is a Business Prof; all they preach over there is profit and loss. Maybe he just wants a piece of the profit."

"Look you two, whatever he wants, find out what it is. If it's money, your job is easy. Say yes, then arrange to meet him and his brother for the payoff in a nice out-of-the way location. The rest is just fire power."

Manci was not convinced Baldridge wanted money. "But what if he wants something other than money? How do we find out what it is?"

"Simple." The voice said. "Ask him.

You two guys have created quite the problem for our organization. A problem that you WILL clean up. Do you understand what I mean?"

"Yes, sir, we understand."

"If you boys don't have resolution within 72 hours, I will have no choice other than to close down the whole operation and eliminate all loose ends.

"The college angle is a license to print money. I don't want to take it apart. Don't make me!"

The phone went dead.

Chapter 93

Karp's eyes were filled with fear as he looked to Manci, no doubt for an answer to this nightmare. "What are we going to do? You know that when the Old Man talks about loose ends, he's talking about us."

"Yeah, I know, but don't freak out on me. Now's the time to use our minds, not lose them. Let's think this through.

"No news from the cops means they are still just concentrating on the murder. They're oblivious to the big thing here.

"We just have to deal with the Professor. I think that we have to assume he knows pretty much what we're doing. Even if he doesn't, we need to cover our asses.

"If he has the records from Albania, he knows everything; if he doesn't, we haven't lost anything by assuming he does."

"Okay, I'm following you." Karp's eyes were getting less burdened with fear. "I agree we have to assume he knows everything. If he doesn't, no big loss.

"We still have to make his death seem like a suicide, though. But what about the brother? He's got to die too, but a suicide probably won't work for him."

"I agree, Dan, but I have a plan. The brother is such a loner; hardly anyone knows him. Best we can tell, his professor brother is the only person he has regular contact with. If he just disappeared, no one would even look. We just need to make sure the body is never found."

Karp was starting to relax. "I like it. Now how do we make it happen?"

"Simple, Dan, we just call him."

Chapter 94

Tarr and Lucky had gotten a good night's sleep and were enjoying a second cup of coffee on the patio, when Tarr's phone rang. "Good morning, Dr. Karp; what may I help you with?"

"Dr. Baldridge, I think it's time you and I had a more in-depth conversation about your future with TMC. You have been a very loyal and productive member of our faculty for many years. I have been discussing your situation with several members of the Board of Trustees. They feel your tenure should be rewarded.

"Three in particular have stated that your unfortunate situation is not of your making. They felt very strongly that you should be adequately remunerated. They don't want you to be destroyed by this thing and I couldn't agree more.

"So, with that in mind, I've been asked to inquire as to your idea of a fair severance amount. Is that something you are prepared to discuss at this time?"

Tarr had put his cell phone on speaker so Lucky could hear both sides of the conversation. As Tarr glanced over at his brother, Lucky held up five fingers and mouthed the word, million.

"This comes as a complete surprise as you might suspect, Dr. Karp. However, I have been bouncing around some numbers with my attorney, just in case I decide to litigate my termination from a tenured professor's position."

"The Trustees mentioned the possibility of future litigation, so it doesn't surprise me, Dr. Baldridge, that your mind has been going in a similar direction. What number did you and your attorney think was a good starting point for discussion?"

Tarr winked at Lucky. "We did come up with a number,

but it isn't a starting point; it is a firm figure. If you want me to ride quietly off into the sunset, it will cost you five million dollars. That's five million, if you settle with me sans lawyer. If I have to get a lawyer involved in anything other than contract review, my price goes up to cover all attorney fees."

"The President whistled as to communicate his astonishment at the figure. Inside however, he wasn't surprised; he just had to fake it. "Wow, that's quite a severance deal."

Tarr and Lucky waited for the 'but'; they knew he never intended to pay the five million anyway. He simply had to play the game.

"Five million dollars is a lot of money, but given the current situation, I don't think the Trustees will consider it out of line. I'll have to make a couple of phone calls and get back to you.

"But there is one other thing. If we agree to the five million, the contract would specify that you turn over to the Trustees any and all college financial documents of any kind in your possession to them. This would include all documents regardless of how you obtained them. Do you understand what I am saying, Dr. Baldridge?"

Lucky could hardly contain his amusement at the conversation. Tarr was trying to quiet him down with a motion of his hand. "I understand completely. I would also expect a wire transfer to an account of my choosing once the documents are relinquished. And of course, any agreement to this would be verbal only. Do you understand?"

"Yes, Dr. Baldridge, of course. I'll get back to you within the hour."

Tarr closed his phone and placed it on the table next to his now cold coffee.

Lucky was polishing off his last sip of coffee. "So, little brother, let me summarize to make sure I understand all of you guy's academic double-speak. You take all the stuff I stole in Albania and turn it over. He in turn wires five million dollars to an account with your name on it. Nothing is in writing.

"Sounds good to me. What could possibly go wrong? I'm sure the Prez is a man of his word."

Tarr and Lucky were both letting out belly laughs when Lucky's phone rang. "Hey, Jack, how they hanging?"

"Better than your old shriveled up set I'm sure. Anything new?"

Lucky told him.

"That sounds like a good deal. Honor among thieves and all that. I tell you what, I've got a little security company business to take care of; think you guys could meet me at my place about ten tonight? We need to do a little planning after Tarr gets the President's next call."

"We'll see you at ten."

Chapter 95

Tarr's phone rang two hours later. "Sorry, Dr. Baldridge, it took a little longer getting hold of the Trustees I needed to talk with. We have an agreement to our aforementioned deal.

"The Trustees Executive Committee is meeting day after tomorrow at one of our donor's ranch. They insist on a private meeting to fulfill the agreement. The meeting is a dinner meeting with only three things on the agenda plus our agreement. Could you make a 10 PM meeting in Aspen day after tomorrow?"

"How do I know you won't try to cancel our agreement permanently after I surrender all the documents?" Tarr let the question hang before continuing. "Why don't we meet at the Grand Junction Mall in Starbucks?"

"You know why Professor. Too many people know the two of us. That means too many eyes. That's why I chose a neutral third party. He loans us his place for meetings all the time.

"Do you really think all his staff could be a part of whatever you think is going on? If it makes you feel better, the owner will be there day after tomorrow. (Karp was lying for Tarr's benefit. The Old Man wouldn't be within a hundred miles of a payoff.)

"The meeting has been scheduled for weeks; we have a potential major donor meeting with the Trustees' Executive Committee. We're negotiating a new building named after this guy's family. There will be at least two lawyers involved and the donor's staff.

"I believe you know where the Ranch is; you've been sneaking around it before. I believe the night you showed up, we were trying real hard to impress a potential quarterback and his family. We put them up for a couple of days there."

"You've convinced me it is safe, but just to make sure, I'll have another person with me. He's a guy I know who's very well informed about international banking, especially numbered accounts and wire transfers."

"Bring anyone you think you can trust, Professor; bring your girlfriend and defense attorney, we don't care. There will be several guests at the Ranch.

"But the final exchange will be with you and your financial expert in a room with V.P. Manci and myself. Just the four of us behind a closed door. The less people witness this, the better."

"It will be just the two of us Dr. Karp. Make sure the five million is in an account and ready to be transferred. No excuses, no delays. Once that is done, you're through with me. No more problems. Try to screw me and you'll live to regret it, but probably not very long."

Chapter 96

Tarr and Lucky immediately began serious preliminary planning, so when they met with Jack later, they had a starting place. The day after tomorrow would come very quickly and they had a lot to do before then.

As they were planning, Tarr's phone rang. Tarr looked at the caller information with interest. "Hey, Tony, I thought I wouldn't hear from you again."

"You were thinking right, Professor, but I've been doing some thinking. Ever since you gave me this bum knee, it keeps occurring to me that maybe I've used up all my luck in this business. Maybe it's time I started thinking about retirement. There's only one problem."

"And what would that problem be, Tony?"

"The one thing keeping me from walking away and never looking back is money. We don't exactly have a 401K here. It's every guy for himself."

Tarr sensed that Tony had a scheme in mind. "So, how would a guy like you, Tony, get enough money to walk away?"

"It usually don't happen. Most of the older guys I know end up being bouncers in one of the Boss's clubs or bartending. I guess it's a living, but it sure ain't much of one."

"You've obviously been giving this some thought, Tony. What do you have in mind?"

"What I have in mind is giving you everything you need to bust this organization apart. You then give me a million dollars."

Tarr was grinning at the phone. He was concerned about just waltzing on to the Ranch and somehow getting to the records he was sure were stored there. He knew they would need a break here and there. This might be just what they needed.

"A million bucks is probably not unreasonable for the info you are talking about delivering, but I don't have that kind of money."

"Professor, I never figured you had a million bucks; I figured you could steal it from the outfit and give it to me, though. Let me tell you what I'm doing now and some stuff I've found out.

"First, let me tell you what I have been doing lately. Because I don't get around so good, I've been given a new job. There's a small pump house out by the irrigation pond, about a hundred yards from the main house. It has always been guarded by four guys from Denver. The rest of us don't have anything to do with them. There's also a little mousey man that works in the house every day.

"Recently, I was assigned to do 12-hour shifts in the pump house, 8:00 PM to 8:00 AM. Denver's been running a little short of manpower lately. I think it has to do with beefed-up security on the Old Man. Anyway, the security set-up on the pump house lost two guys.

"It used to be two men outside and two men inside plus the mousey man. I'm the inside man now and guard the house and mousey man myself. I guess the house boss figured we had enough guys around to protect the place. And since I can still handle a gun, I guess he thought I could handle the inside. I've also been in the family here in Colorado for over 20 years. That earns me a whole bunch of trust."

Tarr's interest was aroused by now. "Tony, why so much security around the pump house?"

"I had wondered that myself. Before I was sent to the pump house, the house boss filled me in and then swore me to secrecy. He said that little house was the most important place on the whole ranch.

"I figured it must be important, but I never knew why. There's a good reason most of us don't know much about the little house. It's where all the records for the family are kept. The little mousey man is an accountant.

"The place is also an escape for the Old Man if something big goes down at the main house. I already knew that, though."

"Tony, back up some and tell me more about the records."

"The house is like a regular house upstairs. It's got two bedrooms, living room, kitchen and a bathroom. There's also a full basement. The basement has a couple of big pumps in one half; the other half is a big waterproof vault. Probably concrete and steel.

"When the accountant is here, he opens the vault and takes out a brief case and a laptop computer. There's also quite a bit of cash. Probably at least a mil. The money is behind a locked steel grill."

Tarr interrupted. "Let me guess, you want the cash?"

"That's right, Professor; whatever cash is in there I get. You get the computer and briefcase. The accountant, Bruce, told me a copy of what is on the computer is in the case. He said the system is designed so the Old Man can grab it on the way by if he has to escape.

"When the accountant isn't here working on the books, everything is locked in the vault."

"Tony, where does the accountant do his work?"

"He brings the computer and case upstairs. One of the bedrooms has been turned into an office."

Tarr seemed satisfied with Tony's explanation of the records. "Now let's back up to the Old Man's escape comment you made earlier."

"When the family first bought the Ranch several years ago and before anyone moved here, a bunch of guys were brought in from Mexico. Me and one other soldier had to watch after them and make sure they had what they needed. Only one of the guys could speak English; he was the boss. I found out later he was also a mining engineer.

"Those guys spent about six weeks building an underground tunnel from the main house to the basement of the pump house. It's an escape tunnel."

"Okay, Tony, give me as much detail on the tunnel as you can."

"It runs from below the bathroom in the Old Man's study to the basement of the pump house. There is a steel reinforced door about ten feet into the tunnel on each end. Both locked."

"How do you access the study entrance?"

"It's in the Jacuzzi tub. There's a false bottom, just turn on the hot water and it pops up. You'll have to go down some stairs. The key to the tunnel doors is under the last step, right side as you face it."

"So Tony, once the Old Man gets to the pump house and gets the computer and briefcase, what next?"

"When you stand in front of the pump house, you will see a small utility, storage-type shed off to one side. There's a four-seater ATV inside. The Old Man and his body guards hop on and take off to the woods. After that, I don't know. I don't think anybody does except the Old Man himself.

"I guess he figures that if the brown stuff hits the fan that bad, he can't trust nobody but himself. But you can bet your ass he's got a plan."

"Okay, Tony, thanks. If I can work this out, you might be thinking about how you're gonna get away hauling all that money. Don't plan on using the ATV, I'll have other plans for that. Just be prepared to leave at a moment's notice."

Tarr turned to Lucky. "What do you think? Can we get in and out of that place?"

Lucky rose from his seat. "I don't make decisions like that without seeing the place with my own eyes."

Tarr looked at his brother walking away. "Shere are you

going?"

"I'm going home to get a few hours' sleep and pick up a few things. Then I'm going to Aspen on a little sneak and peak.

"I'll do some recon tonight, then lay up tomorrow and watch their security. We need to have a good plan for getting in and out of the place. I also want a better feel for security and how good they are.

"I'll meet you tomorrow night about midnight at Jack's. We can finalize our plans then."

Tarr knew better than advising Lucky to be careful or take Jack with him. Lucky was as good as there was in this business. If anyone needed to be careful, it was the bad guys.

Chapter 97

Lucky drove his truck into Aspen a little after Midnight. In the back of the truck was a highly modified dirt bike. In addition to having the highest possible horsepower for the little machine (0 - 60 in 2.35 seconds), it was muffled down to almost no sound at idle.

Finding a place to leave the truck was no problem. He found a condo complex that was not gated; probably where the local retail management people around town lived. A truck like his would not draw any unwanted attention on the street.

Unloading the bike was facilitated by a lightweight ramp. He then walked it out of the complex, just in case some senior citizen was up making his third trip to the john.

Once out of the neighborhood, he mounted the bike, fired it up, and headed toward the Ranch. He had checked it out on GPS and had a good idea what its boundaries were.

Once Lucky got close to the Ranch, he turned on a BLM fire road he had identified on Google Maps. He began a slow drive down the road. Another thing he had identified on the map was a stream that appeared to dissect the Ranch.

Driving very slowly so as to maximize the muffling quality of the engine, Lucky crossed over a small wooden bridge after riding for about 10 minutes. Just what he had been searching for, the stream flowed beneath.

Pushing the bike, Lucky left the road and followed what appeared to be a fairly well traveled game trail paralleling the stream.

He smiled to himself. The game trail was a sign that there was wildlife on the Ranch. From the size of the trail, there were obviously some bigger game such as deer and elk.

Large game made noise as they moved through the brush. That meant any guards posted would be used to hearing it. Also, any motion detectors would prove so annoying, they would probably be deactivated.

All of this was good news to a guy like Lucky planning a sneak and peek, with the emphasis on sneak. He had to get in and out unobserved or the whole place would be put on high alert. High alert would make their job a whole lot more difficult.

About a hundred yards from the fire road, the game trail was intersected by a smaller trail heading away from the stream. This looked like an ideal place to stash the bike. Lucky pushed the bike a few yards down the intersecting trail, then off to the side where he leaned it against a tree. He then covered the bike with a large dark camouflage cotton cloth he had brought for the purpose.

He stepped back a couple of feet from the bike; it was now invisible. He retraced his steps to the main game trail. From this point on, he had to morph into super sleuth Seal mode. After all, it was a sneak and peek, not a 'be seen and have to run' exercise.

It was an exhausting 60 minutes of stealth movement before Lucky saw lights. He had not encountered any sentries or signs of electronic surveillance. That didn't mean no electronic gizmos; just not on a well-used game trail.

Since all the Mafia soldiers were probably urban street killers, it made sense that any sentry patrols would probably be in the open areas surrounding the main house. The electronic stuff would also be concentrated in and around the house. He did remind himself, though, to keep an eye out for cameras.

Lucky now went totally flat on the ground for the sneak on toward the lights. He was especially conscious of sentries who might be just off the trail.

A little later, he smelled the sentry before he identified his location.

Lucky froze when his nose caught the first whiff of cologne.

The guy had probably been told no smoking, but no one thought to tell him not to wear his usual double dose of Old Spice. For a Seal like Lucky, the guy might as well been standing under a spotlight.

From the first time Lucky saw the stream on the map, he knew he might need to get in it. In anticipation of such, he had worn a light weight wet suit under his camo. Time to get wet.

Another two hours of sneaking told Lucky almost everything he needed to know. The stream went all the way to the pump house. This time of year, the stream wasn't more than two feet deep with the banks of the stream being about two feet higher than that.

Lucky had been able to get all the way to the pump house and back unobserved. He had not heard any dogs, but that was no big surprise. With all the wildlife in the area, dogs would be false alarming constantly.

Lucky felt this place was wide open to men trained as Seals. He figured he could get himself and another man back to the pump house with little danger of exposure.

There was one more piece of information Lucky desperately needed: how many men were they going up against? For that, he would need some daylight.

Lucky spent the next couple of hours sneaking and peeking around the entire perimeter of the ranch. He had been right about security. Other than the sentry adjacent to the stream's game trail, there were two guys doing a roving patrol around the perimeter, just outside the tree line. There was a main gate and a secondary gate further on the property. There were two guys on the secondary gate and three on the main. That was a total of eight that he had spotted.

With two shifts required to cover security around the clock, the total jumped to 16. With inside security, the number could be 20 plus shooters.

By the time the sun was up, Lucky had found the highest

spot on the property from where he could see most of it. He had taken a combat nap and was now settling in for a day of watching. The things he did for his little brother.

Chapter 98

It was the night of the exchange. Jack would accompany Tarr as his financial advisor. Lucky and a few of Jack's men would have other duties.

President Karp had convinced Tarr that things would proceed more smoothly if he were allowed to send a car for them. Tarr conceded with two caveats: they would be picked up in Aspen and they nor their briefcases were to be searched. Karp had resisted but Tarr had embarrassed him into agreement.

After all, if two young men like Karp and Manci were afraid of an old crippled up Professor and a geek financial guy, they could have an additional man in the room to watch.

Karp agreed. Tarr and Jack were now in the rear seat of a Lincoln Town Car headed away from the Aspen hotel where they had been picked up. Each of them carried a briefcase and had a small Sig 380 semi-automatic handgun secreted on their body.

Tarr's 'Evidence' was in a briefcase rigged with explosives. Of course, only he, Jack, and the team knew.

Jack's briefcase contained extra magazines for their handguns plus a few equalizers if needed. The equalizers were in fact M67 hand grenades. Weighing less than a pound each, the grenade has a 3-second fuse and yields an injury radius of 15 meters, with a fatality radius of 5 meters.

Jack's philosophy was simple. If you intended to knock down a hornet's nest, bring plenty of hornet spray.

Chapter 99

The rest of the team consisted of Lucky, three snipers and an ex-Navy Seal like Lucky. The team had infiltrated using a stolen BLM SUV. They had driven to within a mile of the bridge crossing the stream. After that each had moved to a pre-designated point around the perimeter.

The three snipers were spaced on high spots that provided coverage of the main house, the small guest cottages, the pump house and the driveway.

Positioning a house, in a spot where you can see enemies coming from a long distance, has an evil twin. You may be able to see them, but likewise they can see you from a great distance. They can also stop anything or anybody from getting to the house.

Three well-trained snipers with the latest semi-automatic rifles in 50 caliber could ruin a lot of days. Add to that enough LAW Rockets to obliterate all out buildings plus a major piece of the main house and you have a very deadly scenario for the supposedly well-positioned house.

Unlike in the movies, not all Mafia enemies arrive in stretch Cadillacs carrying Tommy Guns. Sometimes, hell descends from the hills and you never see the sender; you just experience the wrath.

While the three snipers got into position, the two Seals began their trip to the pump house. They would follow Lucky's previous path. Instead of semi-automatic 50 cals like the snipers, each Seal was fully kitted out with an M-4 assault rifle, a silenced 22 caliber handgun, a combat knife, extra ammo and all the C4 they could carry.

The high Colorado Rocky Mountain serenity was destined

to be interrupted tonight.

Chapter 100

Tarr and Jack's ride rolled to a stop in front of the main gate to the Ranch. The guy in charge did not like this. It went against everything he knew to let strangers in without searching them.

Tarr and Jack had on jeans and light jackets against the cool autumn night. The guard glared at them through the open window. They merely smiled and shrugged their shoulders, as if they also did not know why they were not searched.

The car eased through the main gate. As they approached the secondary gate, Tarr could see through the front windshield that it was open and the guard was waving them through.

The car started through what appeared to be a large meadow. Looking ahead Tarr and Jack could see a winding drive culminating in front of a very large mansion. They could also see the pump house and several additional buildings.

They were met at the front door by a very large man as big as Tarr. He was not a pleasant host. "You guys follow me." He turned and walked into the house's interior.

Tarr could not suppress his need to comment. He started speaking in Jack's direction. "Look at this place. It looks like Italian renaissance humped Cowboy chic and this is their offspring. They ought to coin a new term for this decorating. Something like Mafia Cowboy style.

Jack was laughing. "Dr. Baldridge, you are so crude and terribly unkind. These poor *I-talian* boys are doing the best they can. Although, I expect that any minute now we'll see a 45 Tommy Gun displayed on elk antlers."

They both laughed out loud. Their host turned and gave them a dirty look. "You might want to keep that crap to yourselves or you'll be on the wall hanging by your balls."

Their host stopped in front of a heavy dark oak door. Tarr's guess was that it was a security door, no doubt reinforced with steel in a concrete reinforced frame.

"If this was the study and the Old Man needed to get away, he'd need a door like this to slow down whatever evil was after him.

Opening the door, their host motioned for them to precede him in. As they passed into the room, both were impressed by its early American décor. The Old Man obviously agreed with their assessment of the interior design. He clearly spent most of his time in here.

Tarr looked around. Floor to ceiling bookshelves full of leather-bound books, no doubt many of them first editions. Tarr continued to look around. He saw the requisite large oak desk, a tastefully situated full bar, leather chairs appropriately distributed throughout the room, and a beautiful Persian rug on the floor in front of the desk.

Tarr looked out the large window behind the desk. He could tell by the hue of the glass that it was bullet proof. This was probably a completely hardened room. It would take quite a while to breach, giving the Old Man plenty of time to make it to the bathroom located a few steps from the desk.

It was moot tonight, however, for the Old Man; he wasn't in the room. That should have surprised Tarr, but it didn't. Why would the Family head sit in on a basic transfer and put himself at risk? Better to hear about it later over the phone.

Tarr's visual exploration of the room ended when his eyes met President Karp's. He was seated to one side of the massive oak desk. Seated behind the desk in the power chair was Vice President Manci.

Tarr laughed at Karp. "I always wondered how TMC was so successful under your leadership. You just never seemed to have enough juice for the job. Now I know; you don't. You're the number two man. But why the deception?"

Karp was steaming and Manci was smiling as he responded. "It's pretty simple really; I'm not as accomplished in the art of bullshit, which we all know, is necessary for the President. I'm more a numbers kind of guy who excels at planning. It was simply matching talent to task. He's the face; I'm the brain. Isn't that right, Dan?"

Karp's face was retreating back to its normal color from the crimson of embarrassment. "It takes both to make a place like TMC run. I may not be as smart as Greg, I admit it, but I was sure smart enough to get you in a room with a closed door and no way out."

Manci redirected his attention from Karp back to Tarr. "That is true. Here we all are. You have our evidence. We have Eddie there about two feet to your right with a gun now in his hand. I also need to mention we forgot to set up for the money transfer. We seem to have you and your money man here at a disadvantage.

"Now hand over the evidence and I'll have Eddie kill you quickly so as not to make you endure pain. Mess with me at all or try some lame trick and I'll make sure it takes a week for you to die. And when I say die, I mean after a week filled with the most horrible pain you can imagine."

Tarr never blinked before responding. "Gees, Greg, keep that kind of tough talk going and you might convince us you're the real deal, card-carrying, *I-talian* Mafia boy instead of a bean-counting wanna be."

"Okay, Baldridge, I'm now starting to understand why Dan hates you so much. You're a smart-ass with a very annoying way of phrasing things. Looks like you're going to create a week's work for Eddie."

Karp and Eddie both looked on with the glint of evil humor in their eyes. Jack had remained quiet until now. "Tarr, quit screwing around and show them the dead man's switch on the briefcase."

Tarr feigned confusion. "Oh yeah, I forgot about that. See my left hand. It's holding down a dead man's switch. Shoot me, hit me, do anything to me and I release the switch. When I do, enough C4 goes off to make this room look like a nuclear disaster occurred. Maybe not enough to get through the room's hardened defenses, but enough to kill all of us.

"Now, fire up the computer on your desk and connect to one of your off-shore accounts with enough money to cover our payment. If not, we all go boom."

Karp had risen from his seat by now and taken a step toward Tarr. "Sure you will. Of course, you'll have to leave behind your pretty girlfriend and all those great students you're always going on about. Oh, did I mention your beloved brother and big penthouse, and who knows what else?

"Eddie, shoot this piece of shit in his good leg. But don't kill him, he may not have what we want."

Jack saw Tarr tense, not in fear but in preparation. Jack likewise tensed.

Eddie had been holding the gun down at his side. Before he could physically respond to Karp's command, Tarr struck.

Knowing Eddie had to process the order, send a message from his brain to his shooting hand and then turn toward Tarr and shoot, Tarr was quicker. His walking stick was a blur as his 250 plus pound body brought the stick up in a much practiced manner and struck Eddie.

Instead of slowing the strike as it neared Eddie's nose, Tarr did as he had been taught. He swung with all his power through the target. Anyone able to listen would have heard the stick strike and break the nose.

The nose bone was then carried by the force of the blow into Eddie's brain. Eddie was dead before he hit the floor.

317

Chapter 101

Jack had not seen Tarr strike, he was too busy taking care of the other two. He didn't have Tarr's luxury of killing, he knew their plan depended on taking the other two alive.

Tarr's action caused Karp to automatically take a step forward, which brought him within striking distance of Jack. With no hesitation, Jack drove his knuckles into Karp's exposed throat. The strike was designed to take Karp out of the fight, but not permanently hurt him.

As Karp fell while gasping for air, Jack was already by him and jumping over the desk toward Manci. Manci tried to respond, but like Karp, he was more manager than soldier. Neither had skills anywhere close to Jack's.

Jack's entire body went over the desk and into Manci. He went for the throat to stifle any attempt at screaming. He choked Manci into unconsciousness within a few seconds.

As Jack looked up, he saw Tarr locking the study's door. He looked down at Eddie. "How's Eddie?"

Tarr walked away from the door and looked down at Eddie. "I'm afraid Eddie has taken his last order. Your two guys?"

"They're out but alive. Open your case and give me a couple of flex cuffs and some duct tape. I put three sets in there with the C4."

Tarr watched as Jack cuffed and taped the mouths of TMC's big time administrators.

Jack looked up when he was finished. "Help me get these guys into the bathroom. We need to get them and ourselves down into the tunnel."

Tarr grabbed Karp by his coat collar and easily drug him into the bathroom. While there he turned the hot water faucet to activate the trap door in the tub. It immediately released and popped up.

Jack was dragging Manci into the room as the trapdoor sprang open. He immediately dropped his administrator on top the other, then quickly went down the stairs to the tunnel.

Finding the key to the tunnel door, he had it open before Tarr could ask how he was doing. Jack looked back up the stairs at Tarr. "Help get Karp on the stairs; he should be able to walk by now."

Tarr reached and grabbed Karp by the arm. "Get in the tub and down the stairs."

Before Karp could finish his statement about not going anywhere with them, Tarr jerked him into the tub and dropped him down the stairs. "Bombs away!"

Jack barely had time to jump out of the way. "Hey, be careful you overgrown gorilla."

Tarr reached and pulled Manci into the tub. He was just starting to regain consciousness, as Tarr dropped him down the stairs.

With more agility that one would attribute to a man of his size with a bum knee, Tarr descended the stairs. "I'll start these two down the tunnel while you go back up and set the explosives."

Jack hustled by Tarr and up the stairs. He moved with speed into the study and retrieved his briefcase and Tarr's. He checked to make sure Tarr's case was still set to blow on command.

He took a grenade from his case and rigged it to blow if the study door were opened. He also rigged another to the explosive's case as a backup to the detonator in his pocket.

Before going back down the ladder to the tunnel, Jack reached up and pulled the trap door shut. No need advertising where they went.

Tarr was waiting in the tunnel for Jack. "Everything set

upstairs?"

Jack patted the pocket containing the detonator. "All we have to do is push a button. But before we leave, tell me again why we need these two guys alive."

"We need them primarily for insurance in case we have to have a witness to explain things to Detective Orr. We might also need Manci in case you don't have everything you need to access their accounts.

"Although I have to tell you, Karp hasn't been doing too well. While you were back upstairs, he grabbed his throat and passed out again. You might want to check on him."

Jack bent over Karp, then looked up frowning. "He's dead. I didn't mean to kill him, but just as I started my jab to his throat, he stepped toward me. It threw my timing off. I guess we'll have to rule his death a suicide. My punch would not have been fatal, but his movement added just enough extra to crush his larynx."

Tarr looked down at Karp with disgust. "Couldn't have happened to a better guy. Let's move on down the tunnel.

"How long to move the money once we get the records?"

Jack was helping Manci to his feet. "About five minutes, if we have everything. A little longer if I have to extract it from our friend here."

Tarr looked at his watch. "The pump house should be secure within 3 minutes if Lucky didn't hit a snag. We are almost exactly on schedule, if we move now."

Chapter 102

Lucky had partnered up with an ex-Seal everyone called Snake. Snake was Jack's best reconnaissance man. He was called Snake because there were very few places he couldn't wiggle his way into. Part of his ability was due to his 5'6" size, but mostly it was his coolness under pressure.

Snake and Lucky had no difficulty infiltrating the Ranch. They had crawled out of the streambed and were on their bellies behind the small storage shed adjacent to the pump house.

There were two guards outside the pump house. One covered the front, while the second covered the back. Conveniently enough, neither covered the sides.

Lucky lightly touched Snake's arm. He held up one finger indicating one minute to go. Lucky also pointed his finger at the sentry in the back and then at Snake. Lucky would take the sentry in front and Snake the one in back.

When time was up, Lucky stood and quietly moved to the front side of the house; Snake moved to the rear side.

Snake heard his man coming. The rear sentry moved to the end of his route and turned to go back. That was the moment Snake was waiting for. He pounced quickly and quietly. His left hand grabbed the sentry's head and pulled it rearward. His right hand drove the blade of his combat knife into the man's throat. One down.

Lucky sensed Snake had taken his sentry down. His man was just turning to retrace his steps when Lucky struck. Both sentries died silently within 30 seconds of each other.

It was time to make entry into the house.

Chapter 103

The pump house was not really what the name caused one to visualize. The part of the house you could actually see looked very much like a tract house in any middle-class subdivision. There was a front door, numerous windows, and a back door.

Lucky went into the house through an unlocked front door. Snake had no difficulty gaining entrance through the back.

Lucky had crept to within a foot of Tony who was watching an old western on television. Since Snake had to pass through the living room to find the bedroom office, he waited for Lucky as per their plan.

Lucky had moved behind Tony. He laid the silenced barrel against the back of Tony's neck. Tony's body stiffened but remained in place without sound. Lucky bent in closer to Tony. "Hold up the number of fingers for the people here."

Tony held up two.

"Where is the accountant? Hand motions only."

Tony pointed to a bedroom down the hall on the left. Lucky repeated the message to Snake. Lucky did not remove the gun from Tony's neck.

Consistent with his name, Snake moved quickly and silently across the room and down the short hallway. As he eased up to the office bedroom door, he could hear keystrokes from within. Easing on into the room, he could see the slim, slightly-hunched-over back of the accountant. His hands were now in his lap as he pondered some issue.

Just as he was about to move his hands back to the laptop's keyboard, he felt the coolness of Snake's gun barrel on his neck. He froze in place.

With his left hand, Snake grabbed the rear shirt collar of the accountant and whispered. "Get up slowly." The coolness of the barrel was still on his neck. The accountant did as he was told.

Lucky watched Snake march out the accountant and bring him into the living room. "Flex cuff him, put in earplugs and tape his mouth, eyes and ears."

Snake swiftly followed his instructions, then guided the man to a chair and helped him sit down. He then taped the accountant's legs to the chair legs. Snake then ran a couple of strips to secure the accountant's back to the chair back. He wasn't going anywhere.

Lucky was watching the whole thing. "Did you lock the back door when you came in?" He got the universal one finger response. Lucky grinned, that must be a yes.

Lucky relaxed and removed the gun barrel from Tony's neck. "Okay, Tony, you can breathe now, but before you move, take your gun out slowly and give it to me."

Tony took the gun from his shoulder holster and held it up in the air for Lucky to grab. "Thanks, Tony, you are Tony, right."

"Yeah, I'm Tony. What's the deal taking my gun? I'm on your side remember?"

Snake had not moved from his position by the accountant. His attention however, was totally fixed on Tony. Even though Tony appeared to be sincere, you never knew. And you never trust a person you just met. Lucky had told Snake that his primary job after securing the accountant was to keep Tony constantly under watch unless he, Lucky, had him under control.

Lucky walked around the sofa where Tony had been watching the western. "I know, I know, but I have a rule. Only me and my team have guns. You'll get yours back in a few minutes.

"Right now we need to get down in the basement. Snake, you know what to do."

As Lucky and Tony headed downstairs, Snake went about

the business of booby trapping the doors. They didn't want any surprise visitors.

After finishing his job, Snake took up position so he could see out the front window. Anyone coming his way would be easy to spot.

Lucky and Tony had made their way down the stairs and over to the walk-in vault. "Tony, show me where the tunnel door is hidden."

"It's behind those two file cabinets on the right. The door opens into the tunnel."

Lucky and Tony moved to the file cabinets and wrestled them away from the wall and out of the way. "Can we open the door from this side, Tony?'

"Naw, the Old Man didn't want anyone to be able to sneak down the tunnel and maybe surprise him in his study. That's also why those file cabinets are so friggin' heavy; so nobody will just move them for some reason."

"Well, that makes sense."

Tony had been eyeing the cash in the vault. It was all he could do to look at Lucky when they were talking. Lucky was well aware of this.

"You know, Tony, since we have a couple of minutes to wait, it might be a good time to grab your reward. Can you get into the cage?" Lucky made a head gesture toward the stacks of money.

"Yes I can." Tony didn't have to be told twice. He quickly moved over to the cage, opened it and started stuffing the cash in a large duffle kept there for the purpose. Well, maybe not for the purpose of stealing, more likely for the purpose of hastily moving it.

Lucky's attention was quickly diverted from Tony's ecstasy to the sound of a key in the tunnel door. He stepped behind one of the heavy filing cabinets and aimed his M4 assault rifle at the door. Lucky had lived and survived for many years in a very dangerous profession by adhering to a simple concept: there is no such thing as being too careful.

Tarr was the first one through the door. He had his Sig 380 out front, just in case. Manci was pushed roughly through the door followed by Jack.

Lucky stepped into full view from his area of concealment. "Aren't there two guys? Where's the other one?"

Tarr jerked his thumb toward Jack. "Jack didn't like his singing so he silenced him."

Jack was moving so he could see the entire inside of the vault. "I resemble that remark. How was I to know the guy couldn't take a little constructive criticism?

"His body is back down the tunnel. But enough playful bullshitting, where's the computer and accounts? I've got work to do."

Lucky pointed above his head. "It's upstairs all warmed up and everything. Snake'll show you where."

Jack hurriedly moved toward the stairs. He did indeed have work to do.

Tarr motioned back down the tunnel. "Lucky, do you think you and Tony could drag Karp's body down the tunnel? We can't afford to leave it there. You know why."

Lucky didn't really know why. His little brother was always thinking. Maybe he had a new wrinkle to their plan that involved the administrators, dead or alive. "Sure, come on Tony."

Manci had been watching the exchanges in the basement quietly. "What is this all about, Baldridge? You plan on stealing the money in the offshore accounts? Do you know what the Old Man will do to you? You can't run far enough or dig a hole deep enough to hide.

"Ever hear of a 'turkey' in relation to torture?"

"Yes, I think I might have, Manci. Doesn't it involve cornbread dressing and cranberry sauce?"

"No, smart ass, it's when you are skinned alive and kept breathing during the whole ordeal. That's going to be you guys. You'll live to regret messing with our family and stealing our money."

"Me, steal the family's money? No, that's not going to happen. You see, this was a very elaborate plot conjured up by you, Karp and a Columbian drug cartel to rip off the Old Man and the money. Then you tried to blame it on poor old me and my brother. What a despicable act. You should be ashamed."

"You're crazy, Baldridge, the Old Man is never going to believe that."

"Oh, really. When he actually has time to think about everything, does it make sense that a crippled up old college professor with no military or law enforcement training could take on and kill one of the Mafia's best killers?

"Will the Old Man think the said same professor could organize a hit on his Ranch and overcome 20 or so shooters?

"Will he believe I stole all his money and divided it between two offshore accounts with yours and Karp's names on them?

"Will the Old man then believe almost 20 million dollars were wired immediately to other accounts as payoffs?

"Will the Old Man really believe any of that?"

Manci looked dumbfounded. "How in hell did you do all that?"

"You've forgotten already, I didn't do anything; I was framed. You and Karp did it all."

Chapter 104

Lucky and Tony huffed and puffed a bit as they dragged Karp's body back into the vault and then out into the basement.

Tony was the one doing most of the huffing and puffing. "Okay, boys, I've done my part. When can I take the money and leave?"

Tarr looked at Tony. "Just one more small favor and you can leave."

Tarr told Tony what he wanted. Tony looked at Tarr wild-eyed. "You want me to do that? Are you crazy? I can't do that. If the Old Man found out..."

Tarr interrupted Tony. "Would it be any less easy on you, if he just found out you stole his money? This way, you have a reason for running away and going into hiding."

"I guess you got a point there."

Tony took his phone from his pocket and punched in a number. "Hello, Mr. Barberri, it's Tony from the Ranch. I got something you need to know." Tony was speaking rapidly and running out of breath.

"Hold on, Tony. Slow down; take a couple of breaths."

Tony slowed his breathing and continued with a nervous voice. He didn't need to fake nervous; he was about to tell a lie that would cost him his life, if discovered. "You know I've been inside the pump house for a while now. Well tonight, a couple of thugs sneaked in the house and got the drop on me and the accountant.

"They taped the accountant to a chair all blindfolded and stuff. Then they say they might need the accountant, but they don't need me. One of them drags me downstairs and shoots me in the head."

"Wait a minute, Tony, they shot you in the head, but now you're calling me?"

"That's right Mr. Barberri, they shot me in the head. The shooter used a silenced 22 caliber. Just before he shot me, I heard two more voices in the vault. That made the shooter look up just when he pulled the trigger.

"You can imagine how surprised I was to wake up later. The bullet must have just grazed me. I got a huge headache and blood all over but I'm not hurt that much. I know real hurt; I been shot twice before.

"But I better hurry up. I'm in the basement and everybody else is upstairs. Anyways, I wake up, right, and Mr. Manci and Mr. Karp are over by the vault door. They must have come in through the tunnel. And they got that professor guy and another guy with them.

"Then Mr. Manci tells Mr. Karp they need to hurry; they have to transfer the money before the Columbians get here.

"Does this make any sense to you, Mr. Barberri?"

"Yeah, it's starting to make a whole lot of things make sense. What did they do with the Professor and other guy?"

"They just cold-cocked them. Didn't shoot them or anything. They're on the floor in the vault."

"Now, Tony, that makes even more sense."

"Mr. Barberri, none of this makes sense to me. What's going on?"

"Tony, what's going on is that those two assholes, Manci and Karp, are trying to rip off the family and then blame it on the Professor. The whole deal with the Professor has been a set-up.

"Tony, if you can, I want you to kill Manci and Karp. I know you're hurt, but I would consider it a big favor. Then try to get out and warn the boys; my best guess is the Columbians are gonna hit the Ranch. Now go do what you got to do, Tony."

As Tony was putting his phone back into his pocket, Manci lowered his head and charged him. What Manci probably didn't know about Tony was that he had always preferred a knife to a gun back in his earlier years.

As Manci charged, Tony grabbed the small knife he kept in a case next to the phone. Manci hit Tony in the chest with his head and they both tumbled to the floor, with Manci on top.

Tony struggled some to get the weight of Manci off him and on to the floor. As Manci was pushed off, he landed on his back. Tony's knife was protruding from his chest.

Tony was struggling to get up; his bad knee made it difficult. Tarr stepped over and pulled him to his feet. "Damn, Tony, that's as fast knife work as I've ever seen."

"I'm sorry, Professor, it was just instinct; I didn't really mean to kill him. I hope you didn't need him for anything."

"Well, Tony, he was just insurance. Let's hope we don't need it."

Chapter 105

By the time the two brothers and Tony gathered up Tony's cash and made it upstairs, Jack was coming out of the office bedroom with a computer in one hand and a briefcase in the other. "You boys through screwing around downstairs? What were you doing?"

It was Lucky who responded. "Tying up a few loose ends; we'll fill you in later.

"How about you? Any problems doing what we planned?"

Jack held up the briefcase. "Nope, everything was in here and well organized. You won't believe the info in this case. It'll take us a week to get through it."

Snake had walked up to the group. "Isn't it about time we de-assed this place?"

Tarr looked at Tony. "How you planning to get away with that big bag of money?"

"I've got one of our SUV's not far away. Give me five minutes and I'll be out of here."

"Okay, Tony, you've got your five minutes. And when you leave, leave everything: the Mafia, the country, old friends, all of it. If any old buddies mention seeing you, you'll end up dead. To the Mafia, you're about to become an unknown risk. You know how they'll handle that."

"That's good advice, Professor. Good luck!"

As Tony quickly turned, Lucky stopped him. "How about taking the accountant with you? He won't stand much of a chance if you don't. Dump him by the side of the road where he'll be found."

"I sure will; he and I have gotten to be friends."

After a little knife work on the duct tape, Tony and the

accountant headed for the back door and left.

Lucky opened his pack and took out several bricks of C4. "No need to haul this back. Snake, dump yours too. It'll only take a minute."

Lucky and Snake made quick work of placing the C4 and attaching radio activated detonators. They were soon back with Tarr and Jack.

Jack took his phone from a pocket and made a call. "Go time is five minutes; repeat go time is five minutes; watch for the signal. Then give us covering fire. We're leaving the pump house on a large ATV. Don't forget the sentry by the game trail.

"Okay, you two snake-eaters, lead this big-assed professor and my handsome self out to the storage shed. I figure we fire up the ATV and be ready to leave when all hell breaks loose."

The four-seater ATV was in the shed and easily started. It was obviously well maintained and kept in a state of readiness.

Lucky was driving and Snake riding shotgun. Tarr and Jack were on the backseat. Jack was holding the detonator for the explosives in the study. "Here we go." He pressed the button. Five minutes to the second.

Almost instantaneously, the ground shuddered and the study's window blew out. Hell had arrived at the Ranch.

Without notice, the other end of the main house was struck by a LAW rocket. Another rocket streaked toward a small propane farm containing 10 tanks. The power was about to go out.

With a rumble that could be felt half-way to Aspen, the propane exploded sending flames a hundred feet into the air. The out buildings used as soldier quarters weren't far behind the propane. Each exploded and began to burn.

Men were stumbling out of all structures. Most had rifles and were returning fire. They were shooting at shadows, though. No enemies were within sight.

The sentries on perimeter patrol were the first to determine where the threat was. Before they could even shoot up the hilltops, each was stopped dead by a 50 caliber round.

Around the main house, confusion reigned supreme. Men were running, shooting and yelling. The large caliber firestorm continued its menacing effect.

The men on the ground would probably have felt relief, if they had known the snipers were no longer firing at people. Their job was to destroy as much property as possible. Consequently, every vehicle received attention.

Tony was fortunate; he cleared the gates before hell rained down.

The time allocated to getting the team clear of danger must have felt like an eternity to those below. For a few it was.

Chapter 106

Within seconds after the study exploded, the foursome on the ATV was moving at maximum speed toward the tree line where the stream emerged from the woods.

One of the snipers was tasked with taking out the sentry by the game trail. His secondary target was any roving sentry that might be between the ATV and the game trail.

The ATV was at the tree line in just under one minute. Lucky slowed the small vehicle just enough so he could turn and press the detonator for the pump house explosives. He was rewarded with another lightshow of explosive gases and debris filling the dark mountain air.

Jack had instructed the snipers to engage for four minutes and then fall back to a prearranged rendezvous point. He wasn't sure what response time was by the Sheriff's Department, but they had a tendency to be faster for big mansions.

Seven minutes after leaving the storage shed, the ATV was rolling across a clearing in the woods. It was barely large enough for the medium-sized chopper sitting in its center with rotors moving.

As the ATV pulled up, the snipers also ran up. They however, were out of breath. They, to a man, looked at the ATV with envy.

A little less than two hours later, Tarr, Jack and Lucky were stepping off the chopper at Jack's Glade Park facility.

A couple hours later, the helicopter carrying the remaining team members arrived at the Salt Lake City Airport. There it was towed into a private hanger.

By morning the pilots, Snake, and the snipers would be on their way out of country to new assignments with Jack's company. This was standard operating procedure for Jack. Thoroughly plan, hit hard, then disperse participants to different places around the world's hotspots.

Of course, the three amigos had been at Jack's compound since early last evening playing poker and drinking. They were certain to alibi each other, if the need ever arose.

The next day they took Jack's private plane to San Francisco where Tarr disembarked to join Doni for a week of sightseeing. Lucky caught a commercial flight to Hawaii where there was an old Seal friend he visited. Jack flew on to Seattle, where he had pressing company business.

Chapter 107

Three weeks later, the Baldridge brothers and Jack were sitting in the sunshine enjoying drinks on the cliff house's patio.

As usual all men were enjoying their Jack Daniels on the rocks. Tarr lifted his glass in toast toward the other two. "Here's to my brothers, assholes both of you. But when walking into the unknown, there are no others I would rather have by my side. I didn't have to ask you to cover my back; I knew when I turned around, both of you would be there.

"Thanks guys; this was a hairy one. I couldn't have done it without you. And, Jack, it goes without saying that the assets of your organization were invaluable to the entire operation."

Lucky looked up from the ground where he was staring. "Jack, should we hug the big jerk or kick his ass?"

"Naw, Lucky, he just has to buy the drinks until we're dead. Although I have to say, the three of us probably haven't had this much fun since we were kids. We got to shoot guns, blow up a ton of shit, and sneak around in the bush. Not bad for three guys that are a little past their prime."

Tarr was trying to calculate in his head how much whiskey he owed when Lucky asked Jack, "So what has been going on since that night? I know you've had your ear to the ground."

Tarr jumped in before Jack could answer. "Speaking of that night, what exactly did you do with the accounts? We didn't have much private time to discuss it."

"Well, boys, there was a little over 200 million dollars spread out between a half dozen offshore accounts. The US accounts, I left alone. I had already set up all the receiving accounts in advance, so I didn't have much to do.

"First, I divided the 200 plus million between two accounts:

one in Manci's name and the second in Karp's. Naturally, I bounced it around to several other accounts before it landed in theirs.

"Second, I distributed a little of the money to the people doing the heavy lifting. I transferred some to four different accounts that I made sure can never be traced.

"Account one was a very well concealed account for my company. It had two million deposited. My actual expenses ran almost a million dollars before I even considered the very hefty bonuses that my men get for this kind of work.

"Accounts 2, 3, and 4 are accounts of the three principals. Each now has in a non-traceable numbered account a sum of five million dollars each. I've got your account access information with me.

"The remaining money stays put for the feds to seize.

"Now, before you two start trying to return the money, remember, we had to move a sizable piece of the money into unreachable accounts, so it would look like the Columbians were paid off. Otherwise, how do we sell the deception to the Old Man?

"If we had turned these guys in to the IRS, the reward would have been more than what we moved. Isn't that right, Tarr?"

"Yeah, at the current reward rate of 15-30%, probably a lot more."

Jack smiled. "We just took our reward up front. Now if your conscious doesn't allow you to rationalize the money, wait a couple of years, then start giving it away."

Lucky looked at Tarr. "It makes sense to me. You never know what life has in store. If we ever had to run, an account in a foreign country would make our lives a lot easier."

Tarr shrugged. "What the hell. I'm sure we'll be better stewards of the funds than Uncle Sam.

"What else do you know, Jack?"

"When the Aspen law showed up at the Ranch, they found seven bodies outside on the grounds and several more in the structures. The ones inside the pump house were burned beyond the point of any recognition. The ones in the main house were in better shape, but identification is still going to be difficult.

"Every structure on the Ranch was a total loss. It was obvious some sort of battle had occurred, but with not a single live witness to tell them what happened, law enforcement is at a dead end. It seems everyone that was alive headed for the hills.

"The property, itself, is owned by a Panama corporation. Digging through all the corporate veils involved could take years.

"The cops have a bunch of homicides and nowhere to go. And another thing, a week after we hit the Ranch, the Mob hit the Old Man. I guess it was hard to explain how 200 million dollars of their money just up and disappeared.

"Every Mafia family in the world is probably looking for Karp and Manci. They have no place to hide. All three men began laughing.

"So far, the Denver police haven't connected their homicide with what happened in Aspen. And as you might have figured out, no one has connected TMC with any of it.

"TMC is in the news, however. It seems that four of their trustees plus the President and Vice President have been missing for over two weeks. There is no information as to their whereabouts. Foul play is suspected.

"I figure it's just a matter of time before the TMC disappearances are connected to Aspen."

Tarr was a bit shocked. "So, let me summarize. Everyone that could connect me to this is dead or long gone. We still have control of all the Mob's money, and we have all their records. TMC is in the clear, but probably not for long. Damn!"

"Damn indeed," Lucky added. "How do we get the money and records to the feds without becoming involved in some official way?"

As Jack studied his two friends, he knew they had to finesse this thing. "I've had a couple weeks more than you to think this out. I may have something that will work.

"Tarr, have you heard from Detective Orr? I suspect he feels another interview with you about the murder is overdue."

"Yeah, he called me three times while I was in California. I told him I'd call when I got back to Grand Junction."

"Why don't you call him tomorrow and tell him that a couple of days after you got back to town, you ran by your campus office to pick up some papers. In your office you found a package.

"Tell him you think he might be interested in the contents and you'd like to meet with him."

Tarr looked at Jack. "May I assume you have prepared such a package?"

"Yes, you may and, if I do say so myself, very well prepared."

Lucky looked at Tarr. "Should we ask him how well prepared and let him brag about his super spook skills again?

"I think he has earned a few bragging rights, big brother."

"Let me educate you cave boys on a few skills of the highly trained operative. You will fare well under my tutelage."

Tarr and Lucky flipped off their friend and then settled in for the lesson.

"Listen well, grasshoppers; the master is about to speak. While you guys were away playing in the sun, I had one of my men who specializes in burglaring, mosey on over to Manci's office at TMC.

"He typed you (pointing at Tarr) a note explaining the package. He used the office computer and office stationary. I told him to bring back at least a dozen sets of prints. He even managed to lift a briefcase from the closet.

"He was in and out in less than 15 minutes. No fuss, no

muss.

"I then transferred the lifted prints to all the evidence and the note. The briefcase from the office already had Manci's prints on it. The note was dated the night of the hit on the Ranch.

"Everything is in my truck in a big black tote bag."

Lucky applauded. "Well, aren't you slicker than owl shit on ice? I assume the 'package' clears Tarr, explains the college guys' disappearances and gets all the evidence to the cops."

Jack puffed out his chest in an exaggerated fashion. "Pretty good plan, huh grasshoppers?"

Tarr picked up his phone. "Enough bragging for one day, oh great Master. How about getting us another drink; I've got a phone call to make."

Chapter 108

They were in the same interrogation room as before. Detective Orr was not in a good mood, to put it mildly. "Where the hell have you been, Baldridge? Three times I call and three times you tell me you'll be in touch when you get back to town.

"I should throw your big ass in jail for irritating me. Now talk to me."

"Now, Detective Orr, you know it's not against the law to irritate you. As to where I've been; I can't believe I neglected to mention being on the West Coast during one of your three calls. You know, the mind is one of the first things to go at your age, especially if you are under stress."

"Baldridge, if you don't cut the crap, I swear I'm going to Taser your ass and tell everybody you attacked me."

"Okay, but I really think you need to lay off the caffeine."

Orr just grimaced. "Just show me the package!"

Tarr reached for the large tote bag at his feet. He lifted it from the floor and carefully deposited it on the table. He then slipped on a pair of latex gloves and removed the briefcase. By then Orr was fixated on the case.

"What is it?"

"It's my stay out of jail card. It's the answer to your prayers. It's your future claim to fame. It's your lucky day."

"Shut up Baldridge and cut to the chase."

"In the case, Detective, you will find a note from Thunder Mountain VP Manci, explaining the murder of Dr. Gibbs. The case also contains a great deal of evidence pointing to a major Mafia money laundering operation at TMC.

"And if that doesn't get your detective juices flowing, it also gives you information that will explain the 'Battle of Aspen' a few weeks ago.

"Detective, your mouth is hanging open and it looks like you're starting to salivate. Be careful, a gnat is about to fly into your mouth."

"Baldridge, you better not be bullshitting me or I swear I'm going to put a bullet into your good knee."

"Seriously, Detective, have I ever lied to you? Now, it's going to take some time for you to get through this stuff. Since I skipped breakfast today, I'm going downtown and get some lunch. I'll be back in an hour or so. We can talk more then. And by the way, you're going to need a good forensic accountant to wade through the financials in the case.

"This is big, Orr, real big. You've got some decisions to make about how you're going to handle things, especially things with the feds.

"Now, I'll be back later and please don't tell me I can't go, because we both know I can."

Tarr walked out the door without comment from the Detective. He figured Orr was too shocked to speak.

Chapter 109

When Tarr returned to the police station from lunch, it looked like someone had kicked over a hornet's nest. He bumped into numerous cops as he attempted to weave his way back to the interrogation room.

Before reaching it, though, he heard his name being called. It was Detective Orr pointing at a large conference room and waving him over.

"Baldridge, you're a smart-assed son-of-a-bitch and I'm not sure if I should admire you or hate your guts. With that said, I want to thank you for the 'package'.

"It is big, very big. And by bringing it to me, you have done a big service to Grand Junction and who knows where else."

"Do I get a merit badge or maybe junior detective certificate?"

"I really don't know what to make of you, Baldridge; you treat everything like a game. I assume you know how serious this is."

"Yes, I do. In particular, I'm concerned about the impact and ultimate outcome on Thunder Mountain's students and staff. It could also devastate the economy of Grand Junction. The college pumps a lot of money into the local economy.

"I may be a smart-ass but I'm not a dumb ass. If all this isn't handled correctly, a lot of innocent people are going to be hurt.

"I don't care if you admire me or hate my guts, I just want you to keep all those people in mind. I've seen enough hard-core, asshole detectives in my time to know a good one, when I see him."

"Well, well, Baldridge, should we hold hands and skip into

the conference room?"

"I will, if you will."

"Just shut up and get in the room." His voice was more joking than harsh.

Every cop in town must have been in the conference room. Those not talking were taking notes. That all changed when Tarr and Orr entered the room.

The noise went from jet engine loud to funeral viewing room quiet. Orr led Tarr to the front of the room.

"May I have everybody's attention? I need the room cleared of all non-GJPD personnel not involved with this case. Orr waited until the majority of the people left the room. "I'd like to introduce Dr. Tarr Baldridge, the guy who walked into our interrogation room this morning with the bag of evidence that kicked off this shit storm.

"Dr. Baldridge is an innocent guy who got caught up in a very nasty and convoluted situation. What I intend to do is interview Dr. Baldridge in your presence so he won't have to go over his story a hundred times. I will ask the questions; you will listen and not chime in. If you agree to my requirements, stay; if you don't, please leave."

No one left.

"Dr. Baldridge, is this format comfortable with you?"

Tarr nodded in the affirmative.

"Alright, let's get started. Dr. Baldridge, I have a few questions for the record which is being audio and video recorded. I am not reading you your rights, because you are not a suspect in any criminal activity. Do you understand?"

Tarr replied in the affirmative.

"Dr. Baldridge, where do you work and what is your job there?"

"I work at Thunder Mountain College where I labor in the professorial fields of academic excellence. I've been eradicating ignorance as I find it at TMC for about a decade."

Orr interrupted. "For those of you who don't know Dr. Baldridge, he is endowed with a large dose of smart-assism and is recognized as a bullshit savant.

"In other words, he is full of shit. I have discovered though, that he's pretty smart and not a bad guy. Oh, for those who don't speak in intellectualisms, he's a professor."

The room exploded with laughter as the participants visibly relaxed.

"Okay, Detective, I give. I'll speak plain English."

"Thanks, Tarr. Now for a few questions. How did you come into possession of the bag containing the briefcase?"

Tarr related his previous explanation to Orr.

"What did you do upon finding the bag in your office?"

"I took the bag back to my apartment. My instinct told me to look inside, but the researcher in me said to do it carefully. Once in my apartment, I dug out a pair of latex gloves. I use them when I do dishes. You can never be too careful with your hands."

Once again, the room was filled with laughter.

"I put the bag on my dining room table and carefully removed the briefcase. When I opened the case, the first thing I saw was a note."

Detective Orr held out the note to Tarr. "Would you please read the note, Dr. Baldridge?"

Tarr took the note from the Detective and began to read it.

Dr. Baldridge:

I want to start by saying I am very sorry for what you have been through the past few weeks. I have always respected you and recall our interactions as cordial and always entertaining. (Tarr looked up and wiggled his eyebrows up and down at the audience, much to their amusement.)

When I was recruited to TMC, I came in with my eyes open, fully aware of the money laundering scheme I was tasked with creating. Why would I do this, you might ask? There are many answers, however, the most honest is 'money', lots and lots of money.

Part of my agreement to become involved was that no one would be physically harmed. I didn't mind screwing the government, but I am not a man of violence. I was assured the project was straight forward, white-collar crime, with no desire for nor need to commit violence. Please let people on campus know this, I implore you.

I am leaving the contents of this briefcase for your use as a defense against the accusation of murder against you. After Dr. Gibbs and the student mentioned below, you are the one that this situation will harm the most. Please use this as you will without regard for my future. I signed up for this with my eyes open; you were framed into involvement.

Dr. Gibbs, being the arrogant man he was, thought he could get proprietary information about the inner workings of TMC's financial structure and use it for his personal advancement. He used the promise of an 'A' in his class to get a work-study student in the financial affairs office to procure said financial workings. By now you realize the sensitive nature of such information.

The student involved, Kelsie Daggett, was kidnapped and taken to the Ranch at Aspen, our central location for all our Mafia related activities. Our boss is Philip Barberri, head of the Colorado Family.

Please believe that I never knew I was signing up to work for the Mafia. Once I found out, it was too late. I knew too much.

I'm afraid the student never left the Ranch alive. Once she was thoroughly interrogated, she was left to disposal by Mr. Barberri known to his associates as the Barbarian. It is my understanding, he handled the matter personally and with great enthusiasm. Apparently, he has a proclivity for such action.

President Karp and Mr. Barberri instructed that the student's disappearance be handled in such a way to make it look like she withdrew from school and left the state. As to the fate of Dr. Gibbs, a plan was developed to ultimately have him murdered by a Mafia associate who specialized in such work.

Because you, Dr. Baldridge, had made an enemy of Dr. Karp, when you vigorously objected to our new international extension centers, the murder plan included framing you. Karp was afraid you were too interested in our expansions and might be a real problem down the road.

The same assassin who murdered Gibbs, is the one sent after you. Karp never did figure how you found out, but apparently you did and left town.

The assassin is waiting at the Ranch for your return, so please be careful. Karp really hates you.

You have no doubt discovered the records and financial accounts information left in the briefcase. My understanding is that the IRS will give a 15+% reward for information leading to discovery of financial fraud and recovery of said funds.

To any officials reading this note, please let it be known that Dr. Baldridge's involvement in this matter is the sole reason for it being brought to the notice of the appropriate authorities.

Again, I apologize, Dr. Baldridge. Maybe the reward money will help a little.

I am leaving immediately to a location known only to me. We will never meet again and I will never return to the US.

Karp is leaving too. He thinks we're taking the money and running. That was the only way I could get away with enough money. I talked him into taking it.

I also talked him into bringing in some of his Columbian friends to disrupt operations at the Ranch so we could get away. That's the only way I could get my hands on the financials.

The thing at the Ranch got totally out of hand, though; I barely got out alive. Karp's Columbians were really good at blowing stuff up, but not knowing when to stop. As to Karp, I don't know if he got out or not. We weren't together at the time of the attack.

I transferred the money between two accounts in our names. They won't be hard for the FBI to find and retrieve the money. I did, however, take a little money for myself. Those accounts the FBI will never track. I am an expert at this you know.

You'll know if Karp survived, by any additional activity on his account. If he did, you'll no doubt find him. He really isn't very smart!

Good-Bye

Greg Manci

Detective Orr looked out on a stunned group of cops. "Now you know why I had no need to Mirandize Dr. Baldridge. Before I ask Tarr a couple of follow-up question, I need to talk forensics.

Manci's prints were found on the note and through the additional documents of evidence. The briefcase has been identified as belonging to him and a forensic analysis of his computer has proven the note was typed and printed in his office. Because the internal memory of the computer was expertly deleted and made irretrievable, dating the document proved impossible. He definitely didn't want us finding any clues to his destination.

A forensic accountant has the financial data and is just now starting to get into it. She says it's a goldmine of money laundering evidence.

"Tarr, what is the story on the assassin mentioned in the note?"

"He's the reason I left town for three weeks. It's kind of a long story; do you want abbreviated or full version?"

"We've got time; how about the full version?

"After you came to see me about the murder and the article showed up in the newspaper, I knew I had a serious problem. I just didn't know why.

"After giving the issue considerable thought, I figured it had to be associated with the college. And to set me up like that, the killer had to be a professional. A professional meant it had to be somebody with deep pockets.

"The only people on campus who I had pissed off recently were President Karp and Dr. Gibbs. With Gibbs dead, that left Karp. I decided to keep an eye on him for a while.

"One night he and Manci and a couple of thugs headed east out of town. There was also a trail car. I followed their little parade to a ranch outside Aspen. The caravan entered the ranch through a high end security gate guarded by three armed men.

"After they went through, I pulled up to the gate and told them I was there for the party. I wanted a closer look. Also, I wanted to see if me being at the gate caused a stir. They basically told me to get lost.

"They must have called up to the main house and described me. I left the Ranch heading back toward town. Before I had traveled five miles, a hard charging car was on my bumper flashing their lights at me.

"That's when I knew for sure where my problem originated. I knew I couldn't outrun the car, so I took the first gravel road I came to. They followed and immediately pulled up beside me. There were two very serious looking guys motioning for me to pull over.

"Using my well-developed professorial powers of deduction, I deduced that pulling over might not be in my best interest. Instead I ran them off the road. Have I mentioned yet that I drive a full-sized Hummer?

"When the car started sliding on the gravel road, I nudged them into a roadside ditch. The car flipped and landed very poorly.

"I could see both the guys when I positioned the Hummer with its lights illuminating the wreck. The driver was unconscious; the passenger was beat up some, but ambulatory. He crawled out with a gun in his hand.

"I took that as an unfriendly gesture; so I shot him in the knee with a load of 410 buckshot. I then had him throw me his wallet."

Orr held up both hands in the air. "Whoa there, buddy. You run the thugs off the road; engage one of them who has a gun; and you shoot him in the leg with 410 buckshot? Is that what you're saying? Who are you, James Bond?"

"I shot him in the knee, not the leg, with my Judge handgun. And I prefer being compared to Gibbs on NCIS; he's not so sissy looking.

"Anyway, the guy thought I was going to kill him. He said he was just following orders and they were just going to rough me up a bit, yada, yada, yada.

"I told him I wouldn't kill him if he would call me if anything came up at the Ranch about me. I told him if he didn't, I'd find him later. Remember, I had his wallet. He agreed and I gave him my cell number."

Orr was motioning again. "How was he going to explain the gunshot wound?"

"Because shotgun pellets ruined the knee, he could pass it off as road rash. I guess that's what he did.

"I'm about done with the story, so don't get antsy. The guy called me later and told me about the hired gun coming for me. I immediately called a close female friend of mine who I thought might also be in danger.

"She flew out of town immediately. I hid out for a few days, then left myself. The end."

"Thank God, I thought you were writing a book. Last question: what do you know about the battle at the Ranch?"

Tarr looked at Orr. "That's easy; nothing firsthand. Everything I know I read. Apparently, the night it happened, I was staying with friends on Glade Park. I was catching a ride with one of them to the west coast."

"Oh, one last thing. Did you know the Mafia boss, Philip

Barberri, met a very untimely death recently?"

"Yeah, seems like I heard something about that. Bad things happen to bad men.

"May I assume that sews up the whole TMC money laundering bunch? May I go now? I'm really getting tired of this whole affair. It's way too violent for a peace-loving professor."

Detective Orr motioned for Tarr to follow him out of the room. "I'll walk you to your car. That was one hell of a story. Without the note, it would be unbelievable.

"As a matter of fact, I'm sure you applied a little lipstick to that pig along the way."

Tarr replied as they walked. "There're probably a couple of grains of reality to your supposition; remember, you know the mind slips as you age."

Orr lifted his hands in frustration. "A couple of grains, my ass. No one would be as cool under fire as you seem to be or as unconcerned as you project, unless they had felt the heat before. So, tell me, where did you get the experience for all this, what branch of the feds?

"If you don't answer me, I swear I'll never stop digging into your background until I get an answer. I'll take vacation and hound my federal friends until your name pops out of some sealed file. I will haunt you."

"Okay, Okay, I give. You already know that I haven't always been a professor'? I was an undercover investigator dealing with high-level money laundering. That's the main reason I was able to figure this situation out. I can't go into any more detail.

"If I discuss anything else from my past, I'm subject to federal indictment. I am only saying this to you because of a direct question by law enforcement. I trust it will not show up in your final report."

Orr was almost excited. "I knew it. And no, it doesn't leave this conversation between you and me. It does make me feel a lot better about a few of your embellishments, though. Thanks for telling me."

"I tell you what, Orr; you're a good cop. I'd tell you more if I could. Buy me a drink sometime and maybe something will slip out."

Post Script

The IRS ruled that based on the note and police report, Tarr was entitled to a reward totaling in excess of 27 million dollars.

The money was donated to TMC (Yes, the school survived the scandal.) to establish a scholarship fund for TMC employee dependents. As long as the person remained employed at TMC, all her/his dependent children received full tuition and fees to attend TMC for up to eight regular semesters.

A caveat in the donation contract stated that 50% of the TMC Board of Trustees must be tenured faculty members elected by the faculty-at-large. The caveat was accepted.

Tarr Baldridge was reinstated and is still a tenured Professor of Marketing.

The End

54110021R00219

Made in the USA
San Bernardino, CA
08 October 2017